Atomic Secrets

Janet Asbridge

Published by Janet Asbridge, 2023.

This is a work of fiction. Similarities to real people, places, or events are entirely coincidental.

ATOMIC SECRETS

First edition. October 18, 2023.

Copyright © 2023 Janet Asbridge.

ISBN: 979-8223787105

Written by Janet Asbridge.

Table of Contents

Chapter 1 1
Chapter 2 5
Chapter 3 12
Chapter 4 19
Chapter 5 25
Chapter 6 31
Chapter 7 39
Chapter 8 44
Chapter 9 55
Chapter 10 61
Chapter 11 73
Chapter 12 79
Chapter 13 84
Chapter 14 91
Chapter 15 97
Chapter 16 100
Chapter 17 108
Chapter 18 113
Chapter 19 118
Chapter 20 127
Chapter 21 137
Chapter 22 147
Chapter 23 157
Chapter 24 162
Chapter 25 165
Chapter 26 168
Chapter 27 175
Chapter 28 182
Chapter 29 186
Chapter 30 192
Chapter 31 201

Chapter 32	209
Chapter 33	215
Chapter 34	221
Chapter 37	239
Chapter 42	257
Chapter 43	260
Epilogue	264

For Bob, my chief encourager.

Chapter 1

July 1944

I braced myself as the train shifted and slid into a yawning, black tunnel. My cousin Betty's warped, grinning face reflected in the window like a wraith. She snickered.

"What?" I turned to her, irritated.

Her sharp blue gaze landed on my chest, and she handed me a napkin. The train burst into the sunshine, illuminating a drip of jam on my starched white blouse. I sighed. I had only been able to carry along one change of clothes for our trip across the country. I was going to have to remain stained.

"Beautiful as always, Alice." Betty's voice popped with sarcasm.

Irritation swarmed like a cloud of gnats as I wiped at the drip of jam with a napkin. It smeared into a pink spot. "Mind your own business." It was bad enough that I was hurtling across the country on a train from Wisconsin to Washington State. I didn't need my cousin's sarcasm to make it worse. No longer hungry, I re-wrapped my peanut butter and jelly sandwich in waxed paper and shoved back it into the food carry-on.

Sailors in crisp white uniforms and hats set at a jaunty angle entered our car. Betty dug her elbow into my side. "Ally, look. There goes cute."

Betty was pretty in a long, willowy way, with perfectly coifed hair streaked with gold, and a button nose. Since our first year of high school, all the boys had followed her around like puppies.

Unlike me. I inhaled a crumb and coughed. I took off my glasses and wiped my eyes in time to see the sailors exit our train car.

"Let's follow them," Betty said.

"We don't dare." I put on my glasses and glanced at the stain on my shirt.

"Come on, chicken." She grabbed my arm and pulled.

"Let go!" I pulled my arm free and followed her down the aisle. "You know girls aren't supposed to chase boys. What are we going to say when we catch them?"

"Aren't you curious about where they're stationed?" She pushed on the door separating the cars.

"Not really. I figure we're going to meet enough new people in just a couple of days." I grabbed onto seats to keep my balance.

The sailors had settled at the far end of the car.

"I'm going to drop my hanky when we get close and hope they pick it up." Betty pulled her handkerchief from her bodice.

"Oh, my gosh. Don't you think they're going to know what you're trying to do?"

Betty had always been too bold. Girls were supposed to be quiet and demure, waiting for the boys to come to them. Not the other way around. It just wasn't proper.

Betty's hanky drifted to the floor. A sailor with crinkly dark hair reached down and handed it to me. "Miss, I think you dropped something."

I stammered, "Um, I, it's hers."

Betty feigned surprise. "Oh, thank you. I don't know how I could have dropped it."

The sailor's gaze stuck to Betty. I toyed with my glasses, wishing I had left them back at my seat. If I tripped over something and fell flat on my face, at least I'd look good doing it. They'd see me as a damsel in distress and forget all about Betty.

"So, where are you all being shipped off to?" Betty smoothed her embroidered handkerchief.

A sailor with a short blond crewcut and dimpled chin took off his hat. "We're on our way to the Bremerton Shipyards, and then on to the Pacific to fight the Japs, miss."

"Good luck. I hope you can put an end to this horrible war." Betty fluttered the handkerchief in front of her face as if she was suddenly hot.

"We hope to. Where are you heading?" The blond guy asked.

"We're doing our part for the war, too. At Hanford Engineer Works," Betty said proudly, as if she were personally responsible for Hanford.

"What's happening there?"

"No one knows for sure what they're making out there. But we'll be joining thousands of others building something big to end the war." Betty stared back and flipped her hair.

The blond sailor flexed his muscles. "The only thing that's going to win this war is manpower. Lots of manpower."

My face warmed. When a couple stepped into the car and waited to pass, I grabbed Betty's arm. "We'd better go."

"Bye! Maybe we'll see you around." Betty called as she followed me back down the aisle.

"Your parents would not approve. How can you be so bold?" I whispered.

"Don't be such a stick in the mud. We're on an adventure to the Wild West. Everything is going to be different there, including all the old rules." Betty said.

I sighed, irritated. That change was what scared me. I hated leaving everything I knew and loved behind to move to the Wild West. But after my job hunt back home had met a dead end, I'd resigned myself. When I got to Richland, I hoped to find a secretarial job at Hanford Engineer works so I could earn enough money to return.

Thankfully, we weren't moving to completely uncharted territory. Daddy and Uncle Pete had already gotten jobs and homes in Richland. We were on our way to meet them. And though each of my family members was irritating in their own way, at least I wasn't alone.

I heard my little brother Timmy's airplane noises coming down the aisle and shoved my nose into my book to hide. If I had to read one more comic book about Superman's battle against kryptonite, I was going to scream.

"Yoowwn." Timmy flew his paper airplane at the window and stared outside.

Mother's doe eyes were aglow as she slid into the seat beside me. She touched my shoulder. "Look out the window, Alice. You may never have a chance to see the Rocky Mountains again."

"I don't care about the Rocky Mountains. I just want to go home." I shrugged away from her hand.

"Home is wherever God is, dear Ally."

Mother's tranquil platitude only made me feel more unsettled. She might be right, but Richland could never feel like home.

When the whole train car full of people oohed and aahed as if cued by a bandmaster, I slammed the book shut and pressed my nose to the window. The train was chugging around a bend, revealing craggy cliffs with snow decorating them like doilies. My troubles fell away.

The train straightened, and suddenly we hung suspended in space. Below us, a narrow ribbon of river in the valley below wound its way westward. Fear of my unknown future roared to life, and I clung to Mother's arm.

What were they building at the Hanford Engineer Works in the name of war? What kind of people would be drawn to a brand-new town to do something they didn't understand?

"Good luck. I hope you can put an end to this horrible war." Betty fluttered the handkerchief in front of her face as if she was suddenly hot.

"We hope to. Where are you heading?" The blond guy asked.

"We're doing our part for the war, too. At Hanford Engineer Works," Betty said proudly, as if she were personally responsible for Hanford.

"What's happening there?"

"No one knows for sure what they're making out there. But we'll be joining thousands of others building something big to end the war." Betty stared back and flipped her hair.

The blond sailor flexed his muscles. "The only thing that's going to win this war is manpower. Lots of manpower."

My face warmed. When a couple stepped into the car and waited to pass, I grabbed Betty's arm. "We'd better go."

"Bye! Maybe we'll see you around." Betty called as she followed me back down the aisle.

"Your parents would not approve. How can you be so bold?" I whispered.

"Don't be such a stick in the mud. We're on an adventure to the Wild West. Everything is going to be different there, including all the old rules." Betty said.

I sighed, irritated. That change was what scared me. I hated leaving everything I knew and loved behind to move to the Wild West. But after my job hunt back home had met a dead end, I'd resigned myself. When I got to Richland, I hoped to find a secretarial job at Hanford Engineer works so I could earn enough money to return.

Thankfully, we weren't moving to completely uncharted territory. Daddy and Uncle Pete had already gotten jobs and homes in Richland. We were on our way to meet them. And though each of my family members was irritating in their own way, at least I wasn't alone.

I heard my little brother Timmy's airplane noises coming down the aisle and shoved my nose into my book to hide. If I had to read one more comic book about Superman's battle against kryptonite, I was going to scream.

"Yoowwn." Timmy flew his paper airplane at the window and stared outside.

Mother's doe eyes were aglow as she slid into the seat beside me. She touched my shoulder. "Look out the window, Alice. You may never have a chance to see the Rocky Mountains again."

"I don't care about the Rocky Mountains. I just want to go home." I shrugged away from her hand.

"Home is wherever God is, dear Ally."

Mother's tranquil platitude only made me feel more unsettled. She might be right, but Richland could never feel like home.

When the whole train car full of people oohed and aahed as if cued by a bandmaster, I slammed the book shut and pressed my nose to the window. The train was chugging around a bend, revealing craggy cliffs with snow decorating them like doilies. My troubles fell away.

The train straightened, and suddenly we hung suspended in space. Below us, a narrow ribbon of river in the valley below wound its way westward. Fear of my unknown future roared to life, and I clung to Mother's arm.

What were they building at the Hanford Engineer Works in the name of war? What kind of people would be drawn to a brand-new town to do something they didn't understand?

Chapter 2

"Pasco Station. Arriving, Pasco Station." The station attendant's voice blared.

My eyes were sanded shut against the yellow glare of the overhead light. I forced them open.

Mother held Timmy by the hand. He rubbed his eyes and yawned. Mother said, "Let's get going, Ally dear. Can you carry the food bag too?"

I shoved on my glasses and yawned. "What time is it?"

"Two in the morning."

My mouth felt like the train had been chugging through it all night long as I sat up and tried to get my bearings. The car was alive with people talking and jostling to get into the aisle with their baggage. I licked my lips and pulled the bags from overhead. Mother and Timothy disappeared in the crush, and I waited for an opening.

Sometimes I chafed at Daddy's decisive bossiness, and I was still mad at him for moving and disrupting my life, but Mother was as decisive as a drifting dandelion puff. I couldn't wait to unload all my baggage onto my father and let him enfold me in his take-charge presence. I tried to peer through the blackened windows spattered with dirt and bugs for a glimpse of him.

Finally, a space opened, and I squeezed into the aisle. What if the train left again before I could get off? I sighed, trying to squash my anxiety. They couldn't miss the tall woman with the red hat in front of me. I inched closer and stepped on the heel of her flat. She turned to glare at me before righting her shoe.

"Sorry." I backed off just enough to create a breath of air between us.

At the door, the cool air was a balm for my scratchy eyes. Daddy held Timothy in one capable arm and embraced Mother with the other. He searched the crowd anxiously until his green eyes settled on me. They lit up. "There's our Ally girl." He set Timothy down and raced to hug me.

His familiar pipe smoke smell and scratchy face spoke of safety. "Hi Daddy!"

"It feels like I haven't seen you in ten years. I swear you and Timothy have both grown." Betty and Aunt Edna wandered up looking like weary immigrants. Daddy said, "Edna, Pete stayed home to save on gas coupons. He said to tell you he can't wait to see you."

Aunt Edna unfolded her baggage claim ticket. "Where do we pick up our luggage?"

"Unfortunately, we can't borrow a truck to haul it in until tomorrow. I've arranged to store the bags at the station."

Aunt Edna sighed. Mother carried Timmy into the front seat, and I slid in the back with Betty and Aunt Edna. Betty shut her eyes and leaned against her mom.

Aunt Edna asked, "How long is the drive?"

Daddy clamped an unlit pipe in his teeth. "About twenty minutes. Timmy, you might as well go back to sleep." In the rearview mirror his eyes were lined with red threads. "I can't tell you how good it is to see you all." Our headlights illuminated a low, scrubby bush growing in powdery looking sand. "The houses don't look like much yet, but just you wait. Once we get all moved in, they're going to be great."

The only good thing about the move was that the government was supplying housing for the managers on the project. They were called Alphabet Houses, and we were going to have an A house. I couldn't wait to climb into bed in my very own room.

Mother yawned. "As long as we have beds and a roof over our head, we'll be fine."

"About that...I picked out some furniture last week at the government warehouse, but they haven't delivered it yet." Daddy patted Mother's shoulder. "Luckily, I was able to bring home a small table and chair. I'm sure they'll bring the rest of it first thing in the morning."

Mother's face was awash in shadow, but I could hear uncharacteristic worry in her voice. "Oh dear."

I sucked in my breath, shocked. It was bad enough that we had to leave all our old, comfy furniture back in Wisconsin. Now we didn't have furniture at all. "You mean we have no beds? What will we do?"

"Calm down, Alice." Daddy's voice was firm. "I was able to get new blankets and pillows for everyone. We're going to be as snug as bugs in a rug, each of us in our own room."

The black night beyond the window reflected my uncertainty. A bare house with no beds, no clean clothes, and a few blankets on the floor? I'd sleep in the car. The seat cushion was torn but it at least it was soft. And familiar.

Aunt Edna asked, "Have they delivered furniture to our house yet?" She yawned and her buck teeth caught the light of a lone streetlamp. Betty could sleep anywhere, anytime and already her face hung slack.

"No, unfortunately, but Pete got blankets for you too." Daddy turned onto an empty, dark road. "Your house is right through the backyard from ours. We wanted to get a duplex together, but they assign homes by how many bedrooms you need."

"Pete told me. I guess we can get by without clean clothes until morning." Aunt Edna yawned again.

I stared at the headlights sweeping along the road. Maybe Richland was like its name, rich with green grass, fruit trees, and crops in abundance. As my eyes adjusted to the blackness, I could see a crescent moon drifting above what appeared to be a river. Finally, Daddy turned onto a narrow street lined with houses and stopped the car in front of a one-story duplex.

Uncle Pete appeared on the front porch, grinning like a jack-in-the-box. Nothing could keep him down, even waking at 2:00

AM. He rushed to the car and opened the door. "I don't think I've ever been gladder to see you two beauties."

Betty exited the car sleepily. Suddenly, she let out a whoop. "Where are we? The Mohave Desert?"

Uncle Pete said, "We'll have grass in no time. Just wait till you see our swell house."

"We'll see you tomorrow." Daddy pulled away from the curb. "Oh, yeah. I forgot to tell you. Just as soon as we get moved in, I'll go pick up some grass seed. Isn't it great the government provides everything?"

I groaned aloud. "No beds or clean clothes. An empty house in the middle of the desert? Come on Daddy! This is horrible."

His voice held a false heartiness as he turned the corner and parked in front of a two-story duplex. "It's going to be grand when we're all settled, ladies."

I saw Mother's tears silently pool and spill. Of course, Mother wouldn't complain, but at least the queen of peace was showing some real emotion. If I hadn't been so upset myself, I would have cheered.

I resettled my glasses on my nose and peered up at our new house. A light shone faintly through the front window. It didn't look bad. But I wasn't going to sleep on a rock-hard floor. "But we're not settled, are we?" I spoke bitterly. "You made us move to a house on the other side of the country. The least you could do is make sure it was ready for us."

Daddy and Mother ignored my outburst. "All the houses are given an alphabet letter. Our duplex is called an A house and we've got the right side of it." He opened the car door. "Be careful or your shoes are going to fill up with sand."

I sat stubbornly in the back seat while everyone else got out.

"Sand!" Timmy shouted, "Yippee! Sand for my trucks." He jumped into it and sifted it through his fingers.

Daddy scooped him up. "You can play in it tomorrow." He turned back. "Come on now, Alice. You can't sleep in the car. People will be walking past to catch the bus to work at the crack of dawn. They will be staring at you drooling with your mouth hanging open."

Daddy knew how to get to me. Sand pressed between my toes as I stalked up the short hill to the porch.

He opened the front door and stood back as I stepped into a small foyer. The house echoed its emptiness as I started up the lit staircase. Timothy scrambled around me and took the stairs two at a time. "This one is mine!" He disappeared into the room at the top of the stairs.

Mother and Daddy stopped at the room next to Timmy's. "The biggest room is ours." He deposited Mother's suitcase inside and wiped her silent tears. "Everything is going to work out just fine. You'll see. Come look at the bathroom. There's lots of hot water and a brand-new bathtub." She wandered in silently and shut the door firmly behind herself.

Daddy deposited my suitcase on the floor of the unclaimed room at the end of the hall. "And this is your room. It's a little bit more private."

A folded pink wool blanket, white sheets, and a pillow sat on the shiny wood floor of my room. A small, open window yawned black against the wall.

Timmy rocketed into the room. "Is this yours, Ally?"

Daddy said, "Timmy, go get your little nest ready so you can go to sleep."

Timmy rubbed his eyes and yawned. "A little nest for a big bird." He disappeared.

Daddy touched my cheek. "I know this is hard. It's not the welcome I had hoped for. But it won't be so bad. Like I told your mother, you might just meet a nice young man and settle down right here."

I shook my head. "I'm going home as soon as I earn enough money. I'm not a child anymore and I don't have to stay here." I turned and shook the blanket free from its folds. I would certainly avoid any romantic entanglements unless it was a Wisconsin man who was eager to return home when the job here was done.

The bathroom door opened. Mother called, "Ben, would you come help Timmy get ready for bed? I'm exhausted." I could hear tears in Mother's voice.

It was about time something disrupted her pretend fairy world. In seventh grade, when I told her I couldn't see the chalkboard, she'd only smiled placidly and told me we'd pray about it. Well, God didn't speak loudly enough or something, because I'd spent years feeling stupid and clumsy. Finally, my eleventh-grade teacher insisted that she take me to get my eyes checked. Daddy drove us to the eye doctor, and I wore home a brand-new pair of cat-eye glasses.

At least I'd been able to take typing and shorthand classes my senior year. And I was proud to excel in it. But that hadn't undone the damage I'd suffered. Everyone still thought I was stupid.

I dove into the bathroom and twisted the faucets until I felt a steady stream of warm water. That was one improvement. At home, the water was either burning hot or freezing. Another was the new bathtub gleaming white against the navy-blue linoleum. But none of that was important.

What was important was getting a job so I could move away from this uncivilized place so far away from home. Thankfully, I had typing and shorthand as my ticket back to Wisconsin. I brushed my teeth hard and peered at my red eyes in the mirror on the medicine cabinet.

Back in my room, I stripped to my slip. The floor was hard and slick when I lay down and wrapped the scratchy pink blanket around myself. I closed my eyes, exhausted. They popped open again.

Voices floated through the cracks of the door, Daddy shushing Timmy. "We're right next door, little man. You go to sleep now."

Finally, silence came pouring in the house like fog. Along with the quiet came the sensation that I was still rocking along on the train. I rolled over to try and still it.

Stocking feet came slipping across the hall. The door opened and Timmy appeared with his pillow. "I can't sleep," he whispered.

"No, Timmy. You have your own room now, and so do I."

Timmy pleaded. "Come on, Ally. Please? I'll lie real still. It's too big and scary in my room."

I sighed. "Okay, one more night. Just until we get settled."

Timmy lay down next to me, spoon style. Soon he was snoring his little snuffle. His hot body had stilled the rocking sensation, but anger and fear about my unknown future made it impossible to sleep.

Outside, a wild animal howled, and I pulled my scratchy wool blanket closer. Of course, wolves lived in the Wild West. Their den was probably right next door. They would stalk my every move until they finally caught me.

Chapter 3

A hot sunbeam on my eyelids woke me. I sat up, disoriented. The dirty clothes spilling out of my suitcase and Timmy's blue blanket mounded up next to me on the wood floor brought it all smashing back—the sand in the yard, Mother crying, this desert, the wolves howling.

If we didn't get our furniture today, I was going to mount a full-fledged revolt and go stay in a hotel all by myself. I pushed off my sweaty, twisted sheets and stepped to the window.

The sun had traveled almost halfway up a pale blue sky. I rubbed my eyes, suddenly wide awake. The unadorned houses perched on a bed of sand reminded me of one of Timmy's block towns. A brown hill hunched on the horizon. The sky was enormous.

With a sudden ache, I remembered the familiar streets of Sheboygan where flowers, trees, and church steeples anchored everything in place. In this second story room, I felt suspended on a tightrope. One false move and I could tumble and float endlessly.

Aunt Edna appeared on the back porch of the house directly behind ours with a blanket, careful to shake it high above the sand. I pulled up the window, relieved to see a living, breathing reminder of home.

"Hi, Aunt Edna!" I waved.

Her glasses reflected the sunlight. "Oh hello, Alice. Betty isn't up yet. I'll tell her you're awake when I see her."

I nodded and shut the window. At least my family would anchor me here. I reminded myself again that there had been no jobs in Sheboygan. I couldn't very well live with Grandma and Grandpa just waiting for something to happen. We'd get settled eventually, and I'd get a job to earn enough money to get back home.

I put on the white blouse with the jam stain and paired it with my wrinkled skirt. The hallway was quiet. Mother and Daddy's blanket and sheets were folded neatly on the floor of their bedroom.

Downstairs, I heard the muffled sound of Timmy's voice in the yard and opened the door. Mother stood in the shade of the house watching Timmy dig a hole in the sand with a spoon. Across the gravel street, an empty lot covered in sand and low-growing bushes was flanked on both sides by identical box houses.

"Where's Daddy?"

Mother squinted in the bright sun. "Good morning, Alice dear. He and Uncle Pete went to the train station to collect our stuff." She stepped onto the porch and shook out her shoes. "I'll get you some breakfast."

"Any word on the furniture?" I stepped back to let her in.

"Not yet. I made some oatmeal." She glanced at her wristwatch. "Timmy, let's brush you off. You need to come in now, dear."

Timmy's reddened brow shone with sweat as he pushed into the house barefoot. "Ally, after breakfast, do you want to go across the street with me?"

"No, Timmy. Wolves were howling last night, and they sounded very close."

Mother said, "Your father said they were coyotes."

"Coyotes, wolves—what's the difference?" I followed Mother through an empty L-shaped room.

"Don't worry about coyotes. We have a brand-new home to keep us safe." She gestured. "That's the living room and here's the dining room." She pointed to a small table and chair next to a window near the kitchen door. "You can eat right here."

Timmy hopped on one foot down a small flight of stairs. "What's down here?"

"The basement." Mother put a pink bowl on the counter.

He disappeared and his voice echoed. "Come down here, Ally. It's cool."

My bare feet thumped down the wooden stairs. Sand half covered small windows at the top of the concrete walls. The furnace sat like a beast in the corner. On the other side of the room stood a brand-new wringer washing machine.

"I found the laundry room, Mother!" I leaned against the wall, absorbing its coolness.

She appeared at the top of the stairs. "Oh, good. I may as well start doing laundry. Come get your breakfast now." Mother disappeared.

I took the stairs two by two and sat at the little table. From the back window, I could see Betty's house. "Why did they name this desert Richland? It should be named wasteland."

Mother's brown eyes were unfocused as she set a bowl of oatmeal on the table. "Yes. It's different from home. But we must remember that God is here, too. He'll take care of us, Alice."

I barely tasted the generous helping of sugar and cinnamon Mother had piled on my oatmeal. Yes, God was everywhere, but that didn't mean he didn't have his favorite places. Maybe because it was so ugly, he didn't like it here much and only occasionally dropped by.

Betty burst through the back door, looking crisp and wide awake. "Mom told me to come over and see if you had enough oatmeal for me, too."

Mom looked up from the sink where she was washing the pan. "I just scraped it clean, but I can make you some nice cinnamon toast."

"Sure, that's fine. My dad forgot to go shopping for food." Betty wandered past me into the living room and her voice echoed through the empty house. "I'm going to check out the upstairs."

"It's already hot in here." I took a bite of oatmeal and a cloudy drip landed on my navy-blue skirt. I brushed it with my hand, then got up and grabbed the dishcloth out of the sink to wipe it off. "If we're going to live in the desert, we need a fan. A great big fan. Maybe we can order one from the Sears catalog."

"Hmmm. I don't know. Fans create such beastly drafts." Mother set the clean pan in the dish rack.

I scraped my bowl clean. Mother was always afraid that deadly illnesses wafted in on moving air. What diseases she was afraid of, she never said, but every window in the house in Sheboygan had always been shut tight.

"A draft would feel wonderful right now." After three days on the train, I was feeling especially sticky. "When will Daddy be back?"

Mother pushed a pan of bread covered with butter, sugar, and cinnamon into the oven and wiped her hands on her apron. "I don't know."

"Well, I don't know how much longer I can wear these traveling clothes. They're filthy." I scraped my bowl clean and dropped it in soapy water.

Mother washed it. "Just think about the old days. My grandma used to talk about her one and only going-to-meeting dress."

I wasn't in the mood for Mother's moralizing. Especially today. I started out of the kitchen and ran into Betty.

"You should see my bedroom. It's the biggest one." Betty stepped into the kitchen.

I shrugged. Usually, her competitive nature would have bugged me, but today it made me feel more at home. Betty peered into the oven.

"Go sit down now." Mother shooed her away and pulled the pan of bubbling cinnamon toast from the oven.

"Mmm. That looks delicious." Betty sat down.

"Daddy's here!" Timmy's voice echoed through the empty house.

I hurried outside as Daddy jumped out of a truck piled with trunks and boxes. I spied the box where I'd packed my record player and records at the top of the load. Hopefully, none of the records were broken.

Timmy jumped up and down. "Yippee! I see my toy box! Can you get it, Daddy?"

"Hold your horses, little man." Daddy opened the tailgate.

"I can't wait for clean clothes." I looked for the trunk Timmy and I had packed our clothes in. "What can I do to help?"

"You can carry the lighter boxes." Daddy handed me a box, and I started up the sidewalk. At the sound of squealing brakes, I turned. A moving truck with the words "US Government" on the side was parking front of the house.

I breathed a sigh of relief. At least now I'd have clean clothes and a bed to sleep in.

A bald man jumped out. "Clear the area. We need everything out of the way."

"Come on, Timmy." I set the box back on the truck and grabbed his hand. "Let's go in the kitchen." I couldn't wait to see my new bedroom furniture.

• • • •

AFTER A LATE DINNER of baloney sandwiches and cherries, I ran upstairs to my room. The new government-issued dresser stood as straight as a soldier. My clothes hung in the narrow closet. I'd made the bed with my new linens.

But I'd been too busy helping Mother with the kitchen to really unpack. Without my record player, bedspread, jewelry box, and other homey touches, it could be any stranger's room.

Suddenly, the bleak room in the desert far from home stung me so deep I felt sick. Sagging against the wall near the window, I peered outside, hoping for a glimpse of Betty, Aunt Edna, or Uncle Pete. But only their windows glared back at me like sightless eyes in the setting sun. I wiped my tears and bolted downstairs.

"Sit down with us, Ally. We can finish unpacking tomorrow." Daddy twisted the dial on our big Zenith radio. Static poured out of the speaker. A man's garbled voice faded and died. He finally sat back and lit his pipe. "I guess we're going to have to read the newspaper for war news."

I threw myself onto the shiny damask sofa and groaned. "Of course, there's no radio here at the very end of the world."

Mother leaned back in the wingback chair and closed her eyes. "Maybe it's all for the best. Sometimes the radio makes the war feel too close."

Timmy stared at the radio, undaunted. "Try finding *Captain Midnight*."

"No, Timmy. There is no radio here at all." At least I could listen to my old favorites on my record player. "By the way, I heard what sounded like wolves last night."

Daddy shook his head. "I'm sure they were coyotes."

"What are coyotes like?"

"There's the box with the encyclopedias in them over in the corner. Find the C volume and bring it to me. We can all learn together."

I opened the box and dug through the volumes of the *Encyclopedia Britannica* until I came to C. Timmy grabbed it out of my hands and climbed up next to Daddy on the couch. I crowded next to him and listened as Daddy read. "Coyotes rarely attack humans. If they do, the attack is not serious because of their relatively small size."

The image of the coyote looked like a shaggy, large-eared dog. Except that its eyes were cruel. They glared off the page at me like the predator that it was. I shivered.

Daddy said, "We don't need to worry about coyotes. But we do need to be cautious of rattlesnakes. I hear they are prevalent in these parts and if a bite is not properly treated, it can be fatal. Timmy, you can play in the yard and ride your bike in the street, but I want you to stay away from the vacant lots where the sagebrush can hide them. And if you hear a rattle, back away slowly."

Homesickness crushed me, and I hid my eyes under the crook of my arm to block out the view. Of course, out here in the Wild West, wild animals lived right outside the door. Wild animals that could kill. What other dangers awaited me in this godforsaken place?

Chapter 4

I woke in the darkness to ghosts tapping on the window with a thousand fingertips, moaning to get in. How much creepier could this place get? I pulled the covers over my head and rested my shivers of fear against Timmy's bony back. Wind whipped around and blasted the side of the house. Sharp grains of sand stung the window.

We had finally finished getting the house in order and today, Betty was supposed to drive us to the employment center in Uncle Pete's car so we could apply for jobs at the Hanford Engineering Works. I hoped we could still go in this windstorm.

I had left the window ajar to gather the coolness of the night into my room. Reluctantly, I pushed myself out of bed as another blast of wind hit the house, peppering sand against the window. It was no wonder sand had been mounded up against the basement windows. It was a living, moving thing when the wind blew. I tasted grit as I shoved the window shut and hurried back to bed.

Timmy lay splayed out, arms and legs akimbo. I pushed him over and climbed into sandy sheets as the windstorm howled around the house. Someone got up to use the bathroom and turned on the hall light. It gleamed under the door just enough to illuminate my alarm clock—4:10.

I'd overheard Daddy and Uncle Pete talk about the termination winds. It had sounded ominous and scary, but when I asked, they both just laughed. "You'll find out soon enough." Uncle Pete's mischievous eyes had danced. This wasn't funny.

By five in the morning, the gray light illuminated a fine layer of grime. I peered at Betty's house through a fog of sand. Luckily, the storm appeared to be mostly over. A tiny birch tree, lonely in the bleak landscape, waved like a surrender flag in the small breeze.

I heard Mother and Father's muted voices in the hall. At least my slippers, hidden away in the closet, were clean enough. I threw on my robe and stepped into the hall.

"I left the window open last night and my room's covered in dust." I could hear anger in my voice. It was Daddy's fault that we were in this no-man's-land, perched at the end of the earth.

Mother's face was shadowed, her black eyes bruised and uncertain as she disappeared in the bathroom.

"I'm not sure it would have made much difference if it was closed. Houses get sanded inside no matter what. After this, people will leave in droves." His eyes were stubborn. "Terminating is not an option for us." He turned away and started down the stairs. "Let's clean up the kitchen so we can eat. Your mother is feeling poorly today."

Of course, Mother was struggling. But what about me? "Betty and I are going to apply for jobs today. I can't help very long."

He shook his head. "You're needed here for at least the day."

"Why should I help while Mother hides away, unable to cope with things?" My voice rang with the despair I felt at this new twist of horror.

Daddy whispered, "Alice, you have to make a choice. Will you be the kind of person who hides when the going gets rough? Or will you stand strong and work to change your circumstances?" His eyes were fired with determination. "I hope you will choose the latter."

A part of me was tempted to lie face down on my bed and cry loudly in protest. I shook my head. I wouldn't hide like Mother. I would meet the challenge Daddy laid down. I had a feeling that I was going to need that kind of fortitude in the months ahead if I was going to make it out of here in one piece. "I'll get dressed and be down in a minute."

Timmy didn't stir as I threw on an old house dress and laced up my work shoes. Mother was shutting the door to her room as

I headed into the bathroom. I brushed my teeth so hard my gums stung. Today I would start working on my own future and not be held down by the faults and whims of my parents. If cleaning up the dirt was a part of that, so be it.

My eyes burned as I crunched down the gritty stairs. In the living room, the curved, high-backed furniture with its shiny white upholstery was covered in a blanket of gray. Daddy was sweeping the kitchen.

"This is horrible! I don't know how you can even think about staying here." I rubbed my eyes to try to clear them.

"We don't have the money to move back right now, my dear. My job as an electrician supervisor is important to the operation." Daddy sounded resigned, determined. "Let's get working. It doesn't do any good to complain." He looked at me with pleading eyes.

I sighed "Okay."

Daddy swept the dust toward the center of the room. "You go work in the dining room."

I unhooked the latch on the cabinet, expecting to see puddles of sand filling the dainty, pink-rimmed china cups and plates we'd brought with us from home. Instead, the old dishes stood shiny and formal looking, ready for the next celebration or holiday. My stomach growled.

Timmy appeared, yawning and rubbing his eyes. "What are you doing?"

"You slept through a windstorm. We've got lots of cleaning to do."

Timmy drew squiggles in the sand on the table. "Oh, fun!"

"Here's a rag. You can help me clean the table and chairs. When we get the floor swept, we'll eat some breakfast. Okay?" I set a bucket of clear water on the floor next to him.

"Cool!" Timmy dipped the rag in the water and began smearing dirt around the table.

"Wait! You better dust first." I grabbed the rag from his hand. "I'll sweep."

When the table and floor were clean, Timmy whined. "I'm hungry. I want some cornflakes."

My stomach growled. "Okay. Let's get some breakfast."

Daddy was washing the inside of the pots and pans cupboard.

"We're ready to eat. I hope the cornflakes are still good." I opened the newly washed cupboard and peered into the box. Thankfully, they looked their normal caramel color. During the Depression, we'd eaten strictly oatmeal and eggs for breakfast. Cornflakes were a treat.

"You kids go ahead. I'm going to run to the payphone and call my boss to tell him I'm not coming in." Daddy piled the pots and pans in the cupboard and gathered up his keys. "I'll be back in a few minutes."

Mother arrived, her doe eyes red and puffy from crying. "Good morning, Alice."

"Good morning, Mother."

Her eyes had been red from crying more often in the last week than I'd ever seen in my life. But this morning, she looked totally defeated. I sighed. Even though it made me angry, her reaction was predictable and maybe even understandable. She was the baby of the family and when she and Daddy had gotten married, she'd only had to move down the street. Every day she'd run to Grandma's house for something. Grandma was always at our house, too, ironing and cooking. Mother had never really had to grow up much. She hadn't given me tools for growing up either, but I would change that. In fact, I already was.

Mother was opening and closing the cupboards in the kitchen. She turned and her sad eyes smiled for a moment. "Thank you, my dear Ally."

I nodded as pity papered over my anger. At least I could escape this place when I had earned enough money. Mother had to stay until Daddy had had enough of it and that wasn't likely to happen soon. I touched her shoulder. "Things will be okay. Sunday, we can go to our new church." Today I would help without complaining. And tomorrow, hopefully, I could go apply for a job.

After breakfast, I helped Daddy beat the carpet in the basement while Mother and Timmy dusted the furniture in the living room.

By afternoon, the downstairs was shining. Betty arrived in a dirty muslin work dress and scuffed saddle shoes. "We're already done." She followed me upstairs and hung on the doorframe while I mopped the bedroom floor.

"We're almost done. This 'termination wind' makes me want to terminate before I even start." I sighed. "The next best thing is to get an interview so I can get a job and earn enough money to get out of here."

"Yeah. Maybe we can save enough money to get an apartment in Milwaukee while we look for new jobs. That is, if I don't find Mr. Right, right here. Who knows what could happen? I might be married in a year and then..." Betty smoothed her dusty hair, her eyes dreamy.

"I want a Wisconsin man." If Betty got married, I'd go back when I'd saved up some money. I could live with Grandma and Grandpa. I'd find the perfect man. One who would look past my glasses and think I was beautiful, too.

"You've got a smear on your nose." Betty pointed at the side of her nose. "Right here."

"Yeah. Who cares?" I sighed and pushed the mop. Even when we were kids, Betty had bossed and criticized me. Maybe in this new place I'd be able to escape her shadow.

"Our duplex neighbor came over to see how we were doing. She's really nice." Betty leaned against the doorframe. "Her name is Mrs. Smith, and her husband is a scientist. They've been here for three months now, and she's never seen the dust this bad."

"It better not happen again soon. Once we get jobs, we're not going to be able to clean house all day." I wrung out the mop and shoved it into the last dirty corner of my room.

"Oh, and Mrs. Smith said that there's an opening as a messenger in the 700 Area. She told me to apply and mention her husband's name." Betty moved out of the way as I mopped out the doorway.

Of course, Betty already had a reference. I put the mop in the dirty water and pushed my hair away from my face. "What does a messenger do?"

"They carry letters and other correspondence between offices. It sounds fun." Betty stepped aside, and I carried the bucket toward the bathroom. "I'll get to meet tons of people."

"Yeah, I bet there are a lot of secretary jobs too after this termination wind." I dumped the bucket into the bathtub, and dirty water swirled down the drain. Next was the bathtub.

Betty puckered her lips in the bathroom mirror. "Yeah, probably. But I couldn't stand being a secretary and sitting in one place all day with no one to talk to. It would drive me crazy."

I sighed and rinsed the mop in the tub. "Well, I love typing and shorthand. The idea of working in one place sounds perfect to me." If Betty got the messenger job, she'd be busy in her own world. And I'd be free of her constant criticism.

"Whatever." Betty started out the door. "I'm going home to take a bath and wash my hair." She stopped. "Come over tomorrow morning at seven-thirty. The employment office opens at eight."

"Okay." A bath was the next step for me, too. I was going to have to wash my hair and put it up in pin curls again even though I'd just done it yesterday. But at least the cleaning was done, and tomorrow we could go apply for jobs.

Chapter 5

The next day, I climbed into the passenger seat of Uncle Pete's faded red Ford. Betty sat up taller and started the engine. My teeth chattered with nerves as we started out to the employment center.

"I wish Daddy or Uncle Pete had been able to take us to apply for jobs." I shivered in the early morning air. "So, once we get to George Washington Way, turn left." I couldn't wait to get over with this part of my journey back home. Once I had a job, surely things would settle into a routine that became blessedly mundane.

"Yeah, I know. I've studied the directions to the Employment Center, and I know them by heart." Betty sat up tall at the steering wheel in the ancient Ford, her eyes alert. She'd demanded driving lessons not long before we'd moved. I stomped the floor, willing her to stop at a stop sign. If we got there without mishap, it would be a small miracle.

"We'll be fine. I know what I'm doing. Driving is easy." Betty tossed her head.

"I'm going to ask Daddy for driving lessons too, even though the bus will be picking us up to take us to work every day." I clutched my purse.

"I don't know why you'd ever need to drive. I can take you anywhere you want to go," Betty said.

I shrugged. I wouldn't argue. I'd just learn to drive so I could establish my independence from her. Mother refused to drive, and it would be good to not have to rely on Aunt Edna to take us shopping. Plus, if they had a choir at our new church, I be able to drive myself. Singing helped me forget everything else in the world. Every church had to have a choir, didn't they?

Betty turned onto Jadwin Avenue where parked cars hugged the sidewalk. "Look for it. It's on this street somewhere."

I squinted against the sun glinting off the window of a low cement building. A small sign near the door said Employment Office. "Here it is and people are already waiting to get in the door." I pushed my glasses into place. Maybe I didn't stand a chance.

"I'll go park. You hold a space for me." Betty stopped the car.

I jumped out and hurried to line up on the sidewalk behind a man with a shiny bald spot. He turned, shielding his eyes from the sun. "Are you terminating or applying?"

"We just got here about a week ago. I'm applying for a job as a secretary." I struggled to hold his hooded gaze. Talking with strangers made me quake inside, but I had to get used to it. This place was all about strangers. And if I was lucky enough to get a job as a secretary, I was going to have to conquer my shyness.

"After that last doozy of a storm, you should have no problem."

"Are you applying or terminating?" I asked, proud of my boldness.

"I've been pouring concrete, but I'm hoping to find a job as a bus driver. A little wind won't chase me away."

A bus squealed to a stop nearby. The door flipped open. Chattering women filed off and rushed to line up. Betty appeared and fought her way through the throng.

"Here I am!" I waved at her.

She pushed through. "Excuse me. Excuse me."

"Hey, what do you think you're doing?" A husky woman with hands on her hips blocked the way.

"Oh, sorry. My cousin and I came together, and I had to run back to the car for something. She's been holding my place." Betty smiled her most winning smile.

The woman dropped her arms and gestured with a scowl for Betty to pass.

Betty hurried to my side, then turned around to smile and wave. "Thank you! We really don't want to be separated."

A man in a gray suit opened the office door and gestured to the employees waiting behind him at a long wooden counter. "Terminations on this side. Applications over here." The line shifted and most people rushed to the termination side.

As Betty and I followed the bald man to the application line, I noticed a poster on the wall that said, "Loose Talk, a Chain Reaction for Espionage" and clutched my purse tighter. I didn't know what espionage was, but whatever it was must be bad.

The bald man turned. "It doesn't take long to sign up for jobs, especially for waitress and clerk jobs at the club. They'll take any warm body."

"Oh, I have a recommendation for a messenger job from a scientist I know." Betty smoothed her hair.

"That's a different process. I think you have to interview for that." He glanced at me. "For secretary jobs, too. On account of the secrecy."

"I've heard of the secrecy." Betty leaned in confidentially. "Can you tell us more about that?"

He laughed, showing snaggled teeth. "If it wasn't secret, maybe." His face turned serious. "All I can tell you is that the only thing anybody knows is what's right in front of them."

Betty glanced around. "Being a messenger sounds like fun to me." She raised her eyebrows. "Maybe I'll be able to learn some interesting things."

"Just be careful with what you know." His eyes darted around. "I've seen a lot of people disappear. One day they're here. The next—" He snapped his fingers. "Gone."

I shrunk back. Betty had better not be scheming about how to break the rules and spread secrets. She could get into big trouble. I set my mouth in a firm line. No secret mining for me. I'd do the job set before me and then get out of here as quick as I could.

When I got to the counter, a graying woman peered at me over the top of a pair of half glasses. "Do you want an application for the canteen?"

"No, I want to work as a secretary." I met her square in the eye.

"You have to pass tests for that." She slid a one-page form toward me. "Fill out the application. Then go down that hall to get your picture taken and be fingerprinted. Tomorrow, come back to see if you've gotten an interview." She pointed to a wall of bulletin boards where people were standing three deep and straining to see.

I filled in my personal information and then studied the rest of the application. I didn't dare check the box next to general secretary. The thought of being responsible for a whole office made me quake inside. But I checked the boxes next to typist, stenographer, and file clerk. And then proudly wrote that I could type sixty words per minute.

The next section asked about education and work experience. No work experience. I thought of my typing teacher, Mrs. Riley, with her mean gray bun rapping on her desk to get our attention. Despite my nervousness, I smiled. Just thinking about her demand for perfection gave me a shot of courage. I wrote her name and my school phone number and address on the lines where it requested references. She'd put in a good word for me. As long as they didn't ask any of my other teachers, I'd be okay.

I set the form in the secretarial application box and headed down the hall and stepped into the long, narrow office smelling of ink.

An Army Corps of Engineers soldier motioned me over to a table. "Sit down and write your name and address." His gray eyes were cold.

My hands shook slightly as I filled in the card.

"Now give me your index finger." He rolled my fingertips across an ink pad and stamped them on a card. When finished, he handed me my name and address card and gestured toward the cameraman. "Go get your picture taken."

The red-headed cameraman pointed to the wall. "All right, stand right here and hold your card in front of you so I can see it. No smile please. That's right." The camera flashed, and he glanced at the result. "Got it. Give me your card now. You can go." He motioned towards a door.

I stepped outside into a blinding sun and stopped, disoriented. The message the government sent couldn't be clearer: We can track your every move, so you better keep your mouth shut.

When my vision cleared, I spotted Betty talking to the squared-jawed woman who'd complained when she'd cut in line. She waved me over. "This is my cousin, Ally. We traveled here together, and we live next door to each other in Richland."

"Hi, I'm Annette Barrett." She smiled and her perfect white teeth softened her angular face. "You're lucky to have a house. I live in a barracks with barbed wire around it. They say it's for our safety. I guess the men around here can get pretty lonely. If you know what I mean." She waggled her thick eyebrows.

I wasn't sure exactly what she meant, but I nodded knowingly. Weren't we all lonely out here in the middle of nowhere?

Betty asked, "So, where are you from?"

"Can you guess?" Annette looked at each of us in turn.

Betty spoke what I was thinking. "I don't know, but wherever Bugs Bunny lives in his cartoon world."

She laughed and nodded. "I'm proud to share the same accent with Bugs. I'm from Brooklyn, New York. The best city in the world."

"So, what are you doing way out west?" I blurted.

She shrugged. "It was either this or starve. My family is short on money. Besides, I figure I'm doing my patriotic duty to help end the war."

Betty started talking about Wisconsin and how glad she was to be able to help end the war, too.

Somebody called from the bus window. "Are you coming Annette? The bus is leaving."

Annette said. "Oh, I've got to run. I hope to see you around. Maybe at the recreation center sometime."

We waved goodbye and headed back to the car.

I shut the car door. "She was nice."

Betty nodded and started the engine. "I think we're going to be able to meet all kinds of nice people out here. It's not beautiful or anything, but let's think of this as a new adventure. We might even have fun at the recreation center."

"Maybe." I twisted my purse handle around and around in my hands. "That whole fingerprinting thing was creepy, like they expected me to be a criminal or something."

"Don't worry. We're not criminals and now they know." Betty turned onto George Washington Way.

I sighed. "I guess you're right. I hope I get an interview." If I got a job, I'd work harder than anyone to prove I wasn't stupid. Soon I'd be out of this creepy place.

And sometime, I'd ask Daddy exactly why they needed barbed wire around the women's barracks. Were the men around here as wild as the animals?

Chapter 6

The scent of sickly sweet perfume overwhelmed me as I stepped into the interview office. I sneezed and the other interviewees perched on chairs around the room turned to stare. I fumbled in my purse for my handkerchief and felt myself blush.

"May I help you?" The secretary smiled from her desk. Her warm brown eyes soothed my frazzled nerves.

I dabbed my nose and stepped forward. "I'm Alice Krepsky here for an eleven o'clock interview." My voice came out as a squeak, and I cleared my throat.

"Please have a seat. Mr. Caudill will call you soon."

I perched on the only remaining chair. After examining my green dress for spots, I looked in my folder again to make sure I had the time right: 11:00. How could Mr. Caudill interview all these people in the ten minutes before my interview was scheduled?

A door opened. A sandy haired man with buttons straining against his pressed, white shirt looked at a file folder in his hands. "Gerald Thompson."

The guy next to me leapt to his feet and hurried into the office. That left five of us. I stifled a sigh. Perfection was my goal, just like Mrs. Wiley demanded. As long as nothing happened to my glasses. I reset them on the bridge of my nose. It would be horrible if my new co-workers thought I was stupid and incompetent just because I couldn't see.

I thought of "Brain" Wilson from Kohler whose thick dark glasses were held to his head by a wide elastic band. Everyone teased him unmercifully because of it, especially when he wore a white lab coat over his clothes to school. No, the risk of losing them was better than sealing them to my head. Besides, I would make sure I never took them off except for bed. Nothing could happen to them.

I glanced at a young woman across the room. She smiled and her blue eyes twinkled. Her pug nose made me think of an elf. My lips twitched in an attempt to smile.

The door burst open, and Gerald Thompson charged out triumphantly. "Thank you, sir. I'm looking forward to getting started."

Mr. Caudill grunted and sorted through three file folders, "Mary Clark, Patricia Ward and Alice Krepsky."

I jumped up, suddenly lightheaded. Three of us in competition for the same job? The older woman in the flowery hat probably had loads of experience. The folder in my hand trembled as I followed her into the office. The friendly girl with the elfin nose closed the door behind us.

"I'm Paul Caudill, manager of hiring. Have a seat." He indicated the row of wooden office chairs in front of his desk.

Now was the time to be bold. I sat up tall and set Mrs. Wiley's name and address on his desk. "Here's the name and contact information for a person you can call for a recommendation."

He shook his head and handed it back. "No need for that. You've all passed clearance and have been placed in the typing pool." He folded his hands over his bulging stomach. "Provided you really can type. If you not, you'll be reassigned to something you can do." He handed each of us a large manila envelope and an ID card on a lanyard. "Your first day of work you'll be testing and learning protocol. The bus that will take you to the 700 Area will pick you up near your home." He pointed to a map. "When you get through the Gate House, another bus will take you to the Administration Building. It's all written down for you." He stood and started toward the door. "Any questions?"

I shook my head and jumped up, suddenly feeling as free as summer vacation. Of course, I could type. I was in the typing pool.

I escaped into the bright sunlight and turned to Mary and Patricia. "That was easy! I'm Alice Krepsky. It looks like we'll be working together."

The older woman took off her hat and fanned her red face. "Mary Clark. Happy to meet you." She sounded like she could be from Sheboygan.

"You must be from Wisconsin." I smiled.

She nodded. "Milwaukie. I moved here with my husband a few weeks ago. I've got two sons in the Navy." Her eyes clouded over in worry. "We decided to come here to do our part in ending this war. It can't be soon enough."

Patricia smiled. "I'm Pat Ward and I used to live across the river at White Bluffs."

"I didn't know there was a town around here called White Bluffs." Heat radiated off the sidewalk, and I swung my folder to create a breeze.

"Yeah, there was until the government stole our farm." Her eyes turned as flat as a frozen pond.

"What do you mean?" I stopped my folder in mid-swing.

"Colonel Matthias called everyone to a meeting and told us the government needed our land for the war effort. He didn't explain why and offered a ridiculously low payment. They didn't give us a choice; they just took it." Anger boiled out of her. "My family lost our house, land, orchard, everything." She glanced down the street. "I graduated from Pasco High School in the spring. And I have to get a job and move into the barracks so my family can save on food coupons." She shrugged, suddenly deflated. "I'll be working for the enemy just because these are the only jobs around here."

Mary shoved her hat on her head and her eyes flashed at Pat. "How dare you speak of our government as the enemy! And especially during a war. I'm sure whatever they're doing here is critical." She started toward her car.

I watched her dumpy flowered form climb into the car. "See you on Monday."

She slammed the car door and drove away without a backward glance.

"I'm sorry for your hardship." I looked at my watch and started to back away. "Well..."

"I'm the one who should be sorry," Pat said. "Sometimes I just get so angry. Today, sitting in that office set me off. If my mother was here, she would be quick to tell you how impulsive I am."

I grinned. "You do have a lot to be angry about, I guess."

Pat's face suddenly brightened. "I hope we get to work in the same office. The good thing about all this is making new friends. Do you want to get a root beer? I saw a café down the street when I was coming into town."

"Sure." I smiled, suddenly cheered. I would love to make a new friend.

"It's this way." Pat started walking.

I fell in step beside her. "I was so nervous I could hardly eat breakfast."

"Not me. I've heard they'll take anybody who can pass clearance." Pat stuffed her black pocketbook under her arm. "Especially after that last windstorm." The twist of her lips was bitter. "You know the storms weren't anything like that before they cleared the land for construction."

"It must be hard." I wasn't sure what else to say. Moving away from Sheboygan was nothing compared to having it wiped off the map. She had reason to be bitter. Perhaps I should just listen and commiserate.

"Yeah. My mom and dad are the ones who are really devastated. But my dad may have a chance to go in with a partner on some new land so he can plant another peach orchard. Till then he's working for another farmer outside Pasco." She held up crossed fingers for luck and pushed on the café door. "Here we are."

"Paper Doll" by the Mills Brothers blared from the jukebox in the corner. A large fan blew the scent of hamburgers in our direction. My stomach growled. I perched next to Pat on a metal stool at the counter and looked at the menu. A hamburger was fifteen cents. One shiny dime lay in my flowered coin purse. Maybe five cents had gotten buried. I rummaged around and finally gave up. A soda would have to tide me over until I got home.

A soda jerk with unruly white eyebrows and a sharply creased white hat rested his gnarled hands on the counter. "What'll you gals have?"

"I'll have a root beer, please." Patricia handed him a nickel.

"Me too." I set my dime on the wooden counter. He snatched it up and tossed me Pat's nickel as change.

I stared at the posters of movie stars on the wall. Everyone thought Carey Grant was so dreamy, but Gregory Peck was the one for me. Something about his eyes.

"So, I've been jawing nonstop. Tell me about you." Patricia turned to me curiously.

"By the way, you can call me Ally." The soda jerk slammed two frosty glasses of foamy root beer on the counter. "Mmmm. It's delicious." I turned to her, revived. "I just graduated from high school in Sheboygan, Wisconsin. We had to move here because of the Depression and, of course, to help the war effort."

Pat looked up from her drink. "So, did you move with your family?"

"Yeah." My paper straw collapsed, and I set it aside. I went on to tell her about our new house. You'll meet my cousin Betty too. We're like sisters." I stopped. She'd probably meet Betty soon enough. "Tell me about your family."

"Mmmm." She sucked on her straw. "I have two younger sisters. My mom's always ordering me around. Pat, do this. Do that." She shrugged. "One good thing about moving into the barracks is that she won't be able to do that anymore. Plus, my job will help support the family while my dad gets reestablished. He refuses to work for the government."

"That sounds hard. My mother does everything for my brother and me, so I've never really had to do much work around the house." I hated watching Mother fall apart when the storm hit, but on the positive side, it made me feel capable, like I was a real adult. "I'm not exactly sure how it's going to work now that we're here. My mom's not having such an easy time of it."

"I bet. This isn't exactly paradise." Pat sucked her glass to the bottom and glanced at the wall clock. "We can talk more on Monday, I hope. Right now, I've got to go. My mom is picking me up."

I scooted off the bar stool. "Okay. I've got to meet my Aunt Edna too."

At the 700 Area bus lot, Pat's mom and two little sisters were waiting. "Bye!" Pat chased a sister out of the front seat and climbed in. She waved as they all drove away.

As I waited for Aunt Edna, I studied my ID card, then shoved it back in the envelope with a sigh. I looked uncertain, scared even. I should have pretended confidence.

At least things were starting to look up. I'd already made a new friend without Betty's interference. And with my new job, I'd prove to everyone and myself that I wasn't stupid no matter what my grades in school had been.

I couldn't wait to tell Betty all about my interview. Not that you could even call it an interview. It was more like an informational meeting. All she had to do was show up and whammo, the job was hers. She wouldn't even be able to brag about the recommendation from her scientist neighbor.

Aunt Edna waved to me from their faded red sedan as it slowly coasted around the corner. "Hi, Aunt Edna. I got the job, and I met a nice girl named Pat. She has a sad story, though." I climbed into the front seat.

Aunt Edna said, "Don't we all have a sad story?"

"Maybe." I shrugged. Despite feeling unhappy about the move, my future was looking more promising by the day. "But Pat's story is weird." I told her about her farm being stolen away by the government and her family having to move.

"Well, that is unusual, I must say." Aunt Edna yanked on the steering wheel to turn the corner. "But there are many lives being lost every day in this war. We just have to trust our leaders to know what is best."

A small cloud covered the sun as Aunt Edna's car gathered speed. She was probably right. But Pat's story about her stolen land made me even more curious about what was going on way out here in the desert.

• • • •

THAT EVENING BEFORE bed, Daddy stopped at my room. He stared at the ceiling. "My dear Ally." He stopped and cleared his throat. "I need to say something before you start work." Fiddling with the pipe in his hands, he waited as if unwilling to go on. Suddenly, his face looked fierce. "Many of the men who've come here are wild and unruly and they would love to take advantage of a pretty, young girl like you. That means you must never travel alone. The buses are usually full, so it shouldn't be a problem, but I warn you because you must be very careful." He stood up and brushed his hands as if he'd just finished a distasteful task. "By the way, I've told Timmy that he can't come into your room at night when you're working. If he bothers you, let me know." Daddy turned off the light. "Good night, Alice."

"Okay, Daddy. Good night."

In Sheboygan, the rumor was that Harvey Clink had taken advantage of Mildred Wire. Everyone said Mildred's parents sent her to a home for wayward girls in Chicago to have a baby. She came home alone about six months later, looking tired and sad.

I'd never travel alone. That was for sure.

Chapter 7

I stretched, glad to have some time to lay abed. Tomorrow was Monday, and I'd be awake with the sun to catch the bus on my first day of work.

I looked around my bedroom. With the shades blocking my view of sand and sagebrush and with Mother's handmade doily covering my new dresser, I could almost imagine myself back in Sheboygan. Soon, I'd smell pancakes cooking. After breakfast, we'd walk together across the street to church and meet up with all our friends.

The pungent smell of sagebrush wafting through the open window turned my daydream to reality. Today we'd go meet strangers at our new church. God seemed far from me here in this Wild West. I hoped to find him at church today.

Brakes squealed and car doors slammed outside. I slipped on my robe and headed downstairs. The front-room curtains were open a crack, and I peered through.

A snubbed-nose man opened a truck tailgate. "Wake up, lazybones. Let's get busy." His voice had a slight twang to it.

The guy who popped out of the passenger side looked like a young version of his dad, except his mouth was turned up in an expectant smile.

A gray Ford sedan pulled up behind the truck. One of the sedan's doors opened, and a boy leapt into the sand.

"Jimmy, get out of the dirt." A frowning woman emerged from the driver's seat.

The young man stretched and looked around. "I'm going in to look at the house."

"Doug, take a load with you." His father grabbed an armful of boxes from the back of the truck and stacked them in his arms. "Don't drop them."

"And watch where you're going in this sand, or you'll fall and break your neck." The woman lifted a red-faced toddler from the front seat.

After the family disappeared into the house, I climbed the stairs two at a time. The oldest boy was cute, but his accent suggested Texas and I wanted a Wisconsin boy. Plus, he was either still in high school, or he'd be joining the service any day and disappear.

My pin curls, skewered in place by sharp bobby pins, suddenly became intolerable. I locked the bathroom door behind me and began freeing my head. Smooth, light brown curls bounced around my face and neck. First impressions were important. I'd wear my Patriotic Red lipstick and yellow dress. After church, I'd ask the choir director if I could join.

Timmy pounded on the door. "Ally, get out! I need to go to the bathroom."

"I'm fixing my hair. You're just going to have to wait." I pulled the brush through my hair to smooth the ringlets into waves.

"I have to go!" He pounded on the door again. "Mommy! Ally won't let me in."

"Alice, open the door and let your little brother in right now." Mother's lips were at the door. "You can get ready in your bedroom."

"Oh, all right." I shuffled into my room in my slippers and peered into my hand mirror. The time spent outside helping Daddy plant grass had paid dividends in more ways than one. Soon we'd have a nice green carpet to anchor all the sand in place. And as a bonus, I was tanner than I'd ever been in my life. The glasses that usually defined my face had seemed to fade away.

The outside faucet squealed as Daddy turned on the sprinkler. I set the needle of my record player to "The Boogie Woogie Bugle Boy" by the Andrews Sisters and sang along as I brushed my hair into soft rolls that met the tops of my shoulders. Without my glasses, I looked a bit like Maxene Andrews. She had brown hair and a nose that sloped up like mine. If I practiced enough, I might sing like her too.

• • • •

"LET'S GO, KIDS! HURRY up." Daddy called up the stairs.

I glanced at my reflection in the mirror one last time and closed the door behind me.

"I'll beat you downstairs, Ally!" Timmy scrambled past.

As we crowded onto the porch, the young man I'd seen earlier peered at us over the top of a box. "Hi, Y'all."

Timmy jumped off the porch. "Yippee! We have new neighbors!"

Daddy said, "Hello! I'm Ben Krepsky, and this is my wife, Mary. Our daughter, Alice, and son, Timmy. Welcome."

The young man glanced at me shyly. "Doug Parsons. Glad to meet you. My parents are around here somewhere." He started toward the front door.

"Oh, don't disturb them. We're on our way to church." Daddy opened the car door and waved. "We'll come over and see what kind of help you need when we get back."

"Okay, then. We'll see y'all later." Doug smiled in my direction. As I climbed into the backseat with Timmy, I tried to snuff out the stir of excitement that lit my belly. He was cute. I reminded myself that I didn't want a boy from the South. And there was no way he'd want a girl in glasses even if my tan did disguise them a bit.

As we pulled away from the curb, Mother said, "Ben, I'd like you to go over there and offer to help them plant grass. The more sand we can anchor down, the better."

Daddy stopped at a stop sign. "I'll offer to do it sometime, but not when they're moving things into the house."

"*Ach der Lieber.* I don't know if I can tolerate the dust any longer." Mother's voice had that desperate quality that was becoming so familiar.

"But Mommy, you said you were happy today." Timmy stood up on the backseat and watched the neighborhood go by.

Mother turned and her soft brown eyes glowed at Timmy. "Sit down now, dear."

Timmy jumped up and down. "Oh look, there's the firehouse."

Daddy turned a corner. "The homes here on Duportail Street are D houses."

"Duportail, poopertail, Duportail, poopertail," Timmy sang out.

The D houses looked as if they might fly away in a hard wind. "I just hope the church looks like a real church." I couldn't stand it if the church looked impermanent, too. Churches were supposed to look solid and comforting, like an anchor in a storm.

Mother's eyes were fogged by sadness. "It doesn't matter what the building looks like. It's the worship and the people that make the church."

"Speaking of people, do you remember how scary Mrs. Simpson was when someone sat in her pew? We better be careful to not make anybody mad." Daddy laughed.

"Mrs. Simpson had her faults, just like we all do." Mother adjusted her hat as we turned into the parking lot of the First Church.

Gravel crunched under the tires as Daddy parked the car. "In any case, it's probably best if we sit in the back until we can figure out the lay of the land."

The sharp pinnacle at the front of the long, narrow white building looked insubstantial compared to the tall steeple and bell tower on our homey white church in Sheboygan. Homesickness pinned me to the seat as the rest of the family opened the car doors.

"Come on, Ally," Timmy said.

I rummaged in my purse as if searching for something to hide the tears that sprang to my eyes. "In a minute. Save me a spot."

"Don't be too long." Daddy took Mother's hand and started toward the door.

As soon as they disappeared into the building, I stopped pretending to search and stared out the window at the people streaming into the church. Uncle Pete parked, and Betty hurried into the church ahead of her parents, smiling and saying hello to people as she went.

When the parking lot emptied, I stepped inside, and waited for my eyes to adjust to the light coming through the narrow, stained-glass window at the front of the sanctuary. The congregation stood to sing my favorite hymn, "How Great Thou Art." As I slipped into the pew next to Daddy and sang along, the homesickness poking my heart like a bobby pin loosened.

A man in a black flowing robe stepped to the lectern and introduced himself as Pastor Carver. His large, bulbous nose dominated a rough, pockmarked face, but his eyes were kind and held the light of humor as he told of coming events. Mother smiled faintly when he announced that the quilting club was meeting this Wednesday at 10:00 AM. I was disappointed to hear that choir wouldn't begin until fall.

His sermon made me feel as if he could see the to the depths of my heart. "In Psalm 46:1 God tells us that he is our refuge and strength, an ever-present help in trouble. Therefore, we will not fear though the earth give way..." He laughed and scanned the small crowd. "Didn't you feel like the earth was going to give clean away during that last doozy of a dust storm?"

I laughed along with the crowd. As he continued to speak, the anxiety that had threatened to splinter me ever since I'd left Sheboygan was smoothed away. By the end of the service, I felt whole and seamless. God was with me here, too. He would see me through.

Chapter 8

The serenity I'd felt at church was replaced by anxiety as Betty and I waited at the bus stop the next day. I resettled my glasses. If I didn't pass my typing test, I would never be able to get a job as a secretary. Plus, Pat would think I was stupid just like everybody did back in Sheboygan.

Betty had irritated me to no end when she'd come home gloating about getting the messenger job. Her nose was high in the air when she explained that she'd needed the recommendation from her scientist neighbor to get the job, and that she'd had a real interview. But today, I clung to her like a security blanket.

A man with a newspaper under his arm approached the corner. He nodded his head in our direction. "You gals just starting out?"

"Yes. It's our first day of work. I'm Betty and this is Alice." Betty straightened her hat.

"Harold Drinkwater." He nodded and the grease on his black hair glistened. "The bus will be here any minute. It's never late."

A bus squealed to a stop in front of us. Mr. Drinkwater gestured for us to go first. The bus driver yawned, his eyes red around the rims.

"Hey Ed. Almost done with work?" Mr. Drinkwater asked.

Ed nodded and shut the doors behind us. "My last run."

The bus started moving, and I grabbed seats to steady myself as I weaved past dozing people to a seat in the back. It roared around the corner onto George Washington Way.

"Look, there's Riverside Park and the Columbia River. My dad told me about that." Betty peered past me out the window. "And I heard they were building a big new department store somewhere around here. I can't wait to go shopping after I make some money."

Only Betty could think about shopping for dresses on her first day of work. I tuned her out and rehearsed the information I'd read about checking through at the gatehouse and punching my time clock at Clock Alley.

A billboard ahead showed a picture of a man in a hardhat with his finger to his lips. I read it aloud. "Protection for all. Don't talk. Silence means security." I folded and refolded the top of my lunch sack and whispered. "Another creepy sign."

Betty tossed her head. "I won't have any trouble with it."

"You know people who talk disappear." It would be a miracle if she could stay silent. "I wonder where they go. Some cheaters' prison?" I said, trying to scare her.

The bus stopped at the 700 Gate House and people crushed into the aisle. My legs felt shaky as I stepped off the bus. I took a deep breath for courage. Betty must have felt the same even though she didn't say so, because as we started walking toward the Gate House, she hung onto my arm so hard it pinched. "Ow! Let go a little. It hurts."

"You and I will be fine." Betty loosened her grip.

I spoke aloud to reassure both of us. "Yes, we will."

A guard in uniform with a holstered gun at his waist checked my ID and waved me through to Clock Alley. My hands trembled as I punched my card. A gun meant only one thing. Danger. But danger from what? Or whom? I grabbed Betty's arm, and we moved as one towards a bus that was waiting just inside the gate.

Betty extricated herself from my clinging arm. Her voice was strong as she stepped aboard and announced to the driver. "We're going to the administration building."

"I'll call out the buildings as we go."

I followed Betty down the aisle, trying to stay centered so I didn't trip over elbows and feet straying into the aisle.

"Alice!" Pat grabbed my hand. Her narrow red lips curved up into a smile.

"Hi, Pat! It's good to see you." I squeezed back as pleasure momentarily replaced my anxiety.

Betty tapped my back and cleared her throat.

"This is my cousin Betty, the one I told you about the other day. Betty, this is Pat."

"Hi Pat, nice to meet you." Betty plopped down next to her.

Irritated, I perched on the seat across from them. "Did you get moved into the barracks?"

Pat's mischievous eyes peered around Betty. "Yeah, it's kind of weird with all the barbed wire and stuff. But the gals are nice and now my mom can't use me as her personal servant anymore. Pat, fetch that. Get this. Take your sisters to the park and don't come back till dinner time." She laughed.

Betty beamed in her direction. "I've always wanted a sister. Someone to share clothes with and do each other's hair. It sounds so fun."

"Reality isn't quite what it's cracked up to be," Pat said.

"Aren't you gals nervous?" I bit my nail and stared straight ahead.

Pat said, "Relax. It's not a big deal you know. They take anyone."

I appreciated Pat's effort to reassure me, but it was my first day of work ever. And I had to pass that test. The bus rolled past another large sign that said, "Loose Talk. A chain reaction for espionage." A shiver of anxiety shot down my spine. How many times did they have to remind us?

Betty didn't seem to notice. "Ally and I are going to Riverside Park on Saturday. Do you want to go?"

I sighed and half listened to their chatter. Today felt like a desert too wide to cross and I didn't care whether Betty and Pat became the best friends in the world.

The bus driver announced, "Administration."

From the outside, the administration building looked foreboding and bleak with gray concrete walls and few windows. We exited the bus and found our way to the door. Inside, a spare hallway traveled left and right before us. We stopped to look at our instructions again.

Betty said, "I guess this is where we part company. I'll meet you at the Gate House and we can ride the bus home together."

I nodded and followed Pat down the hall to a door labeled Typing Pool. She pushed open the door with a grimace. "Off to work we go."

A middle-aged woman with chubby cheeks and loose gray pin curls greeted us at the door. "Welcome, I'm Mrs. Chase, secretarial supervisor." She reminded me of my Grandma Krepsky except that her voice rang with authority and her bright eyes snapped with interest as her gaze settled on Pat. "And you are?"

"I'm Patricia Ward."

Her attention shifted to me. I felt myself shrinking under the intensity of her gaze, but spoke up and gripped my purse so she wouldn't see my fingers tremble. "Alice Krepsky. It's nice to meet you."

"We're in Room One. Go on in and sign the paper on my desk. Then find a place at one of the typewriters. We'll begin soon."

We entered a tiny airless room. The three typewriters spaced far apart for secrecy's sake reminded me of test day at school. I signed my name and sat at the desk in front of Pat. Thankfully, the black typewriters with the white letters on round black keys were the same as the ones at school, too. A few minutes later, Mary Clark arrived, looking flushed and harried.

Mrs. Chase followed her in and shut the door. "Welcome. Today, you'll take a series of typing tests to determine whether you belong in the typing pool."

She passed out a list of shorthand sentences. I recognized the first one and smiled. "The quick brown fox jumps over the lazy dog." was a sentence that we practiced over and over in typing class. Easy.

Mrs. Chase said, "Put some paper into your typewriter while I set the timer." She twisted the dial on a kitchen timer, just like old Mrs. Riley used to do. "Go."

The familiar ticking timer and sentences gave me confidence. I finished first, then scanned for errors. I sat back with a relieved sigh. One-hundred-percent accuracy.

Mrs. Chase checked my work and rewarded me with a smile. After a series of tests, she said, "Your final test is to transcribe a full-page letter with an accompanying graph."

I finished both documents rapidly and scanned for errors with a sense of satisfaction. I was in the typing pool.

Mrs. Chase studied my paper and whispered, "Stellar job, Alice."

I felt sure that if anyone looked at me, they'd be blinded by my glow of pride.

When everyone had finished, she stood at the front of the room. "Congratulations to you all. Working in The Hanford Engineer Works typing pool is not without challenges, but always remember that with every document you type, you're helping to end the war." She smiled and deep dimples creased her cheeks. "We'll take a much-deserved lunch break before we dive into some important safety information." She took a silver lunch box out of her desk. "Follow me."

In the break room, knots of chatting people stared at us curiously as we followed Mrs. Chase to an empty table. I got situated and took a sip of orange juice from my thermos.

Mrs. Chase opened her lunch box. "I've been here for six months now, but I started working for Dupont in South Carolina when my youngest daughter went off to high school four years ago. My husband is a scientist on the project. We have three daughters, all of them married, and four grandchildren. Someday, I'd like to move back to South Carolina so we can be near them, but for now, we're needed here."

Mary told her story about her two sons in the war. She turned to us. "We met at our job interview and had a chance to talk." She glared a warning at Pat.

Pat cleared her throat. "I'm from right across the river in White Bluffs. The government took our land for this project and my family moved to Pasco about a year ago. I'll not lie and say it was easy to lose my home. But I'm ready to work, and I'll do the best I can." As she continued about her duties in her large family, I admired Pat's honesty. She wasn't hiding secrets.

When everyone had finished, all eyes turned on me. I swallowed a mouthful of tuna sandwich and told them about my family moving from Wisconsin. "I'm nervous because I just graduated from high school last spring, and I've never worked in an office before." I resettled my glasses.

Mrs. Chase smiled. "You're not going to have any trouble if your tests are any indication." I nodded, elated by the praise. She stood. "Go ahead and finish your lunches. We'll reconvene in Room One in about ten minutes."

"I'm done too." Mary scrambled to put away the remains of her lunch and followed Mrs. Chase.

Pat smiled my way. "The tests were harder than I expected, but I'm glad I passed. Mostly because it looks like I'll be working with you."

I smiled back, grateful for her friendship. "Me too. I hope we're assigned to the same office." I glanced around at the thinning crowd in the break room. "What do you think about Mrs. Chase?"

Pat shrugged. "She seems nice enough. I have to say, though that all the security signs are pretty creepy. Did you notice the one about espionage? I wonder if there's a spy somewhere nearby?"

The man in the business suit sitting alone at the next table rattled his newspaper and glanced our way. I tilted my head toward him and shrugged. I didn't want to get in trouble before we even started. "I'm going to go use the restroom."

• • • •

BACK IN ROOM ONE, MRS. Chase stood near the chalkboard and tapped a wooden pointer against her hand. Gone were her dimples. Her eyes snapped warning. "Here at the Hanford Engineer Works, secrecy and safety are the most important parts of the job." She touched a security poster that read, "Protection for All. Silence Means Security."

"Do not ask questions. Do not share what you learn on the job with anyone. That includes family, your best friend, and other workers on the job." She clarified the government's demand for secrecy, and the concepts of espionage and sabotage in general terms. Then she said, "We'll wrap up this portion of training with this agreement. Read it carefully and only sign it if you promise to abide by the government mandate. If you don't, please leave now. A bead of sweat slid down my back as I studied the document:

> **In signing this form, you, the employee, are taking a pledge of faith and allegiance to the United States of America. You will not disclose any classified information or materials to unauthorized individuals or misuse any material used in the process. Violation of the National Espionage Act or the Federal Sabotage Act is punishable by up to 10 years in prison or up to $10,000 in fines.**

The threat of jail time and fines was irrelevant because I'd never share the government's secrets, ever. I signed the document with confidence. Now, I just had to earn enough money to be able to go back home to Wisconsin.

Mrs. Chase droned on the rest of the afternoon, handing out mimeographed sheets about safety, cleanliness, and office protocol. About the time I thought I might faint from information overload, she said, "Especially when the going gets rough, always remember–you are doing your patriotic duty to end this war and save lives." Her dimples reappeared. "We're done for today. Tomorrow morning we'll reconvene in Room Five, bright and early."

A burst of patriotism carried me toward the bus. I was proud to be able to help my nation end the war. And after my initial bleak, scary impression of the place, it had turned out to be filled with kind, dedicated people. If my work could help save lives, then maybe a few months in the Wild West would be worth it.

Pat stopped short of a small crowd waiting for the bus to arrive. She whispered. "I can't believe I signed something that makes it so I could go to jail for ten years if I don't keep their secrets." She sighed. "You've got to admit, it's creepy."

I nodded. "Yeah, it is weird. But I guess, like Mrs. Chase says, it's best to keep focused on the fact that we're doing our patriotic duty. It's kind of like vowing allegiance to the military, except instead of guns, our weapons are typewriters."

Pat laughed. "Yeah. They weigh about a thousand pounds. You could conk somebody out cold with a typewriter."

We chatted companionably all the way to the Gate House. Betty was waiting when we arrived.

"See you tomorrow, war buddy." Pat waved goodbye.

I laughed, glad to have a friend to help see me through the battle ahead.

Betty was uncharacteristically quiet on the bus ride home, as if the magnitude of secrets she was responsible for keeping had robbed her of the ability to chitchat and even boss me around.

When the bus stopped at our corner, I stepped off with a sigh of relief. "I can't believe I actually feel like I'm coming home."

"And tomorrow is going to be as easy as pie." Betty set off toward home.

"Easy, I'm not so sure. But at least I passed my test." Sand filled my shoes and I stopped to shake them out before hurrying onto the porch.

Doug's door opened and he stepped onto the porch. "Hi."

"Oh, hi." After the long hard day, I must look a mess. I brushed my dusty dress.

Betty cleared her throat.

"Doug, this is my cousin Betty. She lives right through the backyard."

"Nice to meet you, Betty." Doug's smile bloomed.

"Likewise." Betty grinned back. "I hear you got here just yesterday and that you're from Texas."

Doug held Betty's gaze. "Yeah, we're just getting settled."

I was embarrassed that Doug knew I had told Betty about him. He probably thought I liked him. Well, it's not that I didn't. He seemed like a nice enough guy, and he was cute. I glanced at him again. He was fixated on Betty. I sighed. Of course, she still looked crisp and perfect. Somehow, her rose dress looked prettier with a layer of dust coating it. My navy dress looked dirty, and my glasses made me look like a frump.

Betty touched her hair. "So, are you going to look for a job here or what?"

"I just graduated from high school. As soon as my family no longer needs me, I'm going to find a recruiter." Doug stared. "I can't wait to join up and do my part."

Betty gave him a brilliant smile. "We're going to Riverside Park on Saturday. Want to join us?"

"Oh yeah. You bet." Doug cleared his throat. He seemed to have to force his eyes away from her. "But right now, I need to hang some pictures."

"Great. We'll keep in touch." Betty followed me up onto the porch.

"Sure thing." Doug looked Betty up and down before he stepped into the house and shut the door. He looked smitten. Was it love at first sight?

I threw my purse on the couch. "Too bad he's going off to war any day."

"Oh, who knows? Maybe he won't join right away." Betty's eyes were dreamy and unfocused. "He's really cute." She headed toward the back door.

Timmy ran into the living room at top speed. "Mom, Ally is home!"

"Hi, little brother. How was your day?"

White frosting glistened on the tip of his nose. "It was boring without you and dad. Can you read Superman to me?" He grabbed my hand and pulled.

"Maybe later. I just got home." I extricated my hand from his.

Mother appeared in the dining room in her yellow gingham apron. "Hello, Ally dear. Sit down, and I'll bring you a cookie and a nice glass of milk." Mother patted a chair. "We'll eat dinner in about an hour, as soon as your father comes. Swiss steak, your favorite." She bustled into the kitchen.

The familiar smells of oatmeal cookies and Swiss steak almost made me feel like I had been transported back to Sheboygan. The stress of the day fell away as Mother set a plate of cookies and a glass of milk in front of me. They tasted like childhood.

"Did you pass your typing test?" She sat at the table, her brown eyes serene.

"It was easy. And my boss, Mrs. Chase, is kind. She looks a bit like Grandma."

"We got a letter from Grandma today." She slid an envelope across the table.

Homesickness grabbed me as I read her news. Tears surged to the surface and spilled. I stood up.

"Ally's crying!" Timmy's eyes widened.

"Oh dear, I know that letter probably makes you feel homesick. It did me." Tears filled Mother's eyes. She hugged me.

"Yeah." I wiped my eyes again. "Well, I'm going to go up and change and rest a bit before dinner. It's been a long day."

The shades in my room shut out the desert expanse. I stripped off my stockings and too tight girdle gratefully. My old housedress and soft slippers felt like a dream. But even as I tried to drown out my emotions by singing along with the Andrews Sisters to "Don't Sit Under the Apple Tree," an image of the strange document I'd signed played in my head. What were we doing way out here in the desert, where sharing government secrets was punishable by ten years in prison?

Chapter 9

Today was Friday, and I couldn't wait until quitting time. After three weeks on the job, I had settled into a routine. Every day, Mrs. Chase delivered a fresh batch of shorthand notes to my desk. Thankfully, I was able to figure out how to turn them into orderly, legible documents. Nothing I typed made much sense, and a lot of the time I wasn't sure if I was doing them correctly. But Mrs. Chase spent more time frowning over other people's typewriters working out problems than she did over mine, and I was beginning to develop a smidgen of confidence.

Between all the deciphering of what seemed like nonsense, we had two coffee breaks and a half-hour lunch. Then I'd ride the bus home again, feeling like I needed a week instead of an evening to recover.

Even Pat was cowed by the atmosphere that felt at once urgent and oppressive. I hadn't seen a hint of Mrs. Chase's dimples since the first day. She reminded me of a fierce mother eagle feeding us just enough to keep our fingers busy click clacking away all day long.

I tried to ignore her intense eyes on me as I rolled a fresh sheet of paper into the typewriter. It was the second letter of the day, labeled URGENT, written to a Mr. Flint about base metal procurement. I studied the shorthand script and typed. As usual, I could make no sense of what it was about except that base metal was a critical substance to the operation.

Mr. Dirk, the Executive of Interoffice Communications, appeared at the door, scowling. He glared at us over half glasses as he and Mrs. Chase murmured. I felt my already tense shoulders rise. The last time he'd visited, he'd made me so nervous that I'd made a typing error and had to rip the paper out of the typewriter and start over. I took a deep breath. Today, I'd keep my eyes fixed on my work and type extra carefully, so I didn't repeat that performance. When Mr.

Dirk ducked his low brow at Mrs. Chase and departed, I breathed a sigh of relief.

Mrs. Chase's dimples appeared briefly. "In honor of Friday, we'll break early and have forty-five minutes for lunch."

I collected my lunch box, followed Pat out the door and down the hall to the break room where we found a table to ourselves.

"I'm starved."

Pat whispered. "That Mr. Dirk is creepy the way he scowls around. I'll be amazed if I ever see the guy smile. I hereby christen him, Dirt." She raised her thermos and took a drink. "At least the Queen of Secrecy gave us a few minutes extra for lunch today."

"Yeah. After being trapped in that tiny office all day, even the break room feels like freedom." I unwrapped my bologna sandwich. "And it's Friday. I thought it would never come."

"My cousin Pauly asked if we could meet him at the soda shop in Pasco tomorrow."

"I'd love to meet your cousin." I drank some cold tea from my thermos. "I'm so sick of watching Betty and Doug moon over each other. They've only known each other for three weeks, but he's all she thinks or talks about." The jealousy that swamped my heart was familiar and sharp. Betty had always been first in everything. This time it looked like she would be first in love. I reminded myself that I wanted a Wisconsin man anyway, not somebody who would be off to war and then back to Texas.

"I've heard a lot about war brides lately." Her mischievous eyes crinkled at the edges. "Maybe she'll get married?"

I sighed. "With Betty, nothing would surprise me. So, tell me about your cousin Pauly."

"He's twenty-five and finished a stint in the Army right before the war started. He wants to join the Army again, but if he even suggests it, his mom throws a fit." Pat shook her head. "I don't blame her because his two brothers are fighting in France."

"Is he from White Bluffs too?" I asked.

"Yeah." Pat's eyes got that frozen pond look. "His dad owned the *White Bluffs Times*. He lost that, obviously. Now, he's chief editor at the *Pasco Herald*. Pauly works as a reporter for his dad."

"Does he like being a reporter?" In my junior year, we had studied journalism in English class. It was interesting, but I knew I'd never have the courage to interview strangers.

"Yeah, he's a natural born reporter, extremely nosey and outgoing. Always getting into my business." She crumpled her waxed paper and put it back in her lunch box.

I said, "We'll have to ask Betty if she'll take us to Pasco tomorrow instead of the park. It might hinge on whether Doug can go too."

"When do you get a phone installed at your house?" Pat asked.

"Last night Daddy said that it's still a couple of months away." I screwed the lid onto my thermos.

Pat shrugged. "I guess if we don't make it to the soda shop, Pauly can visit with whoever's around. He's good at that."

"When I learn to drive, we can go wherever we want. Did I tell you my dad is giving me a lesson in the morning?"

"Lucky duck." Pat finished off her sandwich. "I've been begging my mom for driving lessons, but she's always too busy with my little sisters. Hopefully soon."

"Maybe when I get my license, I can teach you how to drive."

"Sure! The blind leading the blind." Pat laughed and looked at her watch. "It's time to get back to the nonsense."

"Yeah." I brushed my hands together and stood up. "At least we only have a few more hours to go."

• • • •

BETTY RUSHED OVER AS we waited for the inter-area bus. "Hooray, it's Friday!" She looked me up and down. "It's a miracle. You didn't get even a tiny spot on your dress today."

Pat bounced her purse against her thigh. "Hello to you too, Betty."

"Oh, hi Pat. I don't know if you've ever noticed how messy Ally is, but it's rare for her to go one day without a spot spoiling her clothes." Betty pointed at my head. "Your hair is standing up, right there."

Irritated, I snapped open the clasp on my purse, applied a coat of Patriotic Red lipstick and smoothed my hair. "You don't need to tell me what to do. I'm an adult, you know."

Pat smiled. "Gee, I didn't know you had two mothers, Ally."

"Yeah, she's bossier than my real mother. Bossy, bossy, bossy." I wiped my glasses on the hem of my dress and brushed away some lint.

Betty stood up taller. "Well, even though we were in the same grade, I'm almost a whole year older. I remember when she was still toddling around in diapers at age two. All she did was cry and make messes."

I laughed. "Yeah, and as soon as you could talk, you were ordering me around."

"You gals sound like sisters."

"So how was work?" Betty pulled us away from the little group of people gathering at the bus stop. "Mine was great. I delivered mail to your office area this week, but you two were nowhere to be seen, probably back in your little hidey hole typing away."

I thought about the confining walls of our office and the repetitive work. I didn't dare tell Betty about how restrictive and boring it was. She would rub my nose in it any chance she got.

Pat looked around to make sure no one was nearby. "Well, I love my job. It's interesting reading all the scientific terms and trying to put the pieces of the puzzle together to figure out what they're creating. I feel very close to understanding it all." She winked at me.

"You don't get to learn anything secret delivering those sealed up letters, do you?"

I laughed, glad to have an ally against Betty. "Yeah, and it's a good thing, because if you had our jobs and learned everything we knew, you wouldn't be able to keep your mouth shut."

"Oh, I get to learn plenty, all right." Betty spoke quietly. "I hear conversations about things everywhere I go. The other day, I heard them talking about product. And I deliver to this place where the word 'danger' is written on a door in giant letters. If I went beyond the front office, I'd lose my job for sure."

"Yeah, either that or die of some sort of poisoning." Pat went serious and speculative. "Maybe that's it," she whispered. "They're developing a secret poison to use on our enemies. Something they can put in the water."

"All right. That's enough, ladies. We're not supposed to talk. Remember? I could be a secret spy and you wouldn't even know it," I said.

"Do you really think there are spies around here?" Betty frowned.

"I'm sure of it." Pat nodded. "Hey, my cousin Pauly wants us to join him tomorrow at the soda shop over in Pasco."

"That sounds fun." Betty's face relaxed into a smile. "I've got the car for the whole afternoon and can drive wherever I want. I'm sure Doug will want to go, too." She opened her compact and reapplied her lipstick. "He's such a dreamboat."

Pat smiled. "Pauly will be glad to meet another guy. Pretty much all the guys he graduated with are in the service."

"Doug will be glad to meet him, too. He gets sick of hanging out with his little brothers." Betty smoothed her hair. "He lives right next door to Ally. Did you know that?"

"Yeah, I've heard all about that lots of times now." Pat said.

I rolled my eyes and changed the subject. "Tell us about the recreation hall. I heard they have all kinds of fun things going on there."

Pat nodded. "Bowling is a blast."

"That sounds fun." I had never had much opportunity to play sports, but bowling was the latest thing. It would be fun to try it, especially with Pat.

"Okay. Let's plan a date."

"How about next Friday night? We can get a hotdog at the bowling alley." Pat smiled.

Betty's eyes were far away. "Maybe. Too bad Doug can't come."

I didn't have to wonder what she was dreaming about. If I went bowling with Pat, I'd be free of Betty for the whole day.

Chapter 10

"Ally, wake up." Timmy's breath smelled like syrup.

"Go away." I snuggled under the covers and tried to recapture my dream of singing a duet with someone who looked vaguely like Gregory Peck.

Timmy pulled back the covers. "Daddy said I could wake you up for your driving lesson."

I sat up. "What time is it?"

He twisted the doorknob back and forth. "It's late. Hurry! Daddy said I get to go too."

"I'll get up if you go away."

He left and slammed the door shut. The light through my curtains was bright, and I glanced at the clock—9:00. Today was my first step toward real freedom. Soon I'd be able to drive anywhere I wanted to go. Going to the soda shop with Pat's cousin later in the day would be fun, too. I sat up, suddenly energized. After the long work week, I needed some fun.

In the bathroom, I removed Timmy's wooden boat from the sink and splashed water on my face. One benefit of having a driving lesson this morning was that I could avoid Betty and Doug. Aunt Edna was so old-fashioned she demanded they never spend time alone. Betty asked me to chaperone them every day after work. I hated watching them moon over each other. Even more than that, I detested feeling like a fifth wheel.

I stared in the mirror at a fresh mosquito bite right in the center of my forehead. Daddy must have missed one of the bloodsuckers on his nightly search-and-destroy mission. I scratched the bite and it bloomed. I shrugged. Pauly was too old to be a love interest, anyway. And, hopefully, my Patriotic Red lipstick would distract everyone I met from the ugly spot. In my bedroom, I searched my closet for my favorite casual dress, a blue muslin. Then I brushed my hair one more time.

Daddy sat at the dining room table reading the *Pasco Herald*. "Good morning, sleepyhead." He took a sip of coffee.

I yawned. "Good morning. I feel like I could sleep forever."

"Yeah, I bet you do. Getting off to work early every morning is tough, even for seasoned veterans like me." He set down the paper. "I'm glad you're up, though. As soon as you finish breakfast, I'll drive us to a parking lot behind an office building close to Riverside Park. You can get the hang of the clutch without a lot of other cars around."

"What's this about Timmy coming along?" I sat down at the table. "You know that won't work."

Timmy hung on my arm. "I get to go if I promise to be quiet in the backseat."

Daddy said, "If you can't stay quiet, we'll come straight home without riding the swings at the park. Is it a deal, little man?"

Timmy nodded, grabbed Daddy's hand, and pulled. "Let's go."

"Whoa, boy. Ally needs to eat her breakfast first." Daddy extracted his hand and turned a page in the newspaper.

Mother appeared at the kitchen door with a plate of pancakes. "Good morning, Ally dear. Timmy, you can bring your Superman comic books in the car." She set the plate in front of me. "I need a few minutes of quiet time this morning."

I buttered my pancakes and poured syrup over them. "Okay. But Timmy, did you hear what Daddy said about being quiet? I don't want to crash because you're distracting me."

Mother sat across from me with a cup of tea. "I think I'm gladder that it's Saturday than you. It's so nice having you two at home." She glanced between us, her brown eyes troubled. As usual, she didn't say what was bothering her–probably because she didn't want to disturb our peace. That was fine with me. Her penchant for calm was welcome in a place where everything else was topsy-turvy.

Mother looked heavenward. "I've been praying that you drive well and trusting God to take care of you."

"And don't forget about trusting me and Daddy. I'm sure he's a good teacher and I can learn things, you know." I polished off my pancakes, irritated. "At least now that I have glasses, anyway." Mother spent too much time praying and not enough time doing. God created us with a brain, and he expected us to use it.

She picked up my plate.

Daddy slurped down his coffee and handed the mug to Mother. "We'll be back in one piece. Don't worry."

"I'm not worried, dear." Mother smiled, then disappeared into the kitchen with the mug and plate.

"Yippee!" Timmy raced to the door with his comic books.

On the front porch, Betty and Doug sat close together, holding hands.

Timmy sang out, "Two little love birds sitting in a tree, K-I-S-S-I-N-G. First comes love. Then comes marriage. Then comes the baby in the baby carriage." He blew a raspberry in their direction and climbed into the backseat.

Daddy stopped to greet them.

Betty seemed unfazed by Timmy's chant. She smiled. "Hello, Uncle Ben. Don't crash into any trees at the park, Ally."

"I won't." I climbed into the passenger seat and slammed the car door behind me.

"Those two are getting awfully chummy." Daddy shook his head. "All right now, Alice, watch. Before I start the car, I put my foot on the brake. Like this." He turned the key in the ignition and the car roared to life.

On the way to the park, he narrated his every move. "The hardest part is getting the clutch and the brake to coordinate. If you don't do it right, you'll lurch forward and stall. We'll concentrate on that today. It takes quite a bit of practice."

Timmy erupted when he saw the park. "Oh yay! There are the swings. Are you done yet?"

Daddy turned toward a large, empty parking lot near the office building. "No, we haven't even started. Remember, if you want to swing when we're done, you're going to have to stay quiet. And hang on tight. It might be a bit of a wild ride."

"Thanks for the confidence booster, Daddy." Excitement and nerves propelled me around the car and into the driver's seat.

I placed my hands on the wheel at the ten and two o'clock position and tried to follow Daddy's instructions. Timmy screamed and laughed as we lurched through the parking lot, turned around, then lurched and stalled all the way back to the starting point. By the time I got the hang of it, I was exhausted.

"That was really hard." I slumped back in the driver's seat. "You park the car. I'm done for the day."

"No, you can park. Parking is not half as hard as learning how to use the clutch." Daddy gestured toward the swings. "It looks like there's a good place right in front."

I felt strung together by nerves as I steered the car to a spot close to the swings.

"Good job. That was nice and smooth." Daddy pointed. "Pull forward right here. Now put on the brake."

When I had parked and pulled the keys out of the ignition, I blew out all the breath I'd been holding. "Whew! I'm exhausted."

Timmy shot out of the car and raced to the swings. "Push me, Daddy."

"Ally learned how to drive. Now you need to learn how to pump so you can swing all by yourself." Daddy gave Timmy a push and then began to teach him how to pump his legs.

I settled on a picnic bench in the warm sun. After all the dust, the grassy park was a peaceful oasis. I took a deep breath to relieve my tension. If only I could travel back in time twelve years when the most important thing was learning how to pump a swing. Adulthood was a lot more complicated than I'd thought it would be when I was six and dreaming about marrying my knight in shining armor. He would whisk me away to a home three doors down from my parents' house where I'd live happily ever after.

"Ally, look how high I can fly!" Timmy pumped the swing higher and higher.

Daddy settled on the bench next to me. "Now that Mother's not around, tell me about your first few weeks of work."

I sighed. "I'm assuming you had to sign the document about secrecy too?"

He nodded. "Yes."

"The idea that I could end up in jail was a bit troubling, but after I started typing it doesn't seem like I'm going to be learning any important secrets, anyway. It's all pretty boring stuff like wiring orders and metal production." I yawned.

Daddy sucked on his empty pipe. "Don Drake, a friend of mine, disappeared just last week. I'm not too surprised. He always asked too many questions. I didn't report him, but somebody must have." Daddy shrugged, looking uncomfortable. "Don was a great guy and I know he wouldn't have left without saying goodbye unless he was forced out."

"Do you think he went to jail?" Despite the warm air, I shivered.

"Maybe, or he may have just made them uncomfortable, and they let him go. You need to be careful what you speak and who you speak to about it." Daddy's eyes were serious.

"Betty and Pat and I have been wondering what it's all about. But we talk only when no one else is around."

Daddy looked worried. "Don't do it. It's not worth even discussing theories about it. You never know how someone might interpret your conversation if they overheard."

"Don't worry. I won't get in trouble." I sighed. From now on when Pat and Betty speculated about the reasons for all the secrets, I'd walk away. Daddy was right. It wasn't worth the risk.

"Watch this!" Timmy jumped out of the swing and rolled on the grass.

Daddy clapped. "Yay! Good job, Timmy." He stood up. "We'd better get back to the house. I've got some yard work to do. Do you want to drive home, Ally?"

"No more driving for today. I'm tired."

"I get to sit in the middle." Timmy smelled like cut grass as he scrambled over me to the center seat and squirmed his hot little body close.

At home, Mother met us in the living room with a dust cloth in hand. "How did it go?"

"I stalled the car a few times, but I got the finally hang of it." I smiled. For the rest of the weekend, I'd pretend along with Mother that life here was sweeter than pie. It would be a nice break.

Timmy said, "You should have been there. I learned to pump and even jumped out of the swing all by myself."

"Well, good for you." Mother enveloped him in a hug.

He squirmed out of her grasp. "But watch out, because Ally is going to jail if she keeps talking about the secrets."

"Timothy. Don't tell tales now." Daddy's voice was stern.

I tried to laugh. "You're funny, Timmy."

Mother frowned. "Timmy, you're such a silly boy. Ally is a good girl. There's no reason she'd go to jail."

Daddy forced out a laugh and wandered toward the kitchen. "Ally is the best girl ever."

"Soon you can drive us to the store so we can go shopping, Ally dear. Go upstairs and rest for a while if you want. Lunch will be ready in about half an hour." She followed Daddy into the kitchen.

• • • •

"LET'S GRAB THAT TABLE quick." Pat hurried to a large corner booth in the crowded soda shop. Someone put money in the jukebox and Duke Ellington poured out.

Betty and Doug slid into the booth together. "Ally, you can sit next to us. There's plenty of room." Betty snuggled next to Doug, and he draped his arm around her shoulder. I sat down and there was still a wide expanse of wooden bench between us.

Pat sat across the table and trained her eyes on the door. She glanced at her watch. "Pauly said he'd be here at two-thirty." Her eyes lit up and she jumped to her feet. "Over here!"

A man with wavy brown hair, thick glasses with black frames, and deep laugh lines along the sides of his mouth waved at Pat. He traveled across the room, speaking to someone at almost every table. Finally, he slid onto the seat next to Pat and his laugh lines disappeared in a wide grin.

Pat grabbed his arm and introduced Doug and Betty.

Pauly reached across the table to shake Doug's hand. "Hello, Paul Rodgers. Nice to meet you, Doug and Betty."

"And this is Alice, my friend and coworker that I've told you so much about."

His brown eyes were warm as toast, his hand rough and hard when I shook it, as if he'd done manual labor before writing for the *Herald*. With two slightly different-sized brown eyes, he wasn't handsome, but he exuded warmth and charm. His smile was electric. "Oh, so you're Ally the *Wiscaansin* girl." He spoke the word Wisconsin in an exaggerated Midwest accent. "Do you mind if I call you Ally Oop for short?"

I laughed. "Ally Oop is fine." I felt myself color under his friendly attention and forced myself to hold his warm gaze for a few seconds. "I, I enjoy working with Pat. She's a lot of fun."

"My baby cousin can be a pain. But most of the time, she's all right." He put his arm around Pat's shoulders and hugged.

Pat grinned up at him. "Speaking of a pain. Pauly is always sticking his nose in my business."

"What can I say? Minding your business is a part of mine." Pauly glanced around for a waitress. "How about a couple of large fries and some sodas? I'm buying." He waved to get her attention.

"You don't need to buy." Doug set his wallet on the table. "Let's go Dutch."

"No, I insist." Pauly said.

A noodle-thin waitress showed up at the table with an order book in hand. "What'll ya have?"

Paul said. "Hi, Marlene. I'll have a Pepsi. And we'll have two large orders of fries with catsup."

After everyone had given their drink orders, Betty asked, "Do you like to be called Pauly or Paul?"

"Paul is how I'm known to everyone except family. But hey, you can call me Pauly." He glanced at me. "I hope we can be friends. It's been boring around here since I got home from my stint in the Army. The war started, and all the guys close to my age were drafted or joined up."

Doug leaned forward. "I'm here to help my family settle, and then I'm off to join up too. I can't wait."

Betty stuck her bottom lip out and grabbed his hand.

"I guess I should say until just lately." His voice trailed off as he looked into Betty's eyes. He shook himself as if to clear his head and turned back to Pauly.

Pauly's eyes twinkled as he looked back and forth between the two of them. "I've got two brothers fighting in France right now, and my mom has made it clear to me and to the government that since I've already served, that's enough for one family." He shrugged. "I hate missing out on the action."

The waitress brought plates of fries and drinks to the table. "So, you work as a reporter for the *Pasco Herald*?" Betty asked.

"Yeah. I like talking to people and my dad needs the help."

Betty said, "It must be interesting to work as a reporter. I'm happy to help the war effort as a messenger." I expected her to preen a bit, but her hands were wrapped tightly around Doug's.

"A messenger? What does that entail?" Pauly listened intently as Betty explained her job. When she finally stopped talking, he said, "So, Doug, it sounds like you're from the south."

"Yeah. Houston, Texas. My dad moved out here for a job. He lost his construction business at the beginning of the Depression. Since then, things have been pretty tough."

Pat said, "Yeah. I guess it's been tough for all of us."

Pauly nodded. Betty talked on and on about how great it was in Sheboygan.

When she wound down, Pauly looked at me. "So, what do you miss most about *Wiscaansin*, Miss Ally Oop?"

I shrugged, feeling on the spot, but thrilled by his attention. "I lived in Sheboygan all my life, so it's hard to decide what I miss the most." I stopped to think. "I guess my grandparents. And of course, in Wisconsin we had no boiling temperatures, coyotes, rattlesnakes, or blinding dust storms." I touched the bite on my forehead, feeling self-conscious. "How about you? You must miss White Bluffs like Pat does."

His brown eyes turned serious. "Yeah. It's been rough. Especially not understanding why we lost our homes." He took off his glasses and rubbed his eyes. "Right after my dad took over the *Herald*, some military policemen came into the newspaper and warned him against printing anything about The Hanford Engineer Works.

Including the railroad expansion and all the goods shipped into the area. If we don't comply, we'll get hit with a big fine or worse."

He sighed. "A while back, I took off my reporter badge and started loitering near the gates to the 700 Area in hopes of figuring things out. I wasn't going to print anything, mind you. I was just curious. But the feds noticed, and they've banned me from anywhere near there. I tell you, there's something extraordinary going on."

Betty said, "Yeah. There's no doubt about it—"

"Excuse me." Daddy's warnings blazed in my mind. I didn't dare risk talking about secrets. I slipped into the bathroom, used the toilet, and then examined the mosquito bite in the mirror. It looked even more red than when I left home. And now I had another red spot, except this one was catsup on my dress. I wet a paper towel and rubbed until it was light pink. Hopefully, Betty wouldn't notice. If she did, she'd announce it to the whole restaurant.

Thankfully, when I got back to the table everyone was laughing and Betty barely glanced my way as I slid onto the seat.

Pat said, "Too bad, Ally. You just missed a Pauly joke."

"A Pauly joke? How about another?" I asked.

Pauly glanced at his watch. "How about a rain check on that? It's already three-thirty, and I promised my Dad I'd mow the lawn this afternoon. Afternoon is running out."

Pat laughed. "Pauly, the procrastinator. Your mom is probably stewing about now, wondering if you're ever going to get it done."

"Hey, nobody ever said I was perfect." Pauly stood up and smiled at everyone around the table. "Let's do this again."

"Yeah, this was fun," Doug said, and we all started toward the door.

Pat got up. "I'm going home to visit my family for a while. I'll see you gals Monday morning bright and early. Bye, Doug. Nice meeting you."

Out on the street, the sky to the southwest was dark and ominous. I held my purse tightly in dread as a hot blast of wind and stinging dust slammed us.

"Dust storm!" Pauly put a protective arm around Pat's shoulder and hurried her toward his car.

Betty, Doug, and I raced to the old red Ford. A small tree waved frantically in a nearby church yard as I climbed into the backseat and slammed the door. Betty jumped in the front and squealed as Doug threw himself into the seat next to her. "So much for fun!" She ran her hand through her windblown mop and steered us onto the darkening street.

"Yeah. Hang on. It's going to be a rough ride." Doug's knuckles were white as he clung to the top of the front seat.

The bridge over the Columbia River turned into a tightrope as wind buffeted, forcing us closer to the edge. Below us, black water churned with gray foam.

On the highway, sand peppered the car with each blast of wind. Visibility narrowed to the white strips on the sides of the road. Eerie yellow lights of a car traveling in the opposite direction appeared through the veil of dirt.

"That car looks like it's in my lane!" Betty clung to the steering wheel. At the last minute, the oncoming car swerved over and roared past. "Whew. That was a close one."

Doug looked spring loaded as a tumbleweed rolled into view. "Watch out!" The weed clung to the grille and scraped against the road. Finally, a blast of wind sent it spiraling into the sagebrush.

After what felt like hours, Betty parked the car in front of her house and leaned her head against the steering wheel. "That was the hardest thing I've ever done."

"You did good." Doug patted her on the back. "We made it."

I couldn't speak as I pushed the car door open into the wind. Sand stung my eyes as I raced home.

When I burst through the door, Daddy sagged with relief against the countertop. "Thank God. You made it."

"Barely." Suddenly angry, I bolted up the stairs and slammed the bedroom door behind me before he could ask questions. I climbed under the covers and pulled them close to still my trembling.

Danger lurked everywhere in this horrible place and it was all Daddy's fault that we were here in the middle of it. If it wasn't secrets, spies, and the threat of jail, it was life-threatening car rides through blinding storms.

I hummed tunelessly to drown out the sound of the wind blasting the side of the house and tried to think of good things. There was Pat, the soda shop, and my success on the job. And there was Pauly. He was too old to be a boyfriend, but his gentle teasing and friendliness had created a shiny spot in my heart that no dust could dim.

Tomorrow we'd have to clean from dawn to dusk on our supposed Sunday of rest. I couldn't pretend everything was sweeter than pie, like Mother. But at least, the hope of more fun times with my new friends glimmered just beyond the wreckage.

Chapter 11

Pat opened the bowling alley door. "Here we are." A low rumble punctuated by a chorus of cheers greeted me as my eyes adjusted to the dim light. The smell of fried food caused my mouth to water as I followed Pat to the food counter. "I'm starved," she said. "Let's get some hot dogs and Cokes before we find the gals."

I stood in line with Pat, grateful for my first Betty-free social event. Hopefully, I'd be able to escape her shadow and make my own new friends.

Pat turned to me with a grin. "Pauly said he really had fun on Saturday."

I felt a tiny thrill at the mention of Pauly and turned away so Pat couldn't read my feelings. "I had a good time too." Thankfully it was our turn to order, and I stepped eagerly to the counter.

Hotdog and Coke in hand, I followed Pat to the only group of women in the bowling alley.

Pat said, "Hello, everyone. I want you to meet my friend Ally. Ally, these are my friends and bunk mates." She gestured around the circle of smiling faces.

I recognized the square jawed woman with a red bandana tied around her hair. "Hi, Annette. We met the day we were applying for jobs."

"Oh yeah. I remember you and your cousin." Annette grinned.

I smiled back, hopeful that she'd see me for myself instead of as an appendage to Betty.

Pat and I wolfed down our hot dogs as they took turns warming up. Bowling didn't look too hard. Just step to the line and roll the ball down the lane to topple the pins.

Pat said, "The winner is the one who knocks down the most pins. Annette keeps score. You'll get the hang of it as we go along."

After we'd finished eating, she said, "Come on, Ally. Let's go find a ball and shoes."

We stopped at a rack of balls, and she helped me find one that wasn't too heavy and fitted to my fingers. "You have tiny feet. What size do you wear?" Pat led me to a rack of shoes against the wall.

"A six. Don't you think it's nasty putting on shoes that a hundred other people have already worn?" I looked at the rack of two-toned brown shoes with distaste.

She handed me a pair. "Nah, don't worry about it. They spray something in them to keep them sanitized."

The longer I watched bowling, the more it reminded me of school. Everyone critiqued your performance and tallied your grade on a score sheet. You were good or bad based on how many points you got. Too soon it was my turn, and I stepped to the line feeling jerky and uncoordinated. "I've never done this before."

"Don't worry. You'll get it." Annette showed me how to hold, swing and release the ball while stepping to the line.

I clumsily executed my first swing and rolled a gutter ball. My face heated.

Pat joked. "Ally, with your name, you should be extra good at keeping your ball in the alley and out of the gutter."

The gals laughed and yelled encouragement as I tried again. The ball rolled slowly down the lane before plopping into the gutter. "No!" I laughed.

"You'll get the hang of it." Annette took her place at the line, then executed a perfect swing. The pins exploded and scattered. "Strike!"

Pat said, "No one can beat Annette. I always come in next to last." She got up to bowl and laughed as the pins cascaded into each other as if in slow motion.

Her laughter abruptly disappeared. "Oh, no. It's the slinking lurker, two lanes over."

Annette glanced his way. "Uh-oh, it's the Coyote. I heard a rumor that Wanita was his latest victim."

"Who are you talking about?" When I looked, it was immediately apparent who the Coyote was. He reminded me of the coyote I'd seen in the encyclopedia Britannica. His long, pointed nose jutted above his receding chin. Sideburns stuck out against the sides of his face in brown plumes. I shivered when he glared at me with shadowed eyes.

"His real name is Bart Bundy. He's Exhibit A for why we need barbed wire around the barracks." Pat stood to the line. "Rumor is, he's always on the hunt for any prey he can get."

Annette frowned. "Just stick in groups. It's the girls who drink a bit too much at the dances who really get in trouble."

When it was my turn again, self-consciousness tripped my movements, and I swung the ball clumsily. It rolled slowly down the lane and picked off one end pin. I laughed but stopped short when I saw the Coyote leering my way with a grin that exposed a jumble of crooked teeth.

• • • •

WHEN WE FINALLY STEPPED outside, I was surprised to see the sun burning on the horizon like an electric beach ball. I looked at my watch. "Oh, no! I've got to hurry." I had lost track of time. Hopefully, Daddy wouldn't be too upset.

"It was nice seeing you again, Ally." Annette headed toward a bus at the front of the line.

"Oh, you too! I'm so glad to meet you all." I waved to my new friends. Despite the disaster that bowling had been for me, I enjoyed getting to know them. Especially without Betty around to overshadow me.

Pat called to them as she pulled me toward the front of the bus line. "Ask the driver to wait for me. I'm going to walk Ally to her bus. Got to stick together, you know." At the last bus, she released my arm. "Here's the South Stops bus. See you bright and early Monday morning." She waved and hurried away.

"Bye!" I climbed the steps into the vehicle.

The unfamiliar bus driver's uniform looked starched and brand new. "Where do you want to get off?"

"Casey and Douglas Streets, please." I was surprised to see that the bus was almost empty and settled next to the aisle near the driver. I leaned my head against the seat in front of me, exhausted.

I heard a shout through the open door, "Hey, Bundy, where are you going? Our bus is this way."

"Just taking a joy ride." The Coyote's hard colorless eyes glanced my way as he slunk aboard and settled across the aisle from me. The bus lurched into motion.

I clutched my purse to my chest as armor and stared straight ahead, suddenly missing Betty's large bossy presence. I shot up a prayer, every nerve in my body on high alert.

"Hey—Ally, isn't it? Are you new around here?"

The Coyote had a Wisconsin accent. I kept my eyes glued out the window and pretended not to hear. What a cruel joke. The only guy I'd met out here from my home state happened to be a predator. The sun dropped into a layer of clouds and turned a dark angry red.

He took on a chatty tone. "I heard you talking to your friends. You sound like you're from Wisconsin, too." When I didn't speak, he growled, "You deaf or something?"

The bus driver spoke sharply. "Hey, the lady is riding alone. Maybe she doesn't talk to strangers. Back off or I'll tell my supervisor."

Instead of thanking the bus driver, I opened my purse with shaking fingers, dug around for a hat pin, and planned my exit. If the Coyote followed me off the bus and tried to grab me, I'd have something to stab him with. I'd scream bloody murder, too. The whole neighborhood would hear and come running.

Finally, the bus turned the corner onto my street. I lurched to my feet, gripping the hat pin and the seat in front of me. When we came to a complete stop, I bolted out the door.

Was he following? I panicked, imagining his coyote breath on my neck as I hurried into the street.

Timmy careened to a stop on his bike. "Ally! It's late and Daddy is mad. You'd better hurry."

"Timmy!" I'd never been so glad to see him in my life.

"Let's race."

I didn't need to be coaxed. My black work pumps pinched my toes as I ran toward the glowing lights of home. As the bus roared past, the Coyote leered at me out the window. I shot onto the porch and through the door, breathing hard.

Timmy followed on my heels. "You're fast, Ally."

Daddy looked up with a frown. "It's too late and dark to be riding the bus home, even if it is full of people. Next time, be here earlier, or I won't give you another driving lesson."

My heart hammered so hard I was sure Daddy could hear it. Mother too, if she'd been paying attention. I made a show of casually reclining in the overstuffed chair and clutched my hands together. My voice came out reedy and thin. "Don't worry, Daddy. I didn't realize what time it was. I won't be this late again."

Mother didn't miss a stitch in the sock she was darning. "Did you have a nice time dear?"

"Yeah, I met some nice gals, but I don't like bowling much." Going to a dance was something I'd never do either if I was going to be stalked by guys like the Coyote. I felt slightly dizzy as I stood.

Clenching his empty pipe in his teeth, Daddy frowned. "Are you sure you're okay? You look like you've seen a ghost."

"I'm just awfully tired. It's been a long week. I'm going to bed."

"Okay, dear." Mother smiled at me over her darning.

In the comfort of my room, I sank onto my bed, suddenly limp with gratitude for the bus driver's rescue. And for Timmy showing up on his bike to escort me home.

I stretched and took a deep breath. There was no need to worry about the Coyote or guys like him. From now on, I'd forget about the recreation center unless Betty was with me. Unfortunately, that meant I was still stuck to her like peanut butter on bread.

Chapter 12

I sat down at the break table, glad that Mary had some sort of typing problem to work out with Mrs. Chase so I could talk to Pat alone. I unwrapped my sandwich. "The Coyote followed me home on the bus after bowling. It was so creepy." I shivered, just thinking about it. "He told his friend he was going on a joy ride and then sat right next to me and tried to talk. I ignored him. The bus driver finally told him to leave me alone. But he saw where I live."

"Oh, no!" Pat's open mouth revealed a bite of sandwich inside. "That snake. I wish they would get rid of him." Her frown was sharp. "I've heard that women have complained about him to the authorities, but all they do is pen us up in with barbed wire."

I nodded. "I've decided I don't want to go to the recreation center from now on unless I can get Betty to join me. I'm so disappointed." I took a tiny bite of my tuna sandwich. "Maybe you can ride home with me on Friday nights after work sometimes. My bed isn't very big, but I can sleep on the floor. We have lots of extra blankets. I know my mom would love to cook for you."

"Home cooking sounds great. But I'll sleep on the floor. I can sleep anywhere at any time." Pat's elfin eyes squeezed together in a twinkle. "Pauly will be happy that you don't want to spend all your time at the recreation hall. He really likes you."

I nodded, suddenly feeling shy. "Pauly was fun." The mention of him opened that shiny spot in my heart again. "Can you come home with me tomorrow?"

"Does Saturday work? I'd rather spend the night when I'm not so exhausted from work. Pauly could drop me off and pick me up the next day."

"Great. I have to ask my mom, but I'm sure it will be fine."

Pat nodded. "I can't wait to get away from the barracks–or prison, as it's commonly known."

"You can go to church with us too, if you don't mind missing your own."

Pat's tiny jaw jutted out. "After we left White Bluffs, I only went to church because my mom made me. And since I moved into the barracks, I haven't gone at all. Too sore at God, I guess." Her elfin eyes flashed with anger. "Who knows if he even exists? And if he does, he doesn't care much about me and my family." She shrugged. "But going to church with you will be better than the alternative."

I was shocked into silence. Pat's anger at God was understandable. Having doubts about God, too. But not going to church? In Sheboygan, church was expected, and everyone went except the town drunk. His wife was always making excuses for him, but everyone knew the real reason.

Pat said, "Pauly is a church goer. Maybe he can join us and take me home when it's over."

Mrs. Chase and Mary settled at the lunch table and sighed in unison.

Mary opened her lunch box. "I made Bobby's favorite apple pie last night." She held it up so we could admire it. "He loves cinnamon crumble topping."

Mrs. Chase said, "I haven't made a pie since last Christmas."

The conversation centered on dessert recipes until everyone finished eating.

Mrs. Chase glanced at her watch and stood up. "I'm going to run to the restroom and then we'll get back to work."

When Mary disappeared into the work room, Pat said, "Maybe we can figure out something fun to do on Saturday night too. I know that Pauly would love it."

"That would be great." I grinned, excited at the thought of spending time with Pauly again. Pat closed her eyes and splayed out in her chair as I finished my lunch.

When Mrs. Chase exited the restroom and stood silently behind Pat, I quickly gathered up my lunch things. "I guess we'd better get going."

Pat groaned and stage-whispered, "Aw, do I have to? The queen of secrecy makes it impossible to learn what I'm dying to know, and I'm bored out of my skull. If I didn't need the money, I'd quit so fast."

Helpless to alert her to Mrs. Chase's presence, I tried to make light of it. "Ha! Pat, you're funny."

Mrs. Chase laid her hand on Pat's shoulder. "If you'd like to quit or find another job, please feel free. There's nothing holding you here, you know."

Pat started and blushed to the roots of her hair. "Oh, Mrs. Chase, I'm sorry. I was just blowing off steam. I didn't mean a word of it, really. I like working here with you. Sometimes I just wish I was back in White Bluffs during happier times. That's all." Tears spilled down her cheeks.

"Ally, you go ahead and get busy. I'll be there soon." Mrs. Chase sat down with Pat.

Mrs. Chase wouldn't fire her for just wondering about secrets, would she? Who could work here and not wonder about what we were doing? Besides, Pat was just joking around. Mrs. Chase just had to understand.

Back in the workroom a fluorescent light quivered and buzzed. Poor Pat. First, she lost her home. Then she had to move into the horrible barracks and live behind barbed wire with a bunch of strangers. She always appeared so cheerful. But if her tears were any indication, all the changes and challenges must be weighing heavier on her than I'd thought.

Pat's eyes were red from crying when she returned to the workroom. She blew her nose before rolling a piece of paper into her typewriter. I pushed my glasses firmly onto my nose. If Pat was fired, we'd stay friends no matter what. I knew where her parents lived. I'd chase her down if I had to.

When the clock slid to 5:00, Mrs. Chase stopped by my desk to pick up my completed briefs. After glancing through them, she winked at me. "Thanks for all your hard and accurate work, Alice. I'll see you in the morning."

I felt myself puff and beam at her compliment. "Thank you, Mrs. Chase." I resettled my glasses on the bridge of my nose, grabbed my jacket, and hurried out the door.

I ran to catch up to Pat, who was plodding toward the bus as if she carried the weight of a typewriter on her shoulders. "Wow. I really messed up. Nothing like spilling my real guts in front of the boss."

"Did you get fired?" A drip of rain spit out of the dark sky and landed on my cheek.

"No, but she wants me to retake confidentiality training next week at some other office." She moaned. "If I have to hear it all over again, I'm going to throw up."

Relief flooded through me. "You were just being your funny self. It's too bad you had to do it in front of Mrs. Chase." I chuckled to try to make light of it. "At least you weren't fired. The extra training won't be so bad. Just spend the time daydreaming about all the handsome guys you'll meet when the war is over."

Pat nodded. "I'm the best at daydreaming. In fact, let's do a little daydreaming about Saturday night. What do you want to do?"

"Betty might be able to drive us to the soda shop."

Pat shrugged. "Just hanging around your house with your little brother sounds good to me right about now."

I smiled at Pat. "Ha! You'll be glad to get away from Timmy by Sunday. He can be a real pest. But staying home is fine with me. I can use a break from men like the Coyote and dust storms that nearly kill us. We can listen to records and Betty keeps talking about playing a game of Canasta."

A fun night safe at home with Pat sounded perfect. Especially since I'd get to see Pauly again.

Chapter 13

Saturday after lunch, I carried my plate to the sink. "Pat should be here any minute." I had spent the morning cleaning my room and making it just perfect for her arrival. Hopefully, Betty would be somewhere far away with Doug.

Daddy's eyes glinted at Mother. "We're really looking forward to meeting her. And her cousin, too. Why don't you invite them both over tomorrow for Sunday dinner."

"What a wonderful idea." Mother filled the kitchen sink with hot water and soap and slipped in the lunch dishes.

"I will invite Pat, but I hardly know Pauly." It felt too soon in our friendship to invite him over for Sunday dinner.

"Don't worry about it. He's Pat's cousin, isn't he? Besides, it's a good way to get to know him better." Daddy tamped the tobacco in his pipe and lit a match.

I opened the refrigerator and examined the parcel wrapped in butcher paper. "There isn't enough pork."

"The three of us can fill up on potatoes and gravy and applesauce." Daddy said, as if it was settled.

"I knew everything was going to be just so. Timmy has a friend. And now you have two friends." Mother dried a wet plate and set it in the cupboard.

I sighed. "Pat and Pauly were both kicked out of White Bluffs when the government claimed their land for the war effort. It's interesting to hear their story, but it makes them sad. Please don't ask questions."

Daddy nodded and clenched his pipe in his teeth. "I've not met anyone from White Bluffs yet."

Betty shoved open the back door. "Is Pat here yet?"

"I thought you and Doug were going shopping or something." I hurried into the living room. If only Betty would disappear. Poof, like magic. I peered through the front window. A government moving truck drove past and turned at the stop sign.

"Doug has to help his dad fix the car. They took off to the gas station a while ago. Is Pauly going to stay?" Betty opened the curtain wider and looked up and down the empty street.

"Mother and Daddy want me to invite him over for Sunday dinner." Despite Betty hanging around to spoil things, excitement and nerves flooded me. Was it because I was terrified to invite Pauly for dinner? Or because I would see him again? Maybe a little bit of both, I admitted to myself.

Betty looked sideways at me. "Hmmm. Your face is flushed. Is it because of Pauly? He reminds me of Abraham Lincoln, you know. Kind of homely like that. And he's old. But his personality and smile are great."

An old Abraham Lincoln! I wanted to swat Betty like a mosquito. "No. I'm heading back to Wisconsin as soon as I make enough money."

"You could do worse, though. Doug and I both really like him."

"Who says he likes me anyway?" I resettled my glasses and inspected my dress for spots.

Timmy and Jimmy rode their bikes into the yard and dropped them on the grass. Jimmy scrambled onto the porch and disappeared next door. Timmy burst inside, his cheeks rosy.

"Mother is going to make cookies. I'm sure she'd like some help," I said.

Timmy raced toward the kitchen, and I breathed a sigh of relief. If only I could send Betty off on the cookie-baking mission, too. "Don't you dare say anything to Pat about me and Pauly. I would die if he knew we were even thinking about it. We're just friends."

When Pauly's blue Ford pulled up at the curb, Betty pushed past me out the door.

Pat jumped out of the car holding a small suitcase. "Hi!"

Betty raced down the steps and grabbed it. "You made it. We're so glad you're here."

I followed her out to the sidewalk. "Hi, Pat. It's good to see you."

Pauly stepped out of the car and grinned. "Hi there, Ally Oop."

"Hi Pauly. Thanks for bringing Pat." I smiled up at him. He was taller than I remembered, but he looked nothing like Abraham Lincoln. His warm brown eyes glowed as he looked at me, and I felt a little flutter of pleasure.

Betty swung Pat's bag. "Paul, it's great to see you again. Doug is helping his dad fix the car and they took off to the gas station a while ago. Otherwise, he'd be here too. I know he's anxious to see you."

"Hello, Betty. Maybe we can all meet up at the soda shop again soon."

"My mother asked me to invite you both for Sunday dinner after church tomorrow. Maybe you can see Doug then." I avoided his eyes. "Or maybe you already have something else planned?" My question came out as a squeak.

Betty interrupted before they could reply. "You should say yes. Aunt Mary is the best cook ever."

A mischievous smile played on Pat's elfin face. "That sounds delicious. What do you think, Pauly?" She winked at him.

Pauly's grin widened. "I don't have anything planned for tomorrow after church and I'd love to eat Sunday dinner with you all."

I felt a rush of pleasure. "Fair warning. My little brother will try to trap you into playing a game of Monopoly." I held his warm gaze for a second.

"Oh yeah. I'll play Monopoly just so long as I get to be the car," he said.

I laughed. "You might have to fight Timmy for that." Maybe Timmy would have a new friend, too.

Pat started up the steps. "I'll see you at church tomorrow then, Pauly."

Betty gave him the church address and detailed instructions about how to get there from the main road into town. "We'll save a place for you. We usually sit in the back."

Grinning, he started his car and glanced between me and Pat. "Sounds good. You two don't tell too many girly secrets now."

A bubble of happiness and anticipation rose as I waved him off and turned to Pat. "All right, let's put your suitcase in my bedroom." I reached for it.

Betty grabbed it out of my hand. "I wish I could come for dinner tomorrow, too. It sounds like fun."

I ignored her, thankful that there wasn't enough meat.

Pat surveyed the living room. "Just like I thought. It's a palace."

Timmy came barreling into the living room. "Hi!"

Daddy followed. "Welcome, Pat. This is Timmy. You can call me Ben." Mother appeared in her apron. "And this is Mary. We're glad to meet you. Let's get you settled in Ally's room." He took Pat's bag.

I sighed as Daddy, Betty, and Timmy trooped ahead of us up the stairs. Timmy stood around my room, gesturing as if belonged to him. "This is our record player, and this is the bed where you'll sleep tonight. And Ally gets to sleep right here." He pointed to a makeshift bed of blankets and pillows on the floor.

"No, no. I'm not going to take your bed, Ally. The floor is my favorite." Pat said.

I moved Pat's bag to my bed. "We'll see about that."

"All right, Timmy. Let's go so the girls can sort things out." Daddy hefted him onto his shoulders. "We'll call you when it's dinner time."

Pat paced around the room. "Wow. It's amazing that you have your very own room." She peered out the window.

Betty stood next to her and pointed. "And that's my house. You know Ally and I traveled here together on the train. I'd like you to come over and meet my parents, too."

I fanned out a selection of my favorite records on the bed. "What do you want to listen to?"

Pat chose my favorite. "Boogie Woogie Bugle Boys of Company B." I set the needle and turned the volume all the way up. Betty talked over the music, dominating the conversation. Finally, I looked at my clock in mock surprise. "Ooo! Look at the time. It's three o'clock. I wonder if Doug is home yet?"

"Oh, I can't believe it's so late. Let's play Canasta after dinner." Betty opened the door and the smell of freshly baked chocolate chip cookies wafted into the room.

Timmy yelled from downstairs, "Ally! The cookies are done."

• • • •

THE NIGHT LIGHT IN my room glowed softly, barely illuminating Pat's blanketed form on the floor. "Are you sure you're comfortable down there? I really don't mind giving up my bed for the night."

"I'm supremely comfortable." Pat nestled deeper under the covers. "I had fun with your family."

I could tell both Mother and Daddy liked her. And she hadn't seemed to mind Timmy hanging all over her like a monkey. Betty and Doug sat so close that I thought they might merge into one when we played Canasta.

"Timmy drives me crazy sometimes. My mom, who mostly lives in a dream world, lets him run wild and thinks he's perfect just the way he is. I hope he didn't bug you too much." I rolled over and sighed.

"No, he was fun. Your mom doesn't seem that dreamy." Pat said.

"Oh, she can be. When my seventh-grade teacher told her I needed glasses, she didn't do anything except pray about it for years. I believe in prayer too, but sometimes God expects us to act." I explained how everyone in school thought I was stupid.

"Oh wow. It's hard to believe that anyone could ever think you were stupid." Pat yawned. "I think my mom would have put me in glasses when I was still in diapers if she thought it would make me smarter. She was always after me to study harder and do better in school."

I caught her yawn. "You're lucky."

"I didn't feel lucky. I could never please her."

"That must have been hard. Do you still feel like that?" My eyes burned as I stared at the ceiling.

"Yeah. Now she's after me to find a husband and settle down. It's like she doesn't even realize there's a war on and very few decent guys around."

"Hmmm. Mothers can be hard. Mine still does everything for me. If I actually had to cook for myself, I'd probably starve to death." I pulled the blanket over my head. "And I still live in fear of losing my glasses and everyone thinking I'm stupid."

"Nah. You're Mrs. Chase's golden girl." Pat said. "She's too smart to ever think you're stupid."

I opened the blanket and took a breath of cool air. "Yeah. Typing things I don't understand is starting to bore me to tears, but at least it's easy." Certain words I did recognize–like Manhattan. But it wasn't referring to New York, I was sure.

Pat groaned. "That reminds me of the horrible confidentiality training I have on Monday. I think it's going to be a bunch of us flunkies who are at risk of losing our jobs if we don't change our ways."

"It's better than being in class with a bunch of scared newbies."

Daddy's snore reverberated through the wall. "Sorry. Daddy gets pretty loud sometimes."

"That's nothing. You should try living in the barracks."

I rolled over and peered at my clock, but it was too dark to see the time.

"Thanks for inviting Pauly for dinner tomorrow." Pat said.

"Pauly is a lot of fun." The shiny space inside reserved for him opened up.

"He likes you too." Pat sat up and looked at me. "He thinks you're cute."

The shiny space grew. "Really? My high school boyfriend dumped me as soon as I got glasses." If Pauly thought I was cute, then maybe there was hope for me after all. When I went back to Wisconsin, I'd find my perfect match.

"Ah, all high school boys are shallow cads. They don't know anything." Pat lay back down. "I wish somebody thought I was cute." She sounded wistful.

"Pat, you are a doll. Just you wait. When the war is over, you're going to meet the perfect guy, fall in love, and live happily ever after." I yawned again and rolled over. "What's your dream guy like?"

Pat didn't hesitate. "He's blond, blue-eyed, sweet, and sort of quiet..." She yawned. Soon I heard regular breathing from the makeshift bed on the floor.

As I drifted off to sleep, pictures of Pauly's warm brown eyes played in my head.

Chapter 14

Betty insisted on crowding into the pew with us, so by the time Pauly got to church, he had to squeeze into the narrow place on the end next to me. There wasn't a breath of space between us even when I squished closer to Pat.

Usually, the pure pleasure of singing drove everything else out of my head, but today I couldn't focus. Pauly exuded warmth and some sort of vibration that made the blood in my veins thrum.

What was wrong with me? Just because he thought I was cute meant nothing. Last night, Pat and I had talked so late that my eyes were puffy in a way that even my glasses couldn't conceal. He might think differently now.

Besides, he wasn't a Wisconsin boy. He was a man who belonged here in this desert wasteland. He'd already served in the Army, and I didn't really know anything about him except for his job title and his cousin. And that he was outgoing and funny. And that he thought I was cute, glasses and all. Out of the corner of my eye, I saw that his face was serious as he listened to Pastor Carver.

I resettled my glasses and tried to focus, too. The Pastor said, "In Isaiah, God tells us to 'Forget the former things, do not dwell on the past. See, I am doing a new thing!'" So, I was supposed to forget Sheboygan? Homesickness made it hard to not dwell on the past, but perhaps moving clear across the country wasn't an accident. Maybe God had brought me to this new place and set Pauly right next to me. I squirmed inside as his nearness overwhelmed my senses.

I tried again to focus on the sermon and failed. After church, I would act cool and composed. Pauly needed to know I thought of him only as a friend. Cool and composed, I rehearsed to myself, as Pastor Carver droned on.

When the service ended, Betty hurried over and led Pat and Pauly into the lobby. She introduced them to the Pastor and everyone else while I stood by with a frozen smile, feeling too shy in Pauly's presence to speak.

Luckily, by the time we got home, I had shaken off the crazy spell sitting so close to him had cast. Cool and composed, I reminded myself, as I opened the door to welcome him. "Hi Pauly. I'm glad you could join us for dinner today."

"You have no idea how glad I am to be here." Pauly stepped into the house and breathed in the scent of Mother's cooking. "It smells delicious."

Pat followed him in, and I couldn't help but notice how especially elfish she looked next to his six-foot frame. "My mom would kill me if I didn't offer to help." She disappeared into the kitchen.

Daddy gestured to the couch. "Welcome, Paul. Make yourself at home. Dinner will be ready in just a few minutes." He lit his pipe and puffed. "So, Alice tells me you lived in White Bluffs before they took it over for the war effort."

Pauly's eyes turned to iron as he tersely responded to Daddy's questions. I cleared my throat and frowned in Daddy's direction. Why hadn't he heeded my advice? I moved to stand near his chair to get his attention. But when neither of them even glanced my way, I sighed and followed Pat to the kitchen.

I almost felt as if we'd all been transported back to Wisconsin when I saw Pat setting our pink-and-white china on the white tablecloth. I glanced out the window. Betty's treeless back yard quickly brought me back to reality.

"Wow. Do you always eat a fancy Sunday dinner? At my house, we were lucky if my mom even cooked a meal after church," she said.

"No. You and Pauly are special guests. Mother loves special guests. My dad, however, is grilling Pauly about White Bluffs. Just what he needs on a lazy Sunday afternoon." I took my glasses off and rubbed my eyes. I should have just butted in and steered the conversation in a different direction.

Mother stuck her head in the dining room. "Alice, dear, please come stir the gravy." She handed me the apron with orange flowers embroidered on the skirt and a wooden spoon. "I'll be watching in case it starts to bubble over. Here's the gravy boat and ladle too. It just needs a couple more minutes." She kept one eye on my stirring as she mashed the potatoes.

Pat stood politely at the kitchen entrance. "Is there anything else I can do to help?"

"You can put food on the table." Mother set a heaping bowl of cinnamon apple sauce in her hands.

"Yum." Pat carried it into the dining room.

"Okay, the gravy should be ready now." Mother hurried out the door with a plate of roast.

A spot of gravy splattered onto my apron as I poured it into the gravy boat. I untied it, hung it on the apron hook near the back door, and then carried the gravy boat to the table.

"Dinner is ready," Mother called.

"Paul, you can sit next to Alice. And Pat, you sit here." Daddy directed everyone to their seats, and we bowed our heads for the blessing. As we prayed our family blessing in unison, I stole a look at Pat. She had an amused smile on her face, and her eyes stood wide open.

I spooned some apple sauce onto my plate. As I passed the bowl to Pauly, I couldn't help but notice his large and capable hands. They seemed to exude masculinity. Suddenly, no longer hungry, I trained my eyes on my plate.

"My mom cooks Italian most nights. I can't remember the last time I had homemade apple sauce. It's delicious," Pauly said.

"Do you have an Italian heritage, Paul?" Daddy cut into his small slab of roast.

I sighed. There he goes again, grilling Pauly as if he were interviewing him for a job. Or as a future son-in-law. A bite of pork roast stuck in my throat, and I coughed so hard my eyes teared up. Everyone looked at me in concern as I took a drink of water. I waved away their attention and wiped my eyes with a napkin. Of course, I had to make a spectacle of myself. I wiped at the specks of saliva on my bodice, embarrassed.

If we all wanted to chase Pauly away, we couldn't have done it more skillfully. I sighed. Maybe it was all for the best if I never saw him again anyway. Soon I'd be on my way home. Far from this creepy place—and from my irritating, interfering parents.

Pauly took a bite of pork roast. "Mm. Betty was right when she told us how wonderful your cooking is, Mrs. Krepsky."

"Oh, thank you. I love cooking and I'm so glad you're enjoying it." Mother's doe eyes were soft with pleasure.

"Our little Ally is learning to cook, too. Someday, she's going to be as good as Mother." Daddy took a bite of mashed potatoes and looked with glowing eyes between Pauly and me.

I stifled a groan of embarrassment. What was he talking about? He knew I didn't know how to cook beyond stirring the gravy with Mother watching, so it didn't burn. Pat kicked me under the table and grinned. I avoided her eyes, so I didn't start laughing nervously and never stop.

Pauly grinned. "Well, if she's half as good as you, I'd say she's an excellent cook." His eyes glinted with humor. "Hey Timmy, have you heard the latest knock-knock joke?"

"What's that?" Timmy sat up on his knees.

"You don't know what a knock-knock joke is? Have you been living under a rock?" Pauly grinned. "Here's how it goes: I say, knock knock, and you say, who's there. Got it?"

Timmy nodded. "Yeah."

"Okay, here we go. Knock-knock."

"Who's there?"

Pauly said, "Amos. Now you say Amos who?"

Timmy said, "Amos who?"

"A mosquito just bit me. Get it? Amos, A mosquito? Ha ha."

Everyone at the table groaned and laughed.

Timmy said, "Do another one."

By the time we'd finished dinner, Pauly's charm had succeeded in relaxing us all. I had almost forgotten Daddy's unfortunate comments and had even been able to eat a few bites of my favorite dinner.

Timmy grabbed Pauly's arm. "Let's play Monopoly!"

Mother started collecting plates. "All right. Daddy can help me in the kitchen while you kids go play." She waved us away.

Pauly smiled in my direction. "I get to be the car."

"No, me!" Timmy yelled.

"I told Betty I'd come and get her and Doug when dinner was done." I fled outside and took a deep breath of cool October air. I could kill Daddy for his lie about my cooking skills. My face burned. What did he think he was accomplishing by that? Now I'd never be able to tell Pauly that I could barely boil water without making Daddy look like a liar.

I pushed open the back door at Betty's house and called. "Come on over. We're starting a Monopoly game."

"It's about time." Betty and Doug appeared in the kitchen, holding hands and threaded themselves outside without breaking contact.

Everyone settled around the dining room table. Betty took over the banker job. Pauly seemed to take exaggerated delight in collecting rent from everyone but me. Whenever I landed on one of his spaces, he apologized sweetly as I forked the money over. Timmy got bored and quit.

The house grew hot and stuffy as the game crawled on. Finally, Pauly stood up. "Hey Doug, I think you won fair and square." He stretched and yawned. "I need to get going. Pat, are you ready?"

"Yeah, I guess it's time to go back to prison. Just let me get my things." Pat disappeared up the stairs while everyone gathered round to say goodbye.

As he was leaving, Pauly took my hand and smiled into my eyes. "Thanks, I really enjoyed today."

That delicious thrumming overwhelmed me at his touch. "You're welcome. It was fun."

"How about the soda shop next Saturday afternoon?" He released my hand and turned to Betty and Doug.

Betty said, "Sounds good."

Pat gave me a hug. "Thanks for everything. This really was fun."

I stood on the porch waving until they were out of sight, then escaped to my room. Instead of being put off by Daddy's unfortunate grilling, Pauly had turned our time together into a delightful afternoon. I lay on my bed, staring at the ceiling and reliving every moment of the day.

Finally, I went into the bathroom to rinse my face in an effort to wash him from my mind. What was I thinking? Not even people as nice as Pauly and Pat could convince me to stay here where secrets, dust storms, and barbed wire reigned. But even as I dried my face with one of Mother's embroidered hand towels, thoughts of Pauly were hooked in my mind like burrs on a sock.

Chapter 15

I yawned and laid my cheek on the break room table.
"Tired?" Pat said.
"Timmy kept kicking me." I closed my eyes.
Pat shook her head. "I thought your dad said he couldn't sleep with you when you were working. Why didn't you just kick him out?"
"I was asleep when he climbed into bed. Then when I woke up and saw he was there, I was too tired to make him go back to his room." I closed my eyes. "At least it's Friday and I can sleep in tomorrow."
Pat stirred sugar into her coffee. "You better. Because get this, Pauly found out there's a dance at the Grange Hall in Pasco tomorrow night. He's wondering if we all want to meet him there."
The thought of dancing with Pauly was like a beam of sunshine in my eyes. I sat up. "A dance?"
"It'll probably be mostly a bunch of old farmers. It's their annual fall harvest celebration. But we can make it fun." Pat sipped her coffee.
"Will Pauly bring a date?"
"No dates for Pauly. He broke up with his girlfriend several months ago, and since then he's been avoiding all women. Until now, that is." Pat winked at me.
I shook my head. "We'll see. I'm not sure I want a boyfriend here. I've got my eye on home, you know."
Pat shrugged. "It's just dancing. Doesn't mean you're going to marry him or anything."
"Yeah." I forced myself to eat a few bites of my sandwich. "Who will you dance with?"

"Oh, don't worry about me. I'm used to nobody." Pat tried to sound brave, but I could hear sadness in her voice.

"Maybe someone on leave will be there." I tried to cheer her up.

She shrugged. "Maybe Doug will dance with me once out of pity."

"Betty and Doug will be stuck together like glue." I looked at the clock and put my uneaten sandwich back in my lunchbox. "We better get back to work."

"Is it that time already?" Pat yawned and crumpled her sandwich wrapper. "If for some reason you or Betty can't drive us and we don't show up, I guess Pauly will understand." She lamented. "When, oh when, will you get a phone?"

I shrugged and pushed open the office door. The room smelled stale. Fluorescent lights buzzed overhead. Mary was already at her desk, typing. For the past week, she had been cutting her lunch short to get a head start. I had the feeling that she was in competition about who could finish the most correspondences by the end of the day. But most of the time, Mrs. Chase still stopped her own work regularly to point out Mary's mistakes and problem solve.

For me, the job had become so routine that I could almost do it without thinking. And it was a good thing, because thoughts of the dance with Pauly invaded my head like ants at a picnic. If just the touch of his hand sent my heart thrumming, what would full body contact do? I imagined his strong arms holding me on the dance floor. His chest would vibrate with that deep laugh of his. I shook my head.

I was going to have to guard my heart and mind against the thrill of it because I was not staying here in this wasteland. Plus, if we actually danced like Pat seemed to think we would, we'd have to find something to talk about without someone else directing the conversation. We had nothing in common.

Mrs. Chase stopped at my desk. "Are you feeling all right, Alice?"

I snapped to attention. "Yes, I'm feeling fine." I smiled up at her.

"I see you've typed the second paragraph three times. Maybe you're tired?" She smiled kindly at me.

My face heated. "Oh, Mrs. Chase, I'm sorry. My little brother kept me awake last night."

"Can I get you a cup of coffee? I just put on a pot. It should be ready any minute."

"That sounds wonderful. Thank you. I'd like it black." I hated bitter, black coffee, but today, I'd drink it as penance. Plus, it would be the perfect way to remind myself to keep all thoughts of Pauly and the dance at bay.

Pat kicked me from behind and snickered. I shrugged and started retyping the letter about electrical wiring shipments. When Mrs. Chase brought me an office mug full of coffee, I took a sip and winced. Too hot, too bitter—the perfect reminder to focus. I refilled my cup. And then again.

By the time I climbed on the bus to go home, the caffeine had worn off, leaving me limp and wobbly. I slouched into the last seat at the back of the bus, far from Pat and Betty's chatter. The brilliant orange sunset out the window warred with my dark, confused feelings. I wasn't sure I could stand dancing with Pauly tomorrow without my feelings for him getting stronger. And I wasn't going to stay in this snake-and-coyote-filled wilderness. The dance would only make my feelings worse. No better. I closed my eyes in confusion. He was a good guy and I really liked him. But tomorrow I'd pretend to be sick. That would solve everything—at least for the day.

Chapter 16

The next day, Betty burst into my bedroom. "Are you ready for the dance?"

"I'm not going. I have a headache." I lay on my bed and quickly placed a cool rag on my forehead. I thought about the bandstand in Sheboygan with my family and friends gathered for an evening of fun. That was a real dance—not some old Grange dance with a bunch of farmers.

"Oh, come on. I can't if you don't. My mom barely knows Pat and Pauly not at all. She doesn't trust me with Doug alone in a strange place." She pulled on my arm. "Please? You'll feel better if you get up."

"No, go away." I rolled over. I was not going to live forever in this sandy desert where we all worked like slaves for something we didn't understand. Home beckoned. Even after only two meetings, I liked Pauly too much to hurt his feelings. The only way to avoid getting involved was to stay away from him. I'd explain it to Pat. She'd understand.

"Now, let's see. What can you wear to the dance?" I heard Betty open my closet door. My rust chiffon rustled as she pulled it out of the closet. "This is perfect. There are no stains on it or anything." She reached into my jewelry box. "And here's my favorite necklace. It looks wonderful with this dress. So dainty and thin. Remember when you wore this outfit to homecoming with Alfred? You looked pretty without your glasses."

I sighed. Leave it to Betty to remind me that my glasses made me less than desirable.

"But Paul won't care. He wears glasses too. Wouldn't it be interesting if both of us found men way out here in the Wild West?

We could bring them back home with us when the war was over." I felt the bed dip when Betty sat down next to me.

I peeked at the rust chiffon with the capped sleeves hanging on the closet door and closed my eyes. "I'll freeze in that."

"You'll be fine. I'm wearing my long cream-colored evening gown. Looking beautiful is more important than a little chill."

"I think maybe I'm coming down with something."

"I'll get you a nice cup of tea and some honey toast. That will make you feel better." Betty's perfume faded away.

I sat up and pulled my new Ella Fitzgerald record out of its sleeve. Ella had the best voice ever. While they were having fun at the dance, I'd practice singing along. I quickly lay down when I heard Betty's feet on the stairs.

She balanced tea and toast as she pulled the door open with her foot. "Now sit up. I made the tea nice and strong, and I brought you two aspirin." Betty set it on the nightstand, then put her arm around me and lifted me up.

I groaned and sipped down the aspirin. The Wonder Bread toast was golden and covered with dripping honey. I couldn't resist. I took a bite and then another.

"I knew it. You aren't sick. You're just scared. Now sit up on the edge of the bed. I'll fix your hair. When the aspirin starts working, you'll feel fine." Betty sat me up and began pulling out pin curls. "We're going to have so much fun."

• • • •

FROM THE OUTSIDE, THE Grange was a white boxy looking building with a few tiny windows and a single porch light over the doorway. Inside, someone had decorated the edges of the rough wooden floor with hay bales, pumpkins, cowboy hats, and boots. A table against the wall held a display of squash, corn, and other vegetables. Old-fashioned swing music poured out of modern RCA speakers. A few couples swayed around the dance floor.

An older couple dressed in western wear greeted us at the door. "Welcome. Welcome. Hello, Pat. It's good to see you. Harold is home on leave. He'll be here later. I know he'll be glad to see you, too."

Pat smiled and handed over her coat for checking. "I look forward to seeing him again. Mr. and Mrs. Rafe, these are my friends." Pat introduced Betty, Doug and me.

Mr. Rafe took my coat and hung it on a wooden hanger. Suddenly I was freezing and self-conscious with my naked arms and chiffon dress.

Pat grabbed my arm and led me over to the refreshment center. "Mr. and Mrs. Rafe lived in White Bluffs. Harold is two years older than me. He was always a kind of scrawny outcast. I don't think he ever said two words to me the whole time we were in school together. He joined the army right out of high school." She bit into a pumpkin-shaped sugar cookie.

I scanned the room for Pauly, too nervous to eat. Betty and Doug were already dancing so close that I couldn't see light between them. Most in the crowd were in their forties or older. The women wore simple plaid dresses with large petticoats underneath. The men wore cowboy hats and western shirts. My rust-colored chiffon was too formal and out of place. I grabbed my arms to warm up.

"Cheer up. You look like you've come to a hanging instead of a dance." Pat offered me some hot apple cider. "This will warm you up." She looked perfect in her deep green dress with long sleeves and a wide skirt.

"I should never have listened to Betty. I'm freezing."

"Let's go stand by the potbellied stove and watch the dancing." Pat waved at an older lady on the dance floor. "She's my parents' neighbor. I hope my mom and dad don't show up. That will really kill the mood."

A tall man in an army uniform appeared at the door and scanned the room. Mrs. Rafe pointed at Pat.

"Could that be Harold?" Pat stared. "If it is, he's grown five inches and filled out rather nicely."

Pauly ducked in the door behind him, chatted with Mr. and Mrs. Rafe and shook Harold's hand briskly. I felt a combination of dread and excitement as he and Harold started across the room together. My hot cider wobbled, and I spilled a drip on my bodice. "Oh no!" I wiped at it with my hand.

Pat glanced my way. "You'd hardly notice."

Pauly was all grins. "Hey. Look who I found."

"Harold! It's been ages. How have you been?" asked Pat.

He took off his hat and nodded toward Pat. "Hello, Pat."

"Harold, this is Alice, better known as Ally Oop." Pauly turned toward me. "You look gorgeous."

Flustered, I smiled at Harold. "Hello. Nice to meet you." I turned to Pauly and backed up closer to the stove. "Thank you. I'm freezing in this dress."

"You'll warm up if you get moving." Pauly tipped forward slightly at the waist. "May I have this dance?"

All my arguments against Pauly fled when I looked into his warm brown eyes. He set down my punch and took my hand. I felt that powerful attraction zap between us. Old-fashioned waltz music bleated out of the speakers as he led me onto the dance floor.

"You're shivering. With your permission, I'll hold you close to warm you up."

I nodded and sighed with pleasure as he pulled me into his warmth. He'd called me gorgeous, and at least for the minute I felt it. I rested my head against his chest as he led me around the floor. The song ended, and we barely missed a beat before we began dancing to the next swing band song.

He smiled and nodded at people as we spun past them. I wracked my brain for something to say, but the silence between us stretched like elastic. Where was his comfortable teasing when I needed it? He'd seemed to always be able to turn an awkward situation around, but tonight he didn't even make an attempt. We whirled past Pat and Harold silently plodding around the dance floor. Poor Pat looked miserable. Pauly probably felt the same.

I'd been right. We had nothing in common and he couldn't wait for the song to end so he could go ask someone more fun to dance. He'd called me gorgeous the same way he called me Ally Oop. It was all a joke. I tried to steal myself against the buzz of attraction wafting from his large, warm frame and chided myself for having worried about hurting his feelings by going back to Wisconsin. At least I hadn't told Pat about it. She would have laughed her head off. The waltz ended and I pulled away.

He held my hands. "You've barely stopped shivering. How about another?"

"Okay." I nodded shyly as a slow, old-fashioned western song poured out of the speakers.

Pauly's voice rumbled in my ear. "Sorry for the old-timey songs. I'd hoped we'd be jitterbugging."

"I like any kind of music." Despite my resistance, I relished the feel of his large, warm hand on my back.

"Me too. What's your favorite?" Pauly asked.

Warmth flooded through me. "I love the Andrews Sisters. And Bing Crosby is great."

"The Mills Brothers are at the top of my list." Pauly's grin lit up his face. "I have a huge record collection."

"Me too! Well, not huge. But I'd like to." I said, relieved that we'd made a connection about my favorite thing.

When the song ended, he held onto my hand. "Tell me about your music collection."

I told him about all my records. "Maybe now that I'm working, I can afford to buy some more. Where's the best place to buy them around here?"

"There's a small record store not too far from the soda shop."

We chatted on about our favorite bands and music. Pauly had heard The Glenn Miller Band in person when he was on leave from the Army. He'd been in the glee club in high school but quit because of basketball and baseball. "Since then, I've not sung in any groups at all."

"Oh, I love to sing. At my church, they're putting together a choir for a Thanksgiving celebration, if you want to join." I smiled up at him, then suddenly blushed. Was I being too forward?

"I'll think about that. Hey, I'm thirsty. Let's go get something to drink." He unfolded me from his arms, but held onto my hand as we walked toward the food table where Betty and Doug visited with Pat and Harold.

I was being too forward and now he didn't want to dance with me anymore and probably never would. Oh, why couldn't I have kept my mouth shut about the choir at church? He had his own church, after all.

"Hey, you two were really swinging out there." Pat winked at me.

Pauly handed me a drink of cider. "Our Ally Oop is all warmed up now."

Thankfully, his eyes still glinted warmly at me. I took a long drink. "Yeah. That was fun even though the songs are pretty ancient."

Doug smiled. "It reminds me of the dances we had back in Texas, although there they played strictly country and western."

Betty said, "You should have seen the dances we had in Sheboygan." She described the bandstand and surrounding park in great detail. "Everyone would be dressed to the hilt."

"Kind of like you are tonight?" Pat studied Betty's long creamy chiffon.

"Yeah." Betty examined me and leaned over to whisper in my ear. "You have a spot right here."

I pulled away and turned toward Pat. "Have you been dancing?"

Pat glanced at Harold. "We danced a bit."

Harold said, "Dancing is primitive, but I do it now and again just to be social."

Pauly laughed. "Hey, it's good to act primitive sometimes, right, old buddy?"

Harold stood woodenly, as if he hadn't heard.

Pat grabbed my hand and whispered. "Come with me." She turned to the group. "Excuse us for a minute." As she dragged me toward the restroom, she whispered furiously. "You've got to help me lose Harold. He looks great, but his personality is like a block of wood."

I laughed. "I got a hint of that just now."

Pat disappeared into the only bathroom stall, and I peered in the mirror at the spot on my dress. Just as Pat said, it was hardly noticeable. It would be easy to avoid Betty for the rest of the night. But how could I rescue Pat? Pauly was going to have to ask her for a pity dance or two. That meant I'd have to stay with Harold. At least I didn't have to worry about dancing with him, since he thought it was primitive.

When we returned to the others, an up-tempo song was playing. Pat asked Pauly to dance. I turned to Harold. "What do you do in the Army?"

"I was placed in the Signal Corps because of my high IQ," Harold said in his nasal voice. He shook his head in apparent disgust when Pauly spun Pat so hard that she crashed into a nearby couple.

At first, the offended couple looked alarmed. But I could see Pat apologizing profusely. Then Pauly said something, and they all broke into laughter.

Harold glanced sideways at me. "I'm leaving now. Goodbye."

"Goodbye, Harold." I said, glad that at least now Pat could relax.

The rest of the night flew by. A few of the older men asked Pat to dance. When one of them cut in on Pauly and me, I was surprised by how much I missed him.

When the dance ended, Pauly ushered me out into the black night. A sliver of a moon hung low in the sky. "I'll walk with you to Betty's car." He held my hand as we walked behind Pat and Betty and Doug. Then he opened the back door for me and leaned against the car. He looked into my eyes. "Hey, I wish I could call you. When do you get a phone?"

I blushed with pleasure. "I don't know. I had a good time."

Pat grinned ear to ear. "I can relay messages between the two of you via the barracks phone."

I felt a grin as wide as Pat's steal across my face. I nodded. "Bye! Thanks for the good time."

"Bye." Pauly shut the door gently behind me and waved to the rest of the group.

On the ride home, we all sang snatches of the old-time songs and relived the evening as we drove along the Columbia River. I wasn't sure I'd ever had so much fun.

When I let myself into the house, Daddy was up and reading a book in his housecoat. "I guess I don't need to ask whether you had a good time. You're positively glowing."

"Yeah, but I'm really tired." I made a show of yawning. "I'll talk to you in the morning."

As I stripped out of my rust chiffon, I dreamed about the feeling of Pauly's strong arms around me. He thought I was gorgeous. I couldn't remember why I had ever thought he wasn't handsome. Tomorrow I'd ask Daddy if he knew exactly when we'd get phone service.

Chapter 17

Pauly and I followed Betty and Doug into the crowded theater lobby. "I'm going to the restroom." Betty unhooked from Doug and disappeared into the throng.

"Me too." Doug followed.

"We'll meet you in the car." I leaned toward Pauly's warmth and met cool air. I looked around. Where had he gone?

The smell of burned popcorn pinched my nostrils and I sighed. We had been dating for months, and until today he'd seemed like he enjoyed every minute we spent together. But maybe I'd done something wrong, because during the movie, he had started to withdraw. First, he'd dropped my hand. Then he slumped in his seat, his brooding face illumined in the light of Spitfires exploding on the screen.

Maybe he'd decided he'd had enough of me and my clumsiness. I'd dropped popcorn in my lap. And last week I had knocked over my Coke at the soda shop, soaking his pant leg.

I heard his laugh and turned. A tiny blonde woman gazed into Pauly's face with undisguised admiration. I turned away, surprised at the force of my jealousy. What was wrong with me? I had no right to be jealous. Besides, I was going back to Wisconsin soon. I'd never see him again.

Betty and Doug joined me at the same time that Pauly appeared at my elbow. "Sorry. I stopped to say hi to an old friend and had a hard time escaping. Are you guys ready to go?"

Betty and Doug took the back seat of Pauly's Ford. I hugged my door in the front. As Pauly pulled out of the parking spot, Doug drummed the top of the front seat with his fingers. "That was the best war movie ever."

Pauly didn't reply, his face gloomy in the half light. He was probably trying to figure out how to drop me off quickly so he could go back and find that cute blonde woman.

Betty scolded. "It was good, but it made me realize that you must never become a fighter pilot under any circumstances."

"You know I don't have a choice," Doug said.

"I hope you get a nice, safe assignment in logistics or communications here in the states. Can you request that? I hope you can," Betty said. "I'm going to ask Aunt Mary to pray that you get the safest assignment ever. She prays about everything, you know." Betty prattled on the whole way home.

When Pauly stopped the car in front of Betty's house, Doug grabbed his shoulder. "Thanks buddy, it was good seeing you."

"Yeah. Let's get together at the soda shop next weekend," said Pauly.

I turned my face toward the window to hide my sudden tears as we drove silently around the block. This was it. Our last date. With Pat as his cousin, we'd have to remain friends until I left town. And I'd have to pretend it didn't hurt.

At my house, the glow of a single lamp shone through the front room curtains. "It looks like your dad is waiting up. I'd better be going." Pauly opened his car door and headed around to mine.

"Bye." I jumped out and started up the sidewalk so he wouldn't see my tears.

Halfway to the house, he took my arm and turned me around. "Hey, what's wrong?" He looked at me questioningly.

I sniffed and wiped my eyes. "Goodbye. Thanks for the evening."

"No, no. You're not getting out of here until you explain what's making you cry. I mean I know I've not been the best company. In fact, I was hoping to get out of here before my poisonous mood wrecked our relationship. I guess that didn't work."

"Oh, um. I thought..." I stopped, unwilling to go on.

"Come sit with me and let's talk this out." He opened the passenger door and climbed in next to me. "So, what are you crying about?"

I shrugged. "You acted all mad or something. I thought maybe you couldn't wait to go back and find that blonde woman." I felt my face turn red at my confession.

He smiled and shook his head. "Sheila is married to my oldest friend Dan who's serving in the Navy. By the time she waved at me across the crowd, you had already gone ahead with Betty and Doug. I'm sorry if I hurt your feelings."

He sighed. "Watching the movie and seeing Sheila reminded me that I'm the only one my age who's not contributing anything to the war effort." His face took on that moody cast. "While other men are sacrificing their lives, I'm at the movies with the sweet and beautiful Ally Oop."

Despite his obvious discomfort, I smiled. "But you already served your country and reporting the news is important."

He scoffed. "A reporter is supposed to report the honest facts. But I can't touch one of the biggest stories of the war unfolding right under my nose." Pauly crossed his arms and frowned.

"You mean Hanford." I sighed.

"Why did the government steal my town? People I care about are still trying to find their way out of that bind." He glared past me. "Beyond that, why are they shipping millions of tons of building supplies to a desert out in the middle of nowhere? I'd do anything to break that story." He slumped in his seat, defeated. "The movie brought everything I wrestle with every day into sharp focus." He took my hand. "I just hoped to spare you my foul mood."

I rubbed his thumb. "Pauly, you might not be fighting on the front lines or be able to report what's happening at Hanford yet. But you're helping the people at home who've lost a lot in this war because you're so friendly and kind when you interview them." I studied his shadowed face in the moonlight. "What does your dad think about it?"

Pauly shrugged. "He just figures someday the government will share all and we'll be first in line to report it. He was pretty upset with me when I got in trouble for loitering around the 700 Area and asking questions."

"You mentioned that when we first met, but you never did tell me exactly what happened." I laced my fingers through his.

"The first day I was there, the security people got wind of it and chased me out of town with threats of worse if I ever showed my face again. If I hadn't reformed my behavior, I'm sure they would have come after the newspaper. And maybe I'd be in jail." He lowered his head. "It wasn't worth it. Nobody I talked to knew what was really going on anyway. Just like you."

"Well, I guess it's best if you try to hold onto your dad's perspective. The news will come out someday. And then you'll be the first to scoop the story. In the meantime, I'll try to keep you distracted." I smiled up at him.

His eyes darkened and he pulled me into his arms. Pleasure swirled through me as his lips met mine. Pauly had given me many goodnight kisses. But this was something else. I pressed against his chest, thankful there was no more distance between us. Suddenly, I was aflame with desire and felt my breath coming faster.

Pauly drew back, his eyes glowing at me in the moonlight. "You're something else, you know that Ally Oop? I mean that in a good way. A very good way." He smiled and kissed me again. "Your dad is waiting. I better get you in."

We walked to the porch hand in hand. "Thanks for listening to my ranting."

"Don't ever be afraid to share your feelings with me. I want to listen."

He kissed my hand and sent thrills coursing through my body. "Allie Oop, you're the sweetest. I can't wait to see you at church in the morning." His eyes gleamed with sudden humor. "In fact, a night without you is far too long. I think I'll just sleep right here so I can see you first thing when I wake up." He curled up on the cold porch like a dog, closed his eyes and began snoring.

I laughed. "Get up, silly. You must be freezing down there."

He stole a quick peck on my cheek. "Good night." Sighing, he stumbled toward his car as if held by imaginary chains.

I laughed and waved him off with a full heart. The war would be over soon. In the meantime, I would do my best to keep him preoccupied.

Chapter 18

January 1945

On Monday morning, I rolled paper into the typewriter as thoughts of Pauly played over and over in my mind like my favorite song. I'd just seen him yesterday, but it seemed an eternity. The workweek stretched before me like this desert wasteland where I lived.

During November and December, we'd seen each other at choir practice, but now that was over. I couldn't wait until Friday. Tonight, I'd ask Mother if he could come for dinner on Wednesday. He wouldn't be able to stay long because we both had to get up early to go to work. And we'd have the family hanging around watching our every move, but it would be better than nothing.

My daydreams about Pauly evaporated when a scowling Mr. Dirk showed up and began whispering to Mrs. Chase. Time to focus. I sipped my coffee and began to type. When I finished typing up a request for wiring spools, I glanced up and found Mr. Dirk's beady black eyes zeroed in on me. Startled, I quickly began typing again.

When he started strolling back and forth between our typewriters, my shoulders tensed. Mr. Dirk had never taken any interest in us—just our final product.

I jumped when he suddenly leaned over my typewriter. "Miss Krepsky, may I speak with you for a minute?" His breath smelled of garlic.

I nodded mutely and stood up. Was I in trouble? I was tired and a bit daydreamy after a fun weekend, but that wasn't serious or unusual. I wracked my brain for something I had done wrong as I followed him to the outer office.

"Sit down. I need to ask you a few questions." Mr. Dirk's black wing-like hair sprung above his pale, lined forehead. He sat opposite me at a table. "What do you know about the correspondences you've been typing?" He reminded me of a tethered dog as he barked out his question.

I swallowed, unsure how to answer. Maybe he was trying to trap me into saying something I shouldn't. I twisted my fingers in my lap and decided to be noncommittal. "I don't know anything about them, sir."

"Aren't you curious?" Every time he spoke, the smell of garlic almost bowled me over.

I wanted to yell at him. How could I not be curious? I had tried to squash it, but it was impossible. The whole place was strange. From the nonsensical, half-correspondences we typed, to the government's threat of jail, and Pat's stolen town, the list of unusual activity demanded curiosity. I lied. "Umm. Not really. To be honest, sir, I've just gotten into the routine and don't wonder about what it all means too much anymore."

"What would you do if someone in authority questioned you about your work?" His beady eyes peered into mine.

I looked at my hands. "I guess it would depend on who did the asking. I would be forthright with Mrs. Chase. She's the only one in authority I talk to." I cleared my throat. "And you, sir. Otherwise, we're not supposed to talk about it because of secrecy rules." I felt my heart speed up. For the last few months, I tried to forget about work as soon as I left the office. My job was just weird and mostly boring.

"And why do we need secrecy?"

"Umm. The only thing I know is that whatever the government is building is top secret. It's a part of my patriotic duty to serve and to be quiet about it."

His forehead relaxed, and he stood up. "That will be all for now."

Relieved, I hurried back to my typewriter. Maybe they grilled everyone once in a while to keep us scared into silence. At least he'd seemed to relax a bit when I'd answered the last question. I listened for him to haul Pat or Mary out for questioning. When he didn't, I glanced up. He was gone.

Worry niggled at the back of my mind as I started typing again. Maybe the government had confused me with someone who had broken the confidentiality rules. If they thought I'd spread secrets, I might go to jail. In any case, I'd have to leave Richland—and Pauly. I tried to swallow my anxiety. At least I'd be able to go back home. Sheboygan beckoned pleasantly. Pauly's warm kisses swam to the surface of my mind.

I sighed, conflicted. For now, I'd stay on guard and try to be perfect in my relationship with Mrs. Chase and my work. And despite my growing attachment to Pauly and Pat, I still longed for home.

• • • •

IN THE STREETLIGHT after work, Pat's elfin nose was pink from the cold. "What did Mr. Dirt talk to you about?"

I shivered in my new wool coat. "Confidentiality and job questions. Let's talk about it later. Here comes my bus."

"Skip this one. Let's go for a walk. I can't wait to hear all about it." Pat's eyes flamed with curiosity.

Betty hurried out of the gate. "Hey, Ally! The bus is here. Come on!"

Pat held onto my arm. "We're going for a little walk to talk a bit. Care to join us?"

Betty glanced between us and the bus and frowned. "It's too dark and cold to go for a walk outside." Finally, curiosity got the better of her. "Oh, I guess. What's going on?"

Pat walked along the sidewalk leading toward downtown Richland. She looked at Betty. "Dirt, the Manager of Interoffice Communication, took you-know-who out for questioning today."

"Who?" Betty's blue eyes lit up with interest.

Pat nodded her head in my direction.

Betty sucked in her breath. "What for?"

I glared at them and pretended to zip my mouth closed.

"Are you in trouble?" Betty's spoke loudly.

"No." I sighed and turned away.

"You must be. Otherwise, why would he question you?" Betty asked.

"He asked me what I knew about the correspondences I was typing and whether I was curious about what it meant. He asked what I would do if someone in authority questioned me and why we had secrecy laws."

Betty's mouth hung open. "Why do you think he did that? Isn't he really creepy?"

"Why do you think we call him Dirt?" Pat said.

"I wonder if they got me mixed up with someone else who's spreading secrets. Maybe someone who looks like me?" I shrugged. "But I don't think I'm in trouble yet because Mrs. Chase was extra nice to me today."

"Oh, you know her. Even when I said those horrible things, she was still nice." Pat said.

"I'm freezing, and I don't want to talk about it anymore. If I get in trouble for something I didn't do, I'll talk to Daddy. He could probably straighten it out. If not, I guess I'll be on my way to jail." I started back toward the buses.

"That's ridiculous. Mrs. Chase isn't going to let them send you to jail." Pat followed me.

"Do you realize that in one week and three days Doug leaves for basic training?" Betty stuck her bottom lip out in a pout. "Oh, I don't think I can stand it."

"At least you had time to get to know him," Pat said. "Most guys ship off to training the moment they turn eighteen." She reached the door to her bus.

"Yeah. I know. But don't you see how hard it is to know he's going to war?" Betty's eyes were fogged with sadness.

I'd never her seen so unhappy. Even when she'd been sent to the principal's office for talking too much in grade school.

"At least you can write him letters, and the war won't last forever. You'll be together again before you know it," I said cheerily.

"Small consolation prize. If he gets hurt..." She stopped, unable to speak as a tear dripped down her soft button nose.

A speechless Betty was another first. "Come on, let's get home. You can see Doug tonight and that's something." I grabbed her arm and started toward a South Stops bus. "Bye, Pat."

"Hey, Betty, at least you've still got us," Pat called, then climbed on the bus.

As we found seats on our bus, Betty's problem faded in the light of my own. The government might fire me, but at least I could go back home to Wisconsin. I had enough money saved that I could live until I found another job. Grandpa and Grandma would let me stay with them while I looked. I had my driver's license now, and I could drive to work if need be.

The only problem would be leaving Pauly, my bright sun in this bleak landscape. And, of course, my dear friend, Pat. As we turned the corner toward home, the darkening January sky reflected my sense of foreboding. Nothing good could come of this special attention from Mr. Dirk.

Chapter 19

I stretched my sore neck and glanced surreptitiously at the clock. Only a half hour left.

I stifled a yawn as Mrs. Chase collected my briefs. She leaned down and whispered. "Mr. Dirk and I would like to speak with you alone for a few moments after work. Can you stay?"

Fear hollowed out a pit in my stomach. It had been two weeks since Mr. Dirk's questioning. I'd been able to put it out of my mind, but maybe they really did believe I shared secrets. I'd be mortified if I was fired and sent back to Wisconsin. No one there would be surprised I had failed again. I tried to smile. "Yes, I can stay a few minutes."

Pat must have noticed my distress because she frowned in my direction and mouthed, *"What's wrong?"* I just shook my head and turned back to my typewriter.

At five o'clock, Mrs. Chase said, "All right, girls. We'll stop for today and take it up in the morning." She looked at Pat. "You go on ahead, Pat. Alice is going to stay and speak with me about a few things."

Pat looked questioningly at me and nodded. "Okay. I'll see you later, Ally."

Mrs. Chase put our correspondences in a small safe behind her desk and carefully locked it. "I hope you don't mind taking the bus a bit late. We shouldn't be too long."

My fear expanded as Mr. Dirk stepped inside the room, raindrops glistening on his jacket.

If they think I've done something wrong, I would have to prove my innocence. But how? It seemed impossible. A panicky, sick feeling cramped my gut as Mrs. Chase gathered chairs around her desk.

Mr. Dirk's flat, lipless mouth turned up in what seemed to be his version of a smile. "Mrs. Chase says you are doing an excellent job."

I felt a rush of relief and pleasure. "Thank you, sir."

"One of our secretaries had to quit suddenly and we are searching for a suitable replacement. You are at the top of our list. Is that something that would interest you?" His voice oozed oil.

Shock at the sudden turn of events made me stutter. "I, I don't know."

"It entails taking shorthand notes, typing, mailing correspondence, fielding calls, and generally helping our scientists stay organized."

"I've never had experience as a secretary before. I'm not sure I'd know what to do." I clasped my purse against my chest.

"We're fully aware of that." He leaned back in his chair. "I'd be training you until you learn how things work. We need someone quiet and hardworking. Someone who can follow procedures." His beady black eyes peered at me as if he were examining an interesting lizard. "We think you can be trusted, despite your young age and lack of experience."

He cleared his throat. "I understand you came here with your family and that your father intends to stay, dust storms and all." I felt suddenly exposed. I had told no one beyond Betty and Pat that my dad was determined to stay. When I didn't speak, Mr. Dirk went on. "I've met him. He's a great employee. Works hard. Keeps his head down."

"Mmhmm." Slightly relieved, I nodded. "Thank you. He'd be glad to know that."

"You've passed top secret clearance. Mrs. Chase says you are very bright. We think you are the person for the job."

I almost laughed out loud. They thought I was smart. I sat up straighter.

"You'll get a twenty-five cent an hour raise. Travel time to and from the 100 Area is around forty minutes. Start time is seven o'clock. Quit time is five unless there's an emergency." He passed an application to me across the table. "If you're interested in the job, fill this out and get it to personnel by Monday. If you don't want the job, let Mrs. Chase know as soon as possible."

Today was Tuesday. Just a few short days to decide. I twisted the handle of my purse mutely.

"I hope you'll say yes. Your country needs you." He stood up and grimaced a smile. "I'll be waiting for your call. If you decide to take the job, I'll pick you up and ride with you to the 100 Area. Training will begin immediately."

I struggled to stand, weighed down by the giant decision. "I'll let Mrs. Chase know my decision by Monday, then."

"Thank you, ladies." Mr. Dirk slipped on his black jacket and tipped his scowling forehead in our direction.

"Goodbye and thank you for thinking of me." My voice sounded unsure even to my own ears. Why did they want me? Someone just out of high school who'd graduated with only fair marks.

"Goodbye, Mr. Dirk." Mrs. Chase followed him to the door. When he slipped into the evening, she said, "I'm sorry I couldn't give you more warning. I know it's a big decision."

"Thank you for the recommendation. Most of all, I feel very honored. But I'm not going to lie and say I feel at all competent for the job."

"In this top-secret job, trust is more important than experience. Especially since you're easily trained and agreeable. It's quite a compliment."

"Thank you for your confidence in me." A top-secret job. Did that mean I would be privy to all the secrets surrounding the operation? I felt shaky as I collected my coat and stood in the doorway.

"Hold on. I'll walk with you." Mrs. Chase double-checked the safe, put on a long green coat, and retrieved her purse from her desk drawer.

She matched my stride. Darkness hovered just beyond the bluish lights illuminating the street. "So, what do you think about this opportunity?"

"Leaving Pat behind is one of the hardest things about saying yes to this job. And you, of course." I smiled in her direction. "Riding that long on the bus seems hard too. I don't know..."

"I hope you'll say yes. You're needed." She changed the subject when the bus roared up to a stop in front of the Administration Building and we found seats together. "I hate cooking dinner after working all day. Any ideas for something easy?"

I shook my head. "My mom cooks for me. It's nice to not have to worry about it even though I get irritated that she still thinks of me as her baby."

"I bet she enjoys having you home. I miss my girls so much. I got a letter from Rebecca yesterday." Mrs. Chase chatted about her family until we reached the gate. "Which bus do you take?"

"South Stops. How about you?"

"North Stops. Get a good night's sleep, Ally. I'll see you in the morning."

"Bye, Mrs. Chase." I hurried onto my bus where my favorite driver, Harry, sat behind the wheel.

"You're late," he chided with a smile. "Betty went on home without you. She said something about you having to stay after. I hope there wasn't a problem?" His eyes glinted with curiosity.

"Hi, Harry. No, nothing like that." I took a seat and stared out the window. Under a streetlight, I saw the Coyote slink past. I shivered at his long snout and cold, empty eyes. Thank goodness I hadn't met him face-to-face. But his presence highlighted another problem with taking the job. I would be riding the bus with strangers. I was pretty sure that Daddy wouldn't approve of that. After my experience with the Coyote, I wasn't sure I did either. I'd ask Daddy about it and see what he thought.

Unlike my current job that I could do with my eyes half closed, the new post would require a lot of me. I'd probably be exhausted, and I couldn't let it come between me and Pauly. He was the only thing that kept me going in this dry wasteland.

But with this top-secret job, I'd be able to prove to everyone once and for all that I was smart. I pushed on my glasses. Betty would be so jealous. I'd tell Grandma and Grandpa and they would spread the news around Sheboygan. My old friends would be shocked and amazed. I could just imagine their admiring faces.

An abandoned newspaper lay draped across the seat across the aisle. War headlines caught my eye. Our soldiers on the front lines were dying. Families were grieving. There was talk of an invasion. Something had to be done, and quickly. If what they were doing at Hanford was the key, I had to do whatever I could to make it happen. I was so lost in my thoughts that I didn't even notice when the bus stopped at my corner.

Harry said, "Hey Ally, are you getting off or what?"

I jumped up. "Oh. Yeah. See you tomorrow." Maybe I was selfish to worry about my own comforts. Being entrusted with important government secrets was an honor. Did I dare turn it down?

I rushed into the house and threw my purse on the couch. "I'm home!"

Mother appeared in the dining room with a stripe of flour down her moon cheek. "Betty stopped to tell us you'd be late. Your father will be home in about half an hour. Timmy is at the neighbors. Go rest a bit, dear. I'll call you when dinner is on the table."

As I started up the stairs, Betty opened the front door. "How come you had to stay late?"

I held my peace until we reached my room. I shut the bedroom door behind us.

"You have to promise to keep a secret," I whispered.

"I have a secret, too." Betty looked like she was ready to burst, her eyes bright. "Doug and I are getting married on Saturday. You can't tell anyone. If my parents knew they'd want a big church wedding, and we don't want to wait until he comes home on leave."

"Oh, wow!" All thoughts of my impending job decision were wiped momentarily from my mind.

"We need you and Paul to stand up with us. Doug had lunch with Paul and asked him today. He said yes."

"Of course, I'll stand up for you. Congratulations!" I tried to be happy for her, but misgivings clouded my mind. "Just be careful you're making the right decision. I like Doug and everything, but it seems like you'd get restless waiting for him to come home. And if he was killed—would you be able to bear being a widow?"

"What a horrible thing to say." Betty's eyes were frosty.

I almost said sorry but stopped myself. I didn't always have to try to make things right for everyone. "Oh, come on, Betty. It's only reality. Lots of people are dying in this war." I shoved my feet into my slippers.

Betty shrugged. "He's going to be okay. Besides, whatever we're working on here is going to end the war soon. I just know it." She pushed me out of the way and started going through the clothes in my closet. "You can wear this to the ceremony." She laid my pink wool dress on the bed. "I've ordered bouquets in pink roses and white carnations. We have an appointment with the Justice of the Peace on Saturday at ten." She went on about getting the marriage license. "I told Doug how hard it is for you to keep a secret, and he made me swear I wouldn't tell you until today."

"Hmmm. It seems to me you're the one who has trouble keeping secrets. In fact, I'm surprised I'm just learning about this."

"Obviously, I'm getting better." She beamed at me proudly.

"Which reminds me, I have a secret to share too. I won't tell you unless you promise to keep it—even from Doug."

"All right." She ran her fingers across her mouth. "My lips are sealed."

"Mr. Dirk asked me to be a top-secret secretary in the 100 Area." I watched her face for a look of admiration.

Instead, she feigned a yawn and flopped onto the bed. "Oh, how boring. A secretary. Plus, the 100 Area is so far away. Do you really want to ride the bus that long every day?"

I sighed. Betty's attitude made me want to take the job just to prove to her that I wasn't going to follow her around like a shadow anymore. "I don't know yet. But I do know it's an honor."

She fiddled with a corner of the bedspread. "I'm surprised you'd consider leaving Pat."

"Yeah. That's probably the hardest part. But I get a raise to seventy-five cents an hour."

"Hmm. It's probably going to be a drag." Betty paced around the room, then stopped at the window.

"Maybe, but they said they needed me, and I think I'm going to do it."

She shrugged. "Well, I told Doug I'd come over as soon as I talked to you. I'll see you later, and we can talk more about the wedding. Oh, by the way, I'm not telling Pat until after the wedding happens. You know how word gets around." Her face pinked with excitement, and she slipped out.

• • • •

MOTHER SHOOED US INTO the living room after dinner. "You two have worked hard all day. Go sit down and I'll clean up."

Timmy pulled my hand as we trooped into the living room. "Would you read to me?"

"Not right now, Timmy. I need to talk to Daddy." I extricated my hand from his.

"Aww, come on Ally."

Daddy settled into his favorite chair and looked at me questioningly.

I leaned down to whisper in his ear, "I need to talk to you in private."

He raised his eyebrow. "Timmy, I need you to go and check for mice in the basement. Be still and watch carefully. Then come let us know if you see any tails or whiskers and I'll set some traps."

Timmy grinned. "Aunt Edna has mice, but I didn't think we were so lucky."

"Only come back if you see anything." Daddy smiled as Timmy raced from the room. "Now, what's going on?"

I told him all about my new job offer. "They think I'm smart, Daddy. I can't believe it. And they trust me to be silent about what I learn. Mr. Dirk, The Manager of Interoffice Communication, said he knew you and that you were dedicated to the project."

Daddy frowned. "Mr. Dirk came to my office not long ago. We talked about work and family things for a fair while. It surprised me."

"Oh, he was probably trying to get information from you for my top-secret clearance."

Daddy nodded and sucked on his empty pipe. "Yeah, they need to be very careful about a job like that. I'm sure they talked to people back in Sheboygan too."

"Oh. I wonder who?"

Daddy shrugged. "Teachers, our pastor maybe. You might find out in time."

I pushed my glasses up. "Oh, that's weird. Those people wouldn't say I was smart. Probably just that I did what I was told."

"Mrs. Chase knows you're smart."

"I wonder about riding the bus without Betty?"

Daddy sighed. "The buses are full going back and forth all day, so it wouldn't be dangerous to ride. You'd just have to be careful about not leaving alone between shift changes."

"I'd be very careful." The Coyote slunk into my mind, and I stilled the thought with a shiver.

Daddy bit down on his unlit pipe. "Alice, I'm very proud that you were selected for this honor. But I don't know if it's a good idea." His green eyes clouded with worry. "As a secretary, you're going to be at the heart of all communication and in the know about all of it. I'm sure it holds some risk to be privy to so many secrets."

I said again, "They think I'm smart, Dad. Mr. Dirk said they need me. I'm not sure I can say no. I get a raise too."

He rubbed his eye. "How long before you have to decide?"

"I have to let them know by next Monday, and I start the following week."

Daddy tamped tobacco into his pipe. "You should be getting married and taking care of a home instead of working in a top-secret position. Let's pray about it. But don't tell Mother about this for now."

I shrugged. Mother lived in her pretend world. She wouldn't worry. I didn't dare ask Pauly for advice. Because of all his issues surrounding the operation, he couldn't be a good sounding board. Or Pat, because she just wouldn't want me to leave her. The only thing I could do was pray about it.

Chapter 20

Pauly turned the car onto Fourth Street in Pasco. I stared up at the Franklin County Courthouse, surprised by the ornate brick structure topped by a copper dome and clock. "The courthouse is pretty."

In the backseat, Doug was holding Betty's hand along with her pink rose bouquet. Betty looked beautiful in her simple off-white wool dress. She'd chosen it so Aunt Edna wouldn't get suspicious, but it fell far short of her childhood wedding dress fantasies.

"It reminds me of the oldest, prettiest buildings in Wisconsin. I knew the moment I saw it that this was the place for us to be married." Betty leaned her head on Doug's shoulder.

I nodded, worried. Doug was leaving for the Army in just a few days, and with the church and her parents out of the picture, the whole affair seemed rocky and uncertain.

"I hope my mom and dad won't be too upset." Betty's voice quavered. She cleared her throat. "But if they are, they are just going to have to get over it." She lifted Doug's hand with hers and sniffed her bouquet. "I can't wait till we're all alone on our honeymoon. Our hotel is near the Blue Mountains, you know. Very romantic."

Listening to her prattle on the way to the courthouse had been a bit like listening to one of my records on skip. I could hear her feelings of conflict along with determination in every repetition. Doug had sat mostly silent on the ride, his face white with nerves and anticipation.

Pauly pulled into the parking lot. "I hope you can both forget about anything but your love today."

Doug and Betty took his advice and turned to stare into each other's eyes. I smiled and brushed a spot of lint off Pauly's lapel. As usual, he was helping to make a tense situation more comfortable. "You look so handsome in your suit."

He walked around to open my door. "And you look especially beautiful today, my Ally Oop."

We followed Doug and Betty up the wide staircase. Inside the lobby, I looked around with appreciation. The gold speckled marble walls glowed softly. A shiny gold statue of a woman spilling water from a jar stood on a pedestal in the center of the room. Filigree decorated the inside of the copper dome above our heads.

Betty and Doug stepped to a reception desk. "We are here for the Parsons/Foster wedding at ten o'clock."

The sweet-faced receptionist smiled. "And these are your witnesses?" She gestured toward Pauly and me.

"Yes, Alice Krepsky and Paul Armstrong," Paul said.

She ushered us into a wood-paneled room with a lectern at the top of a short platform. "You may sit here. Judge Marshall will be here any minute."

Even Betty sat silently, clinging to Doug as we waited. Pauly's hand was restless in mine until a thin gray-haired man in a long black robe slipped through a side door and stepped behind the lectern.

"Doug Parsons and Betty Foster, I understand it is your intention to wed in the presence of these witnesses." His voice was friendly, but commanded respect.

Doug said, "Yes, your honor."

Betty nodded.

"You may step to the lectern." The judge turned to Betty. "Do you, Betty, take this man to be your lawfully wedded husband, for better, for worse, for richer, for poorer, in sickness and in health, as long as you both shall live?"

She whispered, "I do."

"Do you, Doug, take this woman to be your lawfully wedding wife, for better, for worse, for richer, for poorer, in sickness and in health, as long as you both shall live?"

Doug's voice was sure and strong. "I do." He slipped the wedding ring on Betty's finger.

The judge said, "I now pronounce you man and wife. You may kiss the bride."

I was amazed by the ease and speed of the ceremony. We quickly signed the paperwork and exited the golden lobby to the cold winter's day.

Sleet stung our faces as we rushed to the car. Pauly revved the engine.

"Heater and fan on high, please!" I shivered and tossed a card into the backseat.

Last night, I had given Betty a lacy nightgown which she'd packed at the very top of her suitcase. Pauly and I pooled our money to pay for their honeymoon suite in Walla Walla.

Betty opened the card and Doug exclaimed. "Thank you! That is very generous."

Betty asked, "How did you know which one was our hotel?"

I rolled my eyes at Pauly. She had only told me ten times. "We wired the money on Friday."

"It's the perfect gift. Especially since we won't be setting up house right away." Betty's voice held a smile.

I grinned toward the back seat. "When Doug is home from the war, we'll throw you a giant reception. It will be so fun, and you'll be showered with gifts."

"Now to the unpleasant task of telling our parents." Betty looked into Doug's face for support.

Pauly asked, "Are you going to tell them together or separately?"

"We've invited each set of parents out to lunch, but they don't know we're all going together. Mary is babysitting my little brothers," Doug said.

"Timmy will like that." I glanced toward the backseat with a smile.

"Drop us off at Doug's house, please." Betty bit her nail. "The next few hours are going to be difficult. Prayers and luck needed."

"Oh, yes. Prayers for all the luck and love and happiness in the world."

Pauly pulled up in front of Doug's house. "Have fun on your honeymoon!" he said.

They climbed out of the backseat, and Betty turned to blow a kiss in my direction.

I watched them disappear inside Doug's house, suddenly weighed down by a sense of responsibility. I turned toward Pauly for support. "I wonder if I should have told her parents?"

Pauly loosened his tie, his warm dark gaze inscrutable. "Betty's all grown up and can make her own decisions without her parents' or your interference."

"Yeah, you're right." But as we pulled away from the curb, I couldn't help but worry whether Aunt Edna and Uncle Ben would be angry at me.

Pauly turned the corner. "You said you had something important to tell me. Let's talk at the park."

Riverside Park was empty except for a shaggy dog nosing through dried weeds on the frozen shore of the Columbia River. With the car windows beginning to fog, it was the perfect place to tell Pauly about my job decision.

But not yet. I snuggled closer to keep warm, unwilling to leave the topic of Betty's wedding ceremony so soon. "After all the years she dreamed about her perfect church wedding, I still can't believe she settled for a Justice of the Peace at the courthouse."

"It wasn't so bad. Short and sweet. No drama." Pauly slipped off his tie and laid it flat in the back seat.

I shrugged and sniffed at my tiny bouquet of pink and white carnations. "These are the only part of her wedding dreams that came true. Pink and white."

I still wanted a white wedding gown and lots of bridesmaids. Dahlias and roses in abundance, and Holly Darmen singing my favorite wedding songs. But I didn't dare share that with Pauly. He'd think I was fishing for a proposal. I loved every minute I spent with him and when he was away, I thought about him. But my goal was to go back home. Wasn't it?

I sighed, happy Betty had found a man she loved with all her heart. They seemed to be a good match for one another. He was quiet and she was talkative. She was bossy and he seemed willing to do what she wished most of the time. Maybe it would all work out. "I wish I could be a fly on the wall at the restaurant when she tells her parents they're married."

He took my gloved hand in his. "Do you think her parents will be mad?"

"They'll probably be more hurt than mad. It will be difficult for them to accept that a Justice of the Peace married them instead of Pastor Carver. And Aunt Edna would have loved the wedding preparations and family celebration. Uncle Pete makes light of everything, but a lot of the time, it seems like a cover for his real feelings."

I thrilled when Pauly pulled off my glove and tucked my hand in his pocket next to his. He said, "For sure, I'd want to go somewhere more romantic than a few days in Walla Walla for a honeymoon. Maybe two weeks at a beach front cottage or a hotel overlooking the Puget Sound."

I shivered in pleasure at his suggestions even though I had no first-hand knowledge of either place and nothing but a hazy idea of what would happen when we got there.

At thirteen, Aunt Edna had told Betty about the birds and the bees. Betty told me all about it. I didn't believe her at first. It sounded like something she'd made up just to make me feel weird. But the closer I felt to Pauly, the more irresistible the idea became. "It sounds wonderful."

He kissed my nose and wrapped me closer. "Your nose is as cold as that dog's on the shore. So, tell me, why did you want to park here?"

I straightened up and removed my hand from his pocket so I could think straight. "I've got something important to tell you." I resettled my glasses. "Last week, Mr. Dirk asked me if I wanted to be a secretary for scientists out in the 100 Area. It's flattering that they want me in a top-secret position. Me, the girl with no secretarial experience who struggled through school. I don't think I can turn it down."

Pauly grinned. "Congratulations. I always knew you were a smart girl. Top-secret, huh? That means you're probably going to be privy to what's really going on."

"Maybe." I felt tender toward his desire to know what was happening and avoided his eyes. I hoped he understood it was even more critical now that I remain circumspect. "The worst thing is that work hours are seven to five o'clock and there's a forty-minute bus ride each way. I'm going to be exhausted, but that doesn't mean we can't still see each other on Wednesdays."

Pauly was silent for a minute then asked, "What does Pat think about it?"

"I haven't told her yet. I hope she'll understand. I just don't think I can say no."

Pauly's brown eyes were serious. "You don't have to do everything people want you to do, you know."

I shrugged. "Yeah. I know." I wanted to ask him if he would respect my need to stay silent about what I was learning, but I didn't dare put a wall between us over my new job before it even started. The dog had disappeared, and the park stood bleak and empty under the low-hanging clouds.

Pauly leaned his shoulder against the car door, and I shoved my hand back into his empty pocket, wanting to recreate the sweet feeling. It was gritty with sand or crumbs. My fingers closed around something smooth and round. "What's this?" I pulled out a small white stone with a faint gold stripe running through the middle. "That's pretty."

"I found it in the desert when I was interviewing some builder about a new house going in. You can have it if you want." Pauly closed my hand around it.

"No, I don't want to take your rock." I pressed it back into his hand.

"I meant to give it to you." Pauly kissed me and I forgot about anything except the feel of his lips and his arms around me. Too soon, he pulled back and touched my chin. "Even though we make some good heat together, your toes must be turning into icicles. We probably should be going."

Heat was a good word for what I felt. Even after all the talk about work, I could fall into his deep brown eyes and never surface. I snapped to attention. "Oh, that's right. I told Pat we'd pick her up and head to the soda shop." Pauly's stomach growled. "I can't believe it's already almost noon." He started the engine.

As we drove to the barracks, I tried to make small talk. But Pauly stayed silent, his face as bleak as the park had been. Was he angry and feeling useless like he had after the movie? Perhaps he was comparing my job in a vital top-secret position to his work at the newspaper, where he was cut off from the truth he wanted to report more than anything. Soon, whatever they were building would end the war, and he'd be able to report it all as the first one on the scene. Until then, I'd pretend to be in the dark about what was really happening even if I was able to figure it out.

When Pauly pulled up in front of the barracks, Pat was waiting on the porch in her red coat with lipstick to match.

She opened the back door. "What are you two all dressed up for? Pauly, I haven't seen that suit since Great Uncle Buford's funeral."

I turned around. "Betty and Doug got married by a Justice of the Peace this morning and they asked Pauly and me to stand up for them."

Pat's eyes flashed hurt. "And I wasn't invited? What am I, dog meat?"

"Nobody was invited. We didn't find out about it until just a couple of days ago, and only because they needed us to make it happen."

Pauly said, "Besides, you hate weddings. Remember when you dropped your flower girl basket and then tripped over it when you were walking down the aisle at Aunt Melinda's wedding?"

Pat waved away his words. "Of course, you have to dig up that old news. If you remember, I was only six years old." She turned to me. "I can't really say I'm surprised about Betty and Doug. She was constantly complaining about how her parents wouldn't let them ever be alone together. So, what was it like?"

"It wasn't exactly my idea of a wedding, but they seemed happy. Elated, in fact. After they meet with both sets of parents over lunch, they're going on a honeymoon in Walla Walla."

Pat studied her nails. "I wouldn't want to be in her shoes, pining away for a husband who might never come back." She sighed. "It's hard to imagine her acting like a wife. Betty the flirt."

"Yeah, I think it's going to be harder than she knows." I slid closer to Pauly.

"Yeah, the war news is pretty bleak," Pauly said. "But hey, Ally here will soon be in a position to personally end this war. Maybe even before Doug gets through with basic."

"Oh, you." I gently slapped his arm and turned around to face Pat. "Before I say more, I want you to know I'm only doing this because they need me so bad. I just don't think I can say no." As I told her all about my new job, I watched her mouth fall open in disbelief.

"How could you leave me? I'll be all alone with the Queen." Pat turned her crestfallen face to the window.

"Leaving you is the worst part of this new job. But remember, Mrs. Chase said something about hiring someone else. Maybe we can make a new friend. Besides, we never get to say two words to each other except for lunch time anyway."

"I suppose you're going to hear all the secrets we've been craving to know about. Oh, if I had only kept my mouth shut, I could be in your position and learn it all." Pat sighed. "I can't believe you'd want to ride the bus so long every day. What if somebody follows you the way the Coyote did?"

Pauly's face turned steely. "Who's the Coyote?"

I ignored his question. "I'm not worried. There are plenty of people riding the bus at that time of day."

Pauly said, "So tell me about the Coyote."

Pat launched into the story, telling it as if she had been the one he'd followed. "I still see him around. One time he asked me where you were."

I shook my head. "Ugh. Luckily, I haven't seen him since then except one time out the bus window."

Pauly parked the car and shifted into park. He was frowning as he opened my car door. "What is his real name?"

"Bart Bundy. Don't worry about it. It's no big deal."

When Pauly opened the soda shop door, a blast of warm air and the smell of grilling hamburgers hit us. My stomach growled. One of Pauly's friends who was home on leave waved us over. Soon we were all laughing, thoughts of work and my new position forgotten for the moment. Maybe Pauly would forget all about the Coyote too.

Chapter 21

On Monday morning, anxiety was my lonely companion as I stared out the bus window at the brown skies and tumbleweeds rolling in the gusting wind. Today, I had to prove that they'd made the right choice when they'd hired me for the job. I pushed on my glasses.

Mr. Dirk sat stiffly next to me without speaking, his mouth pressed into a serious line. I'd said goodbye to Pat and Mrs. Chase only twenty minutes before, but I already missed them almost as much as I'd missed Sheboygan when I first arrived in this bleak desert. Why exactly had I agreed to this new form of torture? There had to be others who were eager to fulfill this top-secret role. Pauly's words played in my head: 'You don't have to do everything everyone wants you to do, you know.' He was right. I didn't. But I was needed. At the theater, newsreels recounted the brave deeds of men fighting the Battle of the Bulge. Many had not survived.

I was needed. Besides, it was the perfect way to prove once and for all that I was smart and capable.

A tumbleweed blew under the bus and scraped along the road. We jounced into a pothole and dislodged it as a blast of dust peppered the windows. Mr. Dirk swayed and tapped his finger against his knee impatiently.

I'd spent the weekend reviewing the Gregg shorthand alphabet. Despite my miserable grades, I was a good speller because I'd studied the spelling lists that Betty had copied off the board. Hopefully, I could finish training quickly and be Dirt free.

A cluster of massive buildings emerged blearily out of the blowing sand. The bus slowed and stopped at a guard station.

Mr. Dirk muscled his way into the throng of exiting workers. I resettled my glasses and waited for my chance to exit. Finally, a man with three chins gestured for me to go ahead. As I stepped off the bus, the wind lifted my hat and sent it tumbling into the hand of a security guard.

Mr. Dirk stood nearby with a scowl. "Hurry now."

The guard handed me my hat as I showed him my ID. "Hang onto that hat now." He winked.

"Thank you." I tucked my hat under my arm. At least not everyone in the 100 Area was a Mr. Dirk.

"Come this way now." He barked, and we followed other workers inside the Clock House. A uniformed guard stood under a sign that said, "STOP Area Badges - Pencils Issued Here." Mr. Dirk said, "You wear these pencils around your neck while you're working and return them at the end of each day."

My badge was similar to the one I'd been issued in the 700 Area. The pencil was cylindrical, but that was where the resemblance to a normal pencil ended. The shaft was cold gray metal and the tip, a bulb of glass.

Mr. Dirk scowled in my direction and spoke gruffly. "Don't waste your time wondering. Just know it's for your safety. If anything unusual registers at the end of the day, you'll be notified and required to take the necessary precautions."

I forgot my pencil reader when we stepped outside. The smokestacks, water towers, and massive structures hulking over us looked like some kind of factory. Nearby, workers disappeared into a low building labeled Change House. Maybe, like Superman, they exited the Change House transformed into superheroes. Superheroes empowered to create a magic something to end the evil war.

Mr. Dirk led the way down the street to a low building and unlocked a door marked Administration / Laboratories. A pale, middle-aged woman with dishwater hair glanced up from her desk. "Good morning, Mr. Dirk." The tidy office was rimmed by the usual safety and security posters. I smiled, grateful to meet another woman.

"Mrs. Frank, this is Ms. Krepsky, our new secretary." Mr. Dirk opened a door marked Offices. "Mrs. Frank is our receptionist and messenger. All typed communication is brought to her for dispersal."

"Hello, nice to meet you." I smiled again.

Mrs. Frank pinched her white lips and nodded.

I followed Mr. Dirk down a hallway of closed doors. "This is your office. Hang your coat in the closet. Take a look around while I get organized."

A phone and typewriter sat on an otherwise spotless desk. A row of filing cabinets stood nearby. I stepped up to view a map of the building with names and departments penciled in on each room. Two laboratories labeled Water Quality Control occupied much of the building.

A man poked his knife-thin face in the door and spoke in a nasal voice. "Mr. Dirk, I'm glad you're finally here. I need to dictate a safety briefing."

Mr. Dirk nodded. When the man disappeared, he handed me a steno pad and pencil. "We'll both transcribe Dr. Holt's safety briefing so I can check your work against mine."

In his office, Dr. Holt's bald spot shone in the overhead light. His kind eyes focused on me. "I'm glad to see our replacement is here."

"Yes, this is Alice Krepsky. She comes highly recommended. Miss Krepsky, this is Dr. Holt."

"Nice to meet you, sir." I sat down, grateful that Mr. Dirk had spoken a good word about me. Maybe working with him wouldn't be so torturous after all.

Dr. Holt smiled. "I'm afraid you'll find the job very demanding. But when you get discouraged, I advise you to view your experiences through the eyes of an adventurer on a quest to unlock a mystery that can save the world."

"Thank you, sir. That's inspiring." I felt myself inflate. I could tell already that I'd enjoy working with Dr. Holt. Mr. Dirk scowled as if he hadn't heard any of our exchange, his pencil poised and waiting.

Dr. Holt cleared his throat. "Safety Bulletin Number 486 Failsafe Shutdown..."

My fingers trembled as I tried to keep up: *Revised procedures for Failsafe Shutdown are as follows...*

My mind skittered along as I tried to understand the message about reactor shutdown procedures. Thankfully, the transcription was short, concluding with dates and the location for training.

"That will be all for now," Dr. Holt said.

Mr. Dirk stood up and slapped his leg with his steno pad impatiently. I felt myself blush as I finished the transcription. I could just hear their thoughts—slow, slow, slow. Maybe she's not so smart after all.

Finally, I stood self-consciously and followed Mr. Dirk to the office. He gestured toward the desk, "Translate your shorthand into longhand and then I'll check it."

I stumbled over my words. "I hope... I mean, a lot of the vocabulary is unfamiliar."

Mr. Dirk cut me off. "We don't have time for idle chit-chat."

He pulled up a chair close to mine and watched as I attempted to spell words like failsafe, radiation, and atomic. I took a deep breath to calm myself and shut off the part of my mind that craved to understand the meaning of the strange new words. I finished the best I could and passed my paper to him.

He pulled a red pen from his pocket, and setting the two transcriptions side by side, he studied one against the other. I felt each slash of his red pen like a wound. When he pushed my slaughtered paper across the desk, I was transported back to middle school when I had felt the like the stupidest girl in the room. "Memorize the words with the red marks."

A dark-haired man with eyes like shiny bullets stepped into the room. "Dirk, may I see you in my office?"

Mr. Dirk nodded. He opened a desk drawer. "Here's where we keep supplies. Type it in triplicate."

When Mr. Dirk left, I aligned a piece of typing paper with two sheets of carbon paper. Studying Betty's spelling words had done me no good here where all the words were strange and meaningless. I was going to have to figure out a way to study them. Maybe I could write down the correct spellings and take them home.

Beyond the worrisome spelling problem, my mind whirred with questions. What was a reactor and why did they need a failsafe shutdown? Why did I have to wear something called a pencil detector around my neck? I sighed, longing for Pat and Mrs. Chase. I hadn't known everything when I'd started there either, but it hadn't mattered because we'd shared a sense of camaraderie. Mr. Dirk was such a machine. He probably never even ate lunch. Mrs. Frank looked like a dry stick, and she acted just as dead. She probably didn't eat either. And if she did, she wouldn't ask me to join her. I swallowed a lump in my throat. I'd probably starve to death.

When I finished typing, I started writing the unfamiliar words on a piece of paper. Mr. Dirk appeared in the doorway, scowling at a paper in his hand. Someone called his name and he retreated. I didn't have time. I was going to have to take home my bloodied notes to study. I felt slightly dizzy from stress as I hurried over and shoved the paper into my purse. When I got home, I'd memorize the unfamiliar scientific terms fast. If I didn't, everyone would think I was stupid. And I'd never be free from Mr. Dirk.

Mr. Dirk reappeared just as I was sitting down at the desk. "Are you done?" He scowled in my direction.

I nodded and handed him the safety bulletin.

"You'll paperclip all shorthand notes to the carbon copy and file it. Put the letter in front. He pulled a giant key ring from his pocket. Keep these keys on your person at all times when in the office. I suggest you wear dresses or sweaters with pockets." His face flushed, as if embarrassed by the mention of my clothing. Maybe Mr. Dirk was human after all.

"Each of the drawers is divided by topic." He stood far back when I looked in the file drawers, as if he was afraid of catching cooties. "Inside the drawer marked Safety, you'll find a file labeled Failsafe Shutdown System. Never leave drawers unlocked nor papers on your desk unless you're working with them. Keep the original for Mrs. Frank and file the rest. I'll check your work when you're done."

I reached into the filing cabinet and tore my fingernail on the sharp edge of the drawer. It hung off my finger as I filed his shorthand notes and the two carbon copies.

If Mr. Dirk saw that I hadn't filed my shorthand notes with the other things, I could be fired after my first hour of work. I ripped my torn finger nail off with my teeth and chewed it as he examined the file. Finally, he slammed the drawer shut and sat down at the desk. "I'll type this letter while you take the failsafe safety briefing to Mrs. Frank for dissemination."

I jumped up, relieved. Even if she wasn't a barrel of fun, maybe I could at least get on Mrs. Frank's good side. Allies here could be critical.

Mrs. Frank sat hunched over, her hair sewn with silver threads. "Mr. Dirk asked me to give you this Safety Bulletin." She squinted at me as if she were a mole coming out of hiding.

"Oh, thank you."

She stood, winced, and held onto the desk for support.

"Are you okay?" I asked.

"I'm okay. I just need a moment. Sitting to standing is the worst." She seemed to gather strength. "You must be wondering..." Her voice trailed off.

"Only if you wish to share." I looked around the neat-as-a-pin office, wondering how someone in such obvious pain could manage keeping things so neat and tidy.

"My horse threw me a few months ago, and I'm still recovering from a back injury. I can't afford to miss work, what with my husband being gone and all." She pinched her lips as if unwilling to go on.

"Oh, I'm so sorry. If there's anything I can do..." I trailed off helplessly. She must be one of the many grief-stricken war widows. I sighed and reminded myself that I wasn't here for fun. I was here was to help end the bloodshed. Dr. Holt's words about saving the world came rushing back to me, and I vowed again to do my best to fulfill my duties here.

As she began to move around, her face cleared. She smiled. "Thank you. Once I get going, I'm all right. I'm going to take this over to the B Reactor. I'll be back in a while."

"Okay. See you later." I hurried back to the office. At least there was a reason for Mrs. Frank's apparent unfriendliness. She might not be a barrel of fun, but she was decent.

The day ping-ponged along rapidly as Mr. Dirk and I scurried between offices taking notes about decontamination procedures, coolant, and chemical separation. And a bunch of references to water. Everything was about water. The more knowledge I gained, the more I felt submerged in mystery. By the end of the day, the names and faces of the scientists and managers were a blur.

At five o'clock, Mr. Dirk gave instructions on locking up. He said, "You are permitted to leave. I have some things to finish up."

I collected my coat and turned to say goodbye, but he was absorbed in paperwork and didn't respond. As I joined a throng of weary men streaming toward the bus, I imagined the stolen shorthand brief burning a hole in my purse. I might as well be carrying kryptonite.

Tonight, I'd study the list even though it had become clear that I probably didn't need to. Many of the words were repeated—especially the word reactor. But what was it exactly? I reacted deliciously when Pauly put my hand in his pocket. But that didn't make me a reactor. Only one thing seemed clear. Since there was such a thing as a B Reactor, there must also be an A and a C reactor. Whatever they were making was enormous.

As the bus pulled away, the Columbia River glowed pink and silver in the dying light. Sand and sagebrush were cast in gold. Men talked quietly and newspapers crackled. As strange and exhausting as the day had been, I felt a certain satisfaction knowing I had done my best on this adventure to save the world.

I smiled at Dr. Holt's words. He'd given me a piece of gold to carry through the dark day. And soon I'd be freed from the barking Mr. Dirk.

For now, I'd remember Pauly's warm hand in mine, his sweet brown eyes and infectious laugh. I sighed. I couldn't wait until Wednesday when he came for dinner.

• • • •

I SET MR. DIRK'S SHORTHAND notes on my nightstand and the record player needle on *Cow Cow Boogie*. As I sang along with Ella Fitzgerald, her smooth, rich voice soothed my frazzled nerves.

Betty opened the door without knocking. "I think I'm going to die a thousand deaths before Doug comes home." She lay on my bed. "You can't imagine how wonderful our honeymoon was. And now we're torn asunder." Her eyes spilled and she wiped them with her fingers.

The shorthand notes seemed to glow like kryptonite as I crammed them into my purse.

"What was that?" She sat up.

"Oh, it's nothing. Just some weird stuff about confidentiality that I'm supposed to study. It's even more important in the 100 Area. They hammer it into your head. You know how it is." I sat on the bed and tried to change the subject. "Now, what were you saying about Doug?"

Betty lay back down and put her hand over her eyes dramatically. "You can't even imagine. I mean, you and Paul care about each other, but until you're married, you have no idea what being in love really means."

"It must be so hard. I can't imagine." If I kept her going, she'd forget all about asking me about my day. Because I couldn't tell her that Mr. Dirt had slashed my papers with so many red marks that it still stung. That the things I was learning about were like from some sort of strange comic book universe. Or that the thing they called a pencil detector I wore around my neck wasn't designed to detect pencils, but instead some sort of dangerous invisible substance. I didn't want to tell her that the only other woman I'd met so far was suffering in pain. I sighed.

Betty must have noticed that I wasn't really listening. "How was work today?"

I shrugged. "I missed Pat and Mrs. Chase and even Mary, but it was okay."

"What was the 100 Area like?" Betty was suddenly charged with curiosity.

"It was like a big factory. I have no idea what they're making out there, but whatever it is, it's something huge." I hoped that would give her just the right amount to derail her questions. "So, tell me more about Doug. Have you heard from him yet?"

"Weren't you listening? I just told you I hadn't heard anything." Betty glared my way. "The good thing is that Pat and I went to the grand opening of the new donut shop downtown after work. We met some ladies that Pat knows. You remember Annette from the day we were applying for jobs. And some of the girls from the bowling alley. We had so much fun." She laid down again and sighed dramatically. "Pat is still mad that you ditched her. Oh, and get this. Mrs. Chase hired this woman named Mildred to take your place. Pat says she never showers, and the room now smells like B.O. They must be getting desperate for typists because they hired her. And of course, they hired you." She crossed her arms. "We're going to meet there again later this week." She stood up. "Well, I've got to go. Maybe I'll see you tomorrow."

"I doubt it. Pauly is coming over for dinner, and we're going to be busy reconnecting." I opened the door and held it for her as she waltzed out.

I slammed the door, smarting like she'd slashed me with a hundred paper cuts. She'd said just enough to make me feel guilty for leaving Pat. Personally responsible for the smelly woman's hiring. Left out. And stupid. Somehow, yet again, Betty had managed to let me know she thought I was stupid even though I'd landed a very important, top-secret job.

Chapter 22

The next day, I set my hand in my pocket to make sure the stolen notes stayed securely inside and watched for Mr. Dirk to climb on the bus. I'd try to slip them into the file cabinet first thing.

The Coyote's colorless gaze speared me the minute he stepped onto the bus. I shrunk toward the window. He slunk onto the seat next to me. "Hello, Ally, right?" His sour smell reminded me of the Sheboygan town drunk.

I nodded. "This seat is reserved for my boss, though. He should be here any minute."

Mr. Dirk stepped aboard. I waved wildly. "Over here! I've been saving you a seat." My stomach sank as he barely glanced my way and continued toward the back. I turned around to see if I could move to a seat next to him, but the whole bus was crammed full.

The Coyote stared past me out the window as we drove past the guard station near the sign that said, Government Property NO TRESPASSING. He ripped the top off a pack of Clove gum. "You want a stick?"

Even his voice was slimy. I shook my head and turned toward the window, trying to suck in the fresh air slipping through the crack. It didn't work. The smell of cloves and alcoholic sourness invaded my nostrils.

"Do you work in the 100 Area now?" He spread his legs so that his wiry thigh touched mine.

I hugged the cold bus wall and nodded. Maybe if I let him know I had a boyfriend he would leave me alone. But that meant I had to talk to him.

His leg jounced against mine as we traveled through a pothole. "What are you doing out there?"

"Secretary." The warnings about him sounded in my head. But even louder was the indefinable, troubling sense that he posed an unknowable danger.

His gum snapped. "I was transferred to the 100 Area a while back. Working swing shift. How about you?"

My nerves felt on fire. "My boyfriend and I both work days."

"You got a boyfriend, huh? What's his name?" He eyed me up and down as if measuring me for truth.

"Paul. I'm going to see him tonight. I can't wait." I sat up taller.

"I don't see you at the recreation hall with your friends anymore. What do you do for fun?"

"Oh, Paul and I mostly just visit at my house. Sometimes we go to the soda shop."

He stared glassily ahead in response, his head swaying with the motion of the bus.

I clutched my purse like a shield as he leaned his head back against the seat and closed his eyes. When he began snoring, I glanced at my watch and relaxed slightly. Hopefully, he would sleep the remaining thirty minutes it took to get to the 100 Area.

I began to review the things I needed to do today. I'd make myself useful and attentive to whatever Mr. Dirk asked me to do, and at my first chance, I'd slip the stolen shorthand notes into the file.

The sleeping Coyote started to tip in my direction.

I pushed him back. "Oh no, you don't."

He fell heavily against my side. His head hit my shoulder. His sideburns tickled my neck. Putrid breath blew in my face with every snore. I pushed him away, but he was dead weight.

I stifled a scream and rummaged around in my purse for a ballpoint pen. Poking his leg with the tip of it only caused his head to slip off my shoulder until it was hanging over my breast. I rammed the pen again into his heavy canvas pants. He snorted, twitched, and resumed snoring. His red neck lay bare, exposed. I prodded it. He swatted at the pen strike as if it were a fly and sat up. His eyes opened a slit.

I weighed whether I should engage him in conversation to try to keep him awake. No. He might think I liked him, and that would create its own set of problems. Soon he was snoring again. His head dipped heavily to my shoulder.

The early sun glowed an angry orange through the clouds at the horizon line. I sniffed back tears and prayed for help. A bead of sweat dripped from his head to my coat. Maybe God really did hate it out here in this dismal desert. Or maybe he was angry at me and punishing me for something. Loneliness blew through me. I missed Pat and Mrs. Chase. The gals would have fun at the donut shop without me. The bus rumbled with strangers except for Mr. Dirk who would bark at me and slash my papers with bloody wounds.

But at least I'd see Pauly tomorrow night. We'd sneak away from the family, and he'd wrap me in his arms. I'd forget all about this horrible ride through the desert with a monster's head mashing my shoulder. Pleasant thoughts of Pauly carried me along to the 100 Area.

When the factory of enormous buildings appeared in the distance and the bus stopped at the Gate House, I stood abruptly. The Coyote startled and rubbed his face.

"Excuse me, please." I began to push past.

"Oh, sure." He stood, his wiry frame blocking my way. "See you this evening, then." He lifted his cap before lumbering off the bus.

This evening I would sit next to someone already seated. It didn't matter who they were as long as it wasn't the Coyote.

When I caught up to Mr. Dirk, he sounded irritated. "Tomorrow, hold the seat next to you open. I had hoped to brief you about protocol on the way to the office."

I felt like screaming, but schooled myself to speak professionally. "Tomorrow morning, I'll wait for you, and we can find a seat together."

The Coyote disappeared into the change house, and I breathed a sigh of relief. Telling him about Pauly had seemed to discourage him. He wouldn't trouble me again.

"We have a meeting in the conference room first thing. Sometimes, group meetings are rapid and difficult to follow, so we'll both take notes." Mr. Dirk opened the door. "Good morning, Mrs. Frank."

She nodded at my smile, her pale face wan under the fluorescent light.

"You need to start carrying the keys on your person starting now." Mr. Dirk handed me the big key ring and I dropped them in my suit jacket pocket next to the stolen notes. He began firing instructions even as I stashed my coat and purse in the closet. "Our job is to capture the discussion around each agenda item. Pay special attention to solutions as they emerge. Others will also be writing notes, but our job is to capture the whole meeting." He handed me an agenda. "Take some time to glance over that. I'll be back in a few minutes." Mr. Dirk headed out the door.

My stomach fluttered uncomfortably as I hurried over to the filing cabinet and shoved the key into the lock.

Mr. Dirk's voice sounded behind me. "You do remember that the file cabinet is to remain locked unless you are getting something out or putting it away?" His normal scowl deepened.

"I, uh. Yes." I felt myself color and sat down weakly with the agenda. The Coyote's smell seemed imbedded in my skin, and all I could think about was washing myself clean in the restroom. When Mr. Dirk indicated it was time to go to the meeting, I hadn't even registered the barest information from the agenda.

"Let's go," said Mr. Dirk. I hurried after him to the conference room. The big wooden table sat empty in the center of the room. "I assume you know how to make coffee." Mr. Dirk motioned toward an electric percolator in the corner.

I nodded and took the pot to a lunchroom that no one seemed to use. I'd watched Mother make coffee and it seemed easy enough, but before I did that I had to try to rid myself of the Coyote's putrid smell. I soaped up a dishcloth and scrubbed my face and neck until it felt raw.

Then I filled the pot with water, dug in the cupboard for the Folgers tin, and used the enclosed scoop to fill the metal basket to the brim. The homey activity reset my brain. With the Coyote's scent wiped clean, the nightmare on the bus faded away.

I'd put the safety briefing back in the file cabinet today while filing something else. And this morning I'd stay invisible, alert, and helpful. I carried the coffee pot to the conference room and plugged it in, then studied the agenda as people came in buzzing and found their places at the table. Dr. Holt sat next to me and smiled.

"I think the coffee is done if you'd like some." I stood up and began filling coffee cups.

A red-haired man in a coat and tie at the head of the table said, "I see we have a new secretary. Mr. Dirk, can you do the introductions?"

I wished I could hide under the table as all the intelligent eyes in the room fell on me. Instead, I tried to smile and meet their eyes as Mr. Dirk made introductions in his barking voice. As the meeting kicked into action, a heated volley ensued about the speed of production and the efficacy of safety procedures. I was at an extreme disadvantage because I had to read name badges of speakers while recording their words. My fingers trembled as I tried to capture the essence of the conversation.

When the meeting ended, my head spun with questions. Even with the safety procedures in place, the operation appeared to be dangerous. Radiation poisoning was a by-product of metal production, but how could metal cause sickness? And what kind of sickness did it cause? Perhaps our mission here was to create a poison we could turn loose on the enemy. If I hung around long enough, I had a feeling that I'd find out the answers to these questions and more.

When the meeting ended, I handed my notes to Mr. Dirk. "I'll clean up here." The morning had already been difficult enough without watching him slash up my notes. Plus, I needed a change of pace from high-intensity concentration. He grunted and left the room as I sloshed coffee from a full cup onto the conference table. As I collected the cups, I realized that no one had tasted more than a sip. I poured a splash of coffee into a clean cup to test it, took a swallow and choked. It was gritty with grounds and bitter.

Tonight, I'd ask Mother to teach me the right way to make coffee. She'd be shocked and impressed that her little girl was required to do something so important as making coffee for a room full of scientists and managers. Daddy would be more than a little troubled about my job if he knew the details. Betty would be green with envy, all while trying to spin it so that my job meant less than nothing at all. Pauly must never know how close I was to all this secret information. If he did, it would only hurt him. I had to play stupid.

Back in the office, Mr. Dirk handed me both copies of the meeting minutes. "Type them in triplicate and file them. Don't give the final copies to Mrs. Frank. We'll leave work an hour early so I can teach you how to access the main procedures vault in the 700 Area. You won't normally need to file things there, but I want you to learn in case I'm absent."

I sat down to type with a sense of relief. I had made a few spelling errors and missed some of the content, but I had kept up for the most part, even with the severe disadvantage of not knowing anyone.

I sighed with satisfaction. Except for the coffee, I was proving I was smart enough to do this job.

Soon, I'd be free from Mr. Dirt. And I'd make sure to never put myself in a position to be accosted by the Coyote again. Before I filed a copy of the meeting minutes, I slipped the contraband shorthand notes about the safety meeting into its proper file.

• • • •

THE SCENT OF CHICKEN and dumplings greeted me at the door along with Timmy, who came running from the kitchen. "Ally, you're finally home. Everybody has been waiting for you. Pauly and Daddy are down in the basement looking at the heater, and dinner is in the oven."

Pauly stepped out of the kitchen, grinning from ear to ear. "You're a sight for sore eyes."

"Oh, hi. You don't know how glad I am to see you. It's been a long day, made longer because Mr. Dirk needed to show me something in the 700 Area." I leaned in for a quick hug. Each minute of delay had felt like an hour.

I kicked off my heels. "I'm going to change out of this suit."

"You look like a proper businesswoman. I like it." Pauly's grin deepened.

"I'll be right back." I hurried upstairs and threw on my most comfortable decent dress and slippers. I glanced in the mirror and reapplied some lipstick.

"Hurry up, Ally!" Timmy opened the door. "Stop worrying about how you look. No one cares about that."

Everyone was already seated at the dining room table when we came downstairs. Pauly reached under the tablecloth for my hand as Daddy said grace. Comfort from his fingers seemed to seal out the memories from the morning bus ride. As long as I was with Pauly, the Coyote couldn't hurt me.

"How was your day, dear?" Mother's doe eyes glowed as she looked between us.

"It was fine. But I need you to teach me how to make coffee. Today I had to make it for a meeting, and it was full of coffee grounds. No one could drink it." I took a piece of chicken and passed the platter to Pauly.

Pauly glanced my way questioningly. Of course he would. Daddy had told him I was the best cook in the world. One of these days I was going to have to come clean and tell him that I didn't even know the barest facts about cooking, even if it made Daddy look like a liar.

"Oh, that's wonderful. My little girl in charge of making coffee." Mother passed the dumplings to Daddy.

"You have no idea how good it is to see you." I turned toward Pauly. "I've been waiting for this all day. How was your day at the newspaper?" I asked, hoping to turn the tide of conversation away from my new job.

"I reported on a Benton County Public Utilities office manager who was pilfering money from the accounting system." Pauly took a bite of dumpling. "This is delicious, Mary."

Daddy shook his head. "I saw your article. It's shameful what people will do for money."

Mother asked, "Did you always know you wanted to be a reporter?"

Pauly shrugged. "I was always good at writing, but I've mostly fallen into it because my dad needs somebody to work for him right now."

Thankfully, my parents kept asking questions about the interesting people and their stories he encountered on the job. When we finished eating, I reminded Mother, "I have to learn how to make coffee tonight because I won't have time in the morning."

"Let's get the dishes done, and then I'll teach you." Mother stacked the plates and handed them to me.

I sighed in frustration as Pauly and Daddy retired to the living room. This evening was already too short. "Mother, please. Just show me now. I want to spend as much time as I can with Pauly."

"Okay, Ally dear. Of course, the amount of coffee you add to the basket depends on how many people you're serving, but never fill the basket to the brim or you'll get grounds in the coffee." I could hear Pauly and Daddy laughing in the living room, and I felt I might wiggle right out of my skin as Mother slowly showed me how many scoops of coffee to use per cup.

Finally free, I sat as close to Pauly as I dared with Daddy in the room. Daddy told us about another Sheboygan boy who was missing in action. I remembered the young man and his family well. The news hit me hard. Almost as bad, Pauly's face took on that now familiar defeated cast. I could almost hear his mind. Here he was, enjoying a pleasurable evening, while men on the other side of the world were dying. I grabbed his hand and clung, wishing I could banish the frustrated thoughts reflected in his face.

A picture of the poison or whatever they were creating at the enormous Hanford complex exploded in my mind. Maybe they would be able to end the war very soon. And along with it, Pauly's angst. I wasn't only sacrificing my comforts for those fighting the battles overseas. I was also sacrificing myself for Pauly's peace of mind.

Too soon, he stood up and turned to me. "You look exhausted, and tomorrow comes early for both of us."

Exhausted was codeword for bad. As he said thank you and goodbye, the memory of the Coyote and his putrid breath on my breasts almost knocked me down. Hopefully Pauly couldn't smell him on me. Suddenly I couldn't wait to scrub myself all over in the tub. "Okay." I walked him to the door.

"I'll pick you up on Friday night and we can go get burgers and fries at the soda shop with Pat. She's dying to see you." Pauly stood back, his eyes troubled. "You look more than just tired. Are you sure everything is okay?"

I nodded and tried to smile. "Mr. Dirk is a grouch, and the bus ride is long. That's all."

"Well, I look forward to seeing you day after tomorrow. And Saturday and Sunday for that matter." He kissed me lingeringly.

I sighed with pleasure. "I can't wait."

When he drove away, I raced upstairs and filled the tub with the hottest water. Slipping into the scented bath felt heavenly. I scrubbed myself all over, then sat back in the water to soak.

My new job was painful, but I was doing the right thing by making this sacrifice. As much for Pauly as for the men dying on the battlefield. And I was proving to myself that I was smart as I quickly learned the procedures and processes for this top-secret position. When the water cooled, I shivered and climbed out of the tub. Tomorrow, I'd cling to Mr. Dirk's side all the way to work. Betty and Pat would laugh so hard if they knew that Dirt was my key to well-being.

Chapter 23

When I stepped into the house after my first week of work in the 100 Area, Daddy and Mother's smiles beamed rays of happy light at me. What was this about?

Pauly stood from the couch, grinning. "Hi. I'm here a bit early. But don't hurry. We've got time before we need to pick up Pat."

"Hi. You have no idea how good it is to see you." I leaned into Pauly for a brief hug. "I need a shower, though. I feel gritty."

"Take your time."

Timmy raced into the room. "Yeah, Ally. Take a long time." He grabbed Pauly's hand. "I didn't see any mice in the basement and I'm tired of looking. Would you play army men with me?"

"My army men are going to whup yours." Pauly knelt on the floor next to the box of army men and blocks.

I ran up the stairs suddenly enlivened after the exhausting workweek. Today I needed Pauly like I needed air, and I couldn't wait to spend the evening with him at the soda shop. It would be good to see Pat too. I dried myself with a clean white towel and wiped a circle in the foggy mirror. My face in the mirror reflected my happy excitement.

Before I left work, Mr. Dirk had told me I'd be on my own on Tuesday. While it made me a little nervous, I agreed. I understood the procedures involved with the job and had learned all the scientists' and managers' names. The people were hard driven and never seemed to stop working even to take a lunch break. But all seemed understanding of the fact that I was new and learning. Soon I'd be Dirt free. I couldn't wait to tell Pat and Betty.

The only problem with freedom from Mr. Dirk was that I'd lose my traveling companion. I'd shrunk under the Coyote's hard, colorless gaze every morning when he'd climbed on the bus. Thankfully, the one day when Mr. Dirk took an earlier bus to work, I'd found a seat next to one of the nice scientists from my office. I could do that again.

I buttoned up my red dress, slipped on my shoes, and hurried down the stairs.

Pauly was holding an army man and grinning at Timmy. "Even the sergeant was covered with spaghetti."

My parents laughed and Timmy jumped on his back. "It's not a spaghetti war!"

Pauly shook him off and turned to me. "You look ravishing tonight."

Betty appeared in the dining room, looking wan. "Pat told me you were going to the soda shop. Can I tag along?" She tried for a smile, but it didn't work.

I sighed, irritated. Betty would monopolize the whole evening with her sorrow. But we couldn't very well say no. She was lonely for Doug and needed companionship.

Pauly nodded. "You're welcome to join us."

"Okay, then. I guess we're on our way," I waved at my parents.

Betty climbed into the backseat. "I got a letter from Doug. He's being sent to the battlefield in France. They're shipping out soon."

Pauly's face took on that now familiar bleakness, and I scooted closer to try to comfort. him.

Betty sniffed loudly. When I turned, she was wiping her eyes.

I asked, "Are you sure you feel good enough to go out? Maybe we can talk tomorrow or something."

Betty twisted her wedding ring. "I thought maybe it would help me to go out, but seeing you two together is just making it worse. Take me home."

We drove back to Betty's house in silence. She opened the door with tears dripping down her cheeks and fled to the door without saying goodbye.

"I feel bad for her, but it's a good thing she won't be around to spoil our evening." I leaned closer to Pauly. The smell of Ivory soap couldn't mask his deeply masculine scent. I breathed him in hungrily as he put his arm around me.

He shifted the car into drive. "Yeah. Let's try to put them out of mind. I've really missed you this week."

"Oh, me too. I thought the week would never end. What were your favorite news stories this week?" I listened contentedly as Pauly reported on the small and large happenings around the community.

• • • •

PAT HURRIED TOWARD an empty booth in the soda shop and waved us over. Pauly stood back while I scooted in first.

Pat looked around. "I just hope someone else sits with us, so I don't have to be the fifth wheel again. I mean, I love you guys, but you know."

"Fred's going to be here." Pauly waved at someone across the room.

"Oh, great. Farmer Fred. Lately, he's paid way too much attention to me. He's a nice guy, but he's almost old enough to be my father."

"Just think of him as a good friend." Pauly held my hand under the table, and I snuggled closer.

Pat sighed and looked at me. "So, my ex-best friend the traitor, how did it go?"

"Oh Pat, don't say that. You're going to break my heart. I've missed you so much. Even Mrs. Chase and Mary."

Pat sighed. "Did Betty tell you about the woman who took over your job? She supports her mother and a bunch of siblings. There's never enough hot water to wash diapers and shower, and so by Friday, she smells ripe. Whew! It's too bad she can type."

"I'm sorry. I was hoping it would be someone fun," I said, feeling guilty for leaving.

Pat sighed. "We all miss you. Even Mary."

"Can you spend the night tomorrow night?" I asked, hoping to bridge the gap that had formed between us.

Pauly grinned. "Do you mean me or Pat?"

I laughed and slapped his arm. If only he could spend the night. My cheeks warmed. Proper girls didn't dream about that, did they?

Pat laughed. "Yes. I accept, even though you are a traitor and I know I'm second choice. We have a lot of catching up to do."

The waitress took our orders. When she left, Pauly put his arm around me, "So what's it like out there in Secretsville, Ally Oop?"

"Oh, I don't know. I'm working at this enormous factory of some kind, and it's surrounded by the unending desert. Secrecy and security measures are worse. No one talks just for fun. It's all work, work, work." I bit my lip. "If I told you anything more than that I'd probably get fired or go to jail. You know how it is." Suddenly, the excitement of the evening drained out of me, and I felt exhausted.

Pat asked, "How is it working with Dirt?"

"The first day he slashed all my errors with red marks until I felt like I was bleeding. It will be so good to be out from under his thumb. He's going to leave me on my own in the office starting next Tuesday. He's such a sour puss. Not mean, exactly. Just hyper-focused. No humanity leaks through at all. The only other woman in the place is like a white shadow. I think mostly because she's in a lot of pain, but it's hard to tell."

"In a top-secret position, the nature of the work must be different too." Pauly's face was alive with interest.

"Yeah. It's a real secretarial job. Very different from just typing."

"You must be learning all kinds of things," he said.

I cared about him too much to shut him out, but I couldn't share either. I just hoped he understood. "Yeah, but it's hard to describe because I don't really understand it all..." I trailed off as the words radiation, plutonium, and reactor spun through my mind. Not to mention the pencil monitor and other bizarre safety measures. "Plus, you know I can't talk about it."

I was grateful when Fred showed up at the table, his large grin highlighting the creases in his cheeks. It was clear he had put a lot of effort into his appearance tonight. His mustache was trimmed, and his hair was slicked back with grease. He smiled at Pat as he squeezed his frame into the seat next to her. She scooted closer to the wall.

I sat quietly as Pauly and Pat reconnected with him, relieved that the subject of my work was forgotten. Hopefully, the next time we met they wouldn't assault me with questions I couldn't answer.

Chapter 24

The yellow crocus pushing through the sand next to Betty's back door contrasted with the dread I felt as I stepped onto her porch the next day. I didn't want to listen to her cry endlessly about missing Doug, but I hadn't seen her all week. It was time to check in. Maybe I could help her feel a bit better. Hopefully she'd wouldn't ask me a bunch of questions about my job that I couldn't answer.

I pushed open the door. "Hello!"

"Hello, Alice. I'm glad you came to visit." Aunt Edna looked up from her darning and frowned. "Betty is having a pretty rough time of it." Her voice rang sharply. "It's not that I didn't try to warn her against getting involved with a young man heading off to war."

I smiled. "Hi, Aunt Edna." I agreed with her, but it would only make things worse if I said so. Best to smile and escape.

Betty opened her bedroom door in her pink chenille bathrobe. She touched her matted hair and peered at me through eyes red from crying. "Come in." She shut the door behind us. "My mom is making everything much worse by harping at me. And my dad is working overtime again today. I've got no support from him anyway." She sat at the edge of her unmade bed and creased and re-creased a letter from Doug.

"Tell me all about it." I slipped off my shoes and sat cross-legged on the bed.

"Doug found out that he doesn't get more than two days of leave between basic training and going overseas. We were counting on spending at least a week together after being apart for so long. I just don't think I can wait till..." She stopped as tears filled her eyes and dripped.

"Can't you spend time with him in Seattle for a few days? It's not that far."

"Daddy said I could take the car if I can get someone to go with me. But still. It's so short." She sniffed and patted her eyes with a handkerchief. "Can you drive with me?"

I couldn't bear to leave Pauly for a whole weekend and made up an excuse. "I can't commit because everyone works overtime, and I could be asked to do it anytime. How about Pat?"

"It sounds like your new job is fun, fun, fun," Betty said sarcastically. "Yeah. I'm sure she'd love a road trip to Seattle."

It was no wonder Aunt Edna was irritated at her. It wasn't as if she didn't know that Doug would be leaving for war from the first time she met him. I sighed. It was just best to listen.

Forty-five minutes later, she seemed to have run out of tears and words. "I know. I should take a shower and get dressed. What are you doing the rest of the day?" She looked at me as if seeing me for the first time.

"Pauly and Pat are coming over this afternoon for a game and dinner. Pat is spending the night. You're welcome to join us for dinner and games if you feel good enough."

"Yeah. I'll probably come over as long as Pat is going to be there."

I escaped into the hall, glad that she was too self-absorbed to ask me any questions about my new job. I didn't need any more prying. "I'll see you later then."

Aunt Edna stood in the kitchen waiting for the kettle to boil. "That girl is going to be the death of me."

"Yeah, I think she just needs us to listen. She seems to feel a bit better. At least she's in the shower. I invited her over for the afternoon."

"Thank you, Alice. You're a good cousin."

I relished her kind words, thankful that she wasn't angry that I hadn't told her about the wedding. After Betty's meltdown, and Pat and Pauly's questioning, I needed it.

Chapter 25

On Sunday at Riverside Park, I walked with Pauly to a bench overlooking the river. We sat down and I put my head on his shoulder, glad for the view of the calm water and the gulls soaring across the dome of blue sky. Friday and Saturday with Pat and the family had been fun, but I was delighted to have him all to myself.

Pauly wrapped his strong arm around me. At times like this, Wisconsin was like a pleasant dream fading fast. I'd always miss Grandma and Grandpa, but Pauly had filled my longing heart to overflowing. I stared at the smooth river reflecting the sky and the low hills in the distance. From this vantage point, even the desert looked pretty.

"I know how much you hate the desert and how bad the dust storms are. But they'll improve once the landscaping is done. I saw some saplings coming into town on a truck the other day. You know it didn't use to be this bad." Pauly fiddled nervously with something in his pocket. "I know you've wanted to go back to Sheboygan more than anything, but..." He trailed off. Suddenly he was on one knee. "I love you, Alice Ann Krepsky and I always will. I know you're planning to return to Sheboygan, and I'll understand if—"

"Stop." My heart felt like it would explode with love and longing as I looked into his uncertain brown eyes. "Sheboygan isn't more important than you. I want more than anything in the world to be your wife. I love you too, and I always will."

His face split into his electric grin. He kissed each finger before sliding on a ring with a tiny chip of a diamond.

I held out my hand to admire it. "It's perfect."

"It looks beautiful on you." Pauly took me in his arms for a long, deepening kiss.

"Ew!" A dirty kid dragging a stick behind him stared at us from the sandy shore.

Our teeth bumped as we laughed. Pauly said, "Hey, kid. What are you staring at?"

A woman across the park called, "Harry! Come back here this instant or I'm going to whip your backside." The kid wiped his nose and ambled off dragging the stick.

Pauly's eyes glinted with humor. "I'm looking forward to a couple of Harrys or Harriets in our future."

"Oh, me too." Thrilled, I leaned my head against his chest.

His voice rumbled in my ear. "I asked your father for your hand in marriage on Friday before you got home from work."

"Hmmm. I wondered why they looked so happy. And why you were there so early."

"Yeah. They wholeheartedly approved. My parents are dying to meet you. Especially since I told them about my intentions."

"I can't wait."

"So, I guess we need to set a date. The sooner the better, in my view." Pauly looked hungrily at me. "What do you think?"

"I want a full church wedding with my grandparents and aunts and uncles here. That means we need some time to plan." A grief-stricken Betty swam into mind. A while back, I would have been filled with glee at the fact that I was going to have a real wedding and she hadn't. But knowing how much she missed and worried about Doug made it a hollow victory. Despite that, I'd pull no stops in planning the wedding of my dreams. "How about we shoot for September when it's not too hot or cold?"

Pauly groaned. "I'm not sure I can wait that long."

"But I've wanted a church wedding for as long as I can remember." I kissed him.

When we finally parted, he said. "I want my girl to be happy. September it is." He stood. "Let's go for a drive. Then I want to take you out to a quiet, romantic dinner."

I grabbed his hand. "I'll follow you anywhere."

Chapter 26

I threaded my way down the bus aisle until I saw Dr. Holt's head, bent over a book. "Good morning, Dr. Holt." I sat next to him.

He nodded a kind smile in my direction and resumed reading. Thankfully, I'd been able to keep a good distance away from the Coyote last week. I'd even been able to avoid his eyes poking daggers in my direction. Thanks to Dr. Holt, I could do it again today and for the rest of the week, too.

Pleasure floated away worry as I held out my hand to admire my engagement ring. Betty would be my matron of honor, and Pat would be my maid of honor. I'd let them fight out who'd be responsible for Pauly's ring and who would hold my bouquet as the wedding vows were spoken. For my dress, I wanted a fitted lacy bodice, a big flouncy skirt, and tiny cap sleeves. Maybe Daddy would drive us to Spokane for a shopping trip. Mrs. Dalgrin from church was the obvious choice to play the organ.

When the bus roared off toward the 100 Area with neither Mr. Dirk or the Coyote aboard, I wrenched my mind from the deliciousness of wedding plans and Pauly. Correct spellings of scientific words associated with the project sparked in my head, and I felt a burst of confidence and pride. I could do this job. I'd already proven it, and I'd prove it again.

The way to ending the war was as clear as a frosted window on a cold day, but it wouldn't last forever, partly because of my effort and sacrifice. I glanced at Dr. Holt. I'd choose to think of it as an adventure.

By the time we reached the 100 Area, blasts of wind had begun kicking up dust. As I walked with Dr. Holt to the office, I wanted to ask him questions about himself and his life, but the secrets of the job felt like a heavy barrier to any kind of normal conversation. At my old job, my new ring would have caused the gals to go crazy, and Mrs. Chase would have to shush us to get us to settle down. But at least we'd finally gotten a phone installed at home. Tonight, I'd call Pat and ask her to be my maid of honor.

Mrs. Frank's desk stood empty in the foyer. In the office, Mr. Dirk sat hunched over something at the desk. "Good morning." I went to the closet to hang my coat.

He greeted me with a grunt. "I've prepared a list of procedures in case you forget something. I've included my phone number. Keep it locked." He beckoned me to the file cabinet as I shrugged out of my coat. "Feel free to call me if you have problems."

I peered into the file drawer. "Thank you." I wanted to show him my ring, but instead shoved my hand in my jacket pocket with the keys.

He stood. "Mrs. Frank called in sick today. That means we need to go make some information deliveries."

My coat was still warm when I pulled it off the hanger. If Mr. Dirk wasn't such a machine, he would have told me to keep my coat on. At least I could brag to Betty that I was now a part time messenger. Not that she'd even care anymore. Mr. Dirk fought to open the door into the wind. I crushed my hat to my head as sand stung my face. Just five minutes before, it had been relatively calm. Now it looked as we were in for a full-on dust storm.

Mr. Dirk yelled above the sound of the wind. "First stop, Change House."

The wind pushed us into the Change House and slammed the door behind us. Men eating dinner at a long table stopped to stare.

Mr. Dirk led me into a lounge scattered with low-slung couches and magazines on tables. Talking men in overalls exited a door marked Change Room/Showers and disappeared out a side door.

Mr. Dirk motioned to a bulletin board. "Messages go here." He pushed a tack into the corkboard to post the briefing. "Someone else oversees their removal, so don't even try to guess what's not needed. Next, we'll take the 100 Area bus to the B Reactor."

The words B Reactor made my heart race. According to the meetings I'd sat in, the B reactor was where the danger was. The place where my pencil monitor might detect dangerous levels of metal poison. Everyone seemed healthy enough, but perhaps they hid away the ones who were sickened and unable to function. Maybe that was why Mrs. Frank was absent. I sighed, picturing her at home, coughing. Would I be next?

Mr. Dirk led the way onto a bus marked Inter-Area. "Buses run throughout the 100 Area at all hours of the day and night."

We passed a guard tower where a man in uniform peered at our bus moving along the street. The vehicle stopped in front of a multi-level concrete building. Next to it sat a smokestack belching white smoke.

"This is B Reactor." Inside, Mr. Dirk led me down a narrow hallway to a bulletin board. He posted his message under the word Urgent, then motioned to the other side of the board. "Training notices go here."

A door marked Danger opened, and a man in white protective clothing lumbered out. I shrunk back as he passed by in the narrow hallway. If radiation poisoning was catchy like the flu, I'd surely caught it from contact with his white safety suit. My heart raced as I thought of carrying poison home to my family and Pauly. The white-suited man disappeared behind a door with a Silence Means Security poster on it.

On the bus back to the administration building, Mr. Dirk said casually, "On days when Mrs. Frank is absent, you will be required to work as a messenger in addition to your other job, and that will create longer hours. I'm sure you've understood that overtime is a part of the job. Everyone does it. You'll make time and a half."

I bit my lip. Right now, I didn't care a lick about the money. I did care about seeing Pauly and planning for my wedding. Before I took the job, no one said anything about overtime. Now people talked about it all the time. I sighed. At least we had a phone, and I could call to let them know if I'd be late.

Thankfully, the day shot past like a bullet. At 4:55, I yawned and finished up a letter to a Mr. Smith about metal slugs. Soon I'd be home waiting by the phone for Pauly's call. After that, I'd call Pat and invite her to be my maid of honor. I'd wait a few days to tell Betty. Hopefully, by then, she'd have had time to get over the worst of missing Doug.

Mr. Dirk interrupted my reverie. "Post these two bulletins at the Change House on your way out." He shoved two of my typed documents into a file folder and set it on my desk. "Tomorrow you're on your own. Questions?"

I shook my head. Hopefully, I'd never have any questions ever, then I'd never have to hear him bark at me again. I put on what I hoped was a polite face. "Thank you for all your help, sir. I'll be sure to call you if I have a question."

His stiff face cracked into a smile. "You've learned quickly, and the scientists and managers have told me they're happy with your work."

"Thank you, sir." A wave of pride washed over me. Suddenly the Coyote, the stressful job, required overtime, secrecy, and dust storms in this otherworldly place were worth it. No one could ever think I was stupid again, and I was doing something important. My work could save lives.

"Go ahead, now." He waved me off and turned back to the file cabinet. Maybe Mr. Dirk did have a human bone in his body after all.

I put on my coat. "Goodbye, sir. And thank you again."

In the Change House, a wolf whistle rang out from one of the men scattered around at the tables. I felt myself blush and hurried into the lounge area where I carefully posted the notices.

When I turned around to leave, the Coyote's hard, leering eyes stared into mine. "Fancy meeting you here."

I flashed my engagement ring, turned back to the bulletin board, and pretended to study a posting. A cold shiver ran up my back at his dark presence lurking behind. I re-pinned a training notice to buy time.

A man burst out of the change room. "Hey, Bundy. Stop staring like a dog with your tongue hanging out. We gotta go."

I waited to be sure they were gone, then I ran toward the buses, my black heels pinching my toes with each step. A rock seemed to rise up out of nowhere on the uneven roadway. I tripped and went sprawling. My knees and hands stung as I lay stunned.

A shadow fell over me. "Are you okay?" The man's voice above me was gentle.

"I think so." I examined my stinging knees and hands. "Just a few scrapes. No harm done." Embarrassed, I tried to smile through my tears.

"There, there now." The balding gentleman dusted off my hat and patted my arm. "In shoes like that, it's best to walk around here." He touched his hat and continued on his way.

"Thank you!" I waved and walked to the bus stop. Fear had caused that accident. I was going to have to get over it, or something else worse could happen. The buses to and from work were always full. I could make sure there were always people between me and the Coyote. Besides, what could be worse than his putrid breath on my neck? I'd survived that. I stepped out of the gate just as my bus started to pull away. I raced after it. "No! Wait!" It didn't even slow. I swallowed a giant lump in my throat and turned.

A guard near the Clock Alley rubbed his red nose. "Another bus in a half hour. You might as well wait inside where it's warm." He gestured to the Clock Alley.

I sniffed back the tears that threatened to bust open like a Wisconsin downpour and glanced at my watch. A half hour wasn't much in the grand scheme of things. "Okay. Thank you."

In the Clock Alley, I discovered a brightly lit waiting room with a black phone hanging on the wall. I gratefully put the receiver to my ear and dialed my new phone number. Timmy answered in just one ring. His chirpy voice sounded like he was in the next room.

I wiped my eyes. "Hi, Timmy. I missed my bus and I'll be about a half hour late. Tell Mother, please."

He yelled into the receiver. "Ally is going to be late."

I heard Mother's voice in the distance asking a question.

"How late?" Timmy asked.

"A half an hour." I listened to Timmy relay my message. A man in a long coat entered the room and stood nearby.

Timmy said, "Hey Ally, today..."

The man behind me cleared his throat. "I've got to go, Timmy."

"Bye!"

I perched on a hard wooden chair. My skinned knees and hands were nothing a band aid wouldn't soothe. This weekend, we would ask when Pastor Carver was available to marry us, and we'd set a date. I'd get to meet Pauly's parents.

But as the minutes crawled by, I felt fenced off from those I loved—Pauly, Pat, my parents and Timmy—even Betty. What was I doing in this dangerous place all on my own? I perched on the edge of my seat with my purse clasped to my breast. I thought I heard the Coyote's voice from the other room and whispered, "Oh, God, please help."

When the bus finally pulled up, I stuck like glue to the stranger who'd used the phone after me. When I sat next to him on the empty bus, he unfolded his newspaper in my face.

I sat at the edge of my seat and watched each passenger climb aboard. Thankfully, we roared off without the Coyote aboard.

Chapter 27

The next weekend, Pauly opened his parents' front door, and the scent of tomatoes and spices enveloped me. I shivered with nerves as he hung my coat on a rack near the front door. Making a good first impression could set the stage for the rest of my life.

"Are you cold?" He put his arm around me. I shook my head and leaned into his comforting warmth.

White doilies and family pictures decorated the tables in the living room. Newspapers and magazines were stacked on the end of a coffee table. One wall was dominated by a full bookcase. A picture of Jesus on the cross hung near the doorway of a small dining room.

"Mom, Dad, we're here," Pauly called.

A round woman with a salt-and-pepper bun and a worried frown appeared in the doorway. Jowls hugged her smile as she examined me from head to toe. "Hello, Ally. I'm Beatrice."

A skinny, gray-haired man with Pauly's infectious grin appeared behind her and roared, "Welcome, Ally." He took my hands in both of his and scrutinized my face. "Our Pauly is smitten, and I can see why."

I felt myself blush under his intense gaze. Beatrice scowled and slapped her husband's arm. "Manners, Robert. Can't you see the girl is nervous? Shoes off, Pauly. Who knows where you've been tramping around today?" She turned to me. "You'll find out as soon as you're in charge of taking care of our king Pauly here that he still has a few things to learn about cleanliness and order." Her sharp words contrasted with the sweetness of her gaze fastened on her son.

"Hey, I'm not that big of a slob." Pauly slipped out of his shoes.

I followed suit, my toes in my nylons cold and exposed.

"Now, now, Bea, you're going to chase her off. Keep your shoes on, Ally, and have a seat." Robert gestured toward the living room.

I smiled at Beatrice. "Mrs. Armstrong, do you need some help in the kitchen?"

"Sure. But before that, let me see that ring on your finger." I held it out. "Our Pauly getting married." Bea examined the ring and my face. "Grandchildren can't be too far behind."

My face heated.

"All right, Mom. Now, how about supper? I'm starved." Pauly put his arm around me.

"Come with me, Ally, but call me Bea like the rest of this family."

"You're going to love my mother's spaghetti." Pauly called as I followed her to a warm yellow kitchen.

Spaghetti! I'd only seen pictures of it in advertisements. I couldn't imagine how I'd be able to navigate the long strings without splattering myself with tomato sauce. Maybe I would only pretend to eat. I was too nervous to be hungry anyway.

"Here. You can put the salad on the table." She handed me a molded salad with vegetables shining through the clear green gelatin. I set it on the red gingham tablecloth and admired the homey white dishes with tiny red flowers around the rim. Back in the kitchen, I watched her fill a large serving platter with the long, saucy spaghetti and spoon meatballs on the side. "It smells delicious."

"This is Pauly's favorite dinner." She gleamed as she handed me the platter to carry to the dining room.

His favorite dinner. And I'd never even eaten it before. Maybe I'd come clean and confess I had no idea how to cook. And maybe Bea, as scary as it seemed, would be willing to give me cooking lessons. I could learn how to cook Pauly's favorites. If I could only get through this dinner without creating a scene of flying noodles and red spots all over my starched white blouse and pale yellow cardigan.

Bea hollered, "Come on, you big lugs. It's dinner time."

Pauly and his dad stepped into the dining room laughing about something. Pauly held my chair. Bea opened the top of a foil-wrapped parcel and steam escaped, filling the air with the lovely scent of fresh garlic bread. We all joined hands, and the family recited a blessing over the food.

Robert glanced at me. "Now you got to understand. This spaghetti here was as foreign as Mars when we first got married. But after that first taste..." He kissed his fingertips and selected a piece of bread. "I couldn't get enough. What are your family origins?"

I slid a small spoonful of spaghetti and two meatballs onto my plate. "My dad's family is from England or somewhere like that. I have to admit, I've never eaten spaghetti." Mother's German heritage was best ignored what with the war going on. Especially when I was trying to make a good impression. I helped myself to a large portion of Jell-O salad. That was something I could eat without making too big of a mess. I watched as Pauly twisted his fork in the spaghetti. "So, you just wind it around the fork like that?" I asked shyly.

Robert said, "It takes a while to figure out how to eat it without making a mess. In fact, I'd suggest using your napkin as a bib." He stuffed his napkin in his neckline. "Like this, you see?"

I smiled gratefully at his rescue and shoved the napkin into my white blouse. Pauly, who was uncharacteristically quiet, seemed content to let us get to know each other without interruption. Or maybe he was too consumed by his favorite food to talk.

I concentrated on rolling the spaghetti around my fork. It slipped off. Finally, I got a few strands to my mouth and the flavors burst in my mouth. "Mmm. This is delicious." I smiled at Bea.

"My parents didn't approve of Robert because he was neither Catholic nor Italian. So, we moved way out west where it didn't matter if you were Catholic or Protestant, Italian or Irish."

"Oh, that must have been hard, leaving all your family behind."

"Ally had to leave a lot of her family behind when she came out west, too." Pauly said skillfully, building a bridge between us.

"Yes, then it's something you understand." Bea nodded.

Robert winked at me. "I knew something serious was in the works when our Pauly here started going to church clear over in Richland."

"Tell me about your family," Bea said.

I told her about everyone and explained about how we came to Washington. "I was so glad to meet Pat. And not just because she introduced me to Pauly. She's a lot of fun."

"Oh yes, we love our Pat. She's quite the character," Robert said.

I turned to Bea. "I hope you can teach me how to cook all of Pauly's favorites."

She flushed with pleasure and her worry lines erased. "I'd be glad to teach you. Lasagna and calzone, not to mention pizza. All of Pauly's Italian favorites."

Maybe I wouldn't even need to confess that I didn't know how to cook. I'd cook Italian food.

"So, the wedding is in September," Bea said.

Pauly spoke up. "I'm hopeful that Robbie and Tony can both put in for leave and be home in time to stand up for me."

Bea's face was pained as she crossed herself. "With God's divine intervention."

A pall fell over the table.

Finally, Robert spoke. "As much as we hated losing our home in White Bluffs, we're hopeful that whatever is happening where you work will be effective in ending the war and bringing our boys home." His eyes twinkled the same way Pauly's did when he was telling a joke, but his joviality seemed forced. "We're counting on you personally to end it with that top secret job of yours. Any idea when that might happen?"

I laughed. "You're going to have to wait forever if you're counting on me to end the war. Everything is so hush, hush. I have no idea of what's really going on, and I don't dare say a word about the things I do know for fear of losing my job or maybe even going to jail."

Bea passed the spaghetti and nodded appreciatively as I took another helping.

"That's what I've heard on the newspaper end, too. Our turn will come soon enough." Robert gave Pauly a look.

Bea said, "Our Pauly wishes he was over there fighting too, but he knows how much he's needed at home. He's a good boy, our Pauly."

"And a crackerjack reporter too when he's not wasting time shooting the breeze with every Tom, Dick, and Harry," said Robert.

"You mean to say that my deep and meaningful conversations with all kinds of people help me do my job well." Pauly smiled.

By the time dinner was over, my napkin was fairly splattered with tomato sauce. I removed it, and my shirt was still a pristine white. I sighed with relief. Pauly smiled and winked. The rest of the evening flew by.

When it was time to leave, I hugged my future family with real affection. "Thank you so much for the delicious dinner. I really enjoyed myself." On the way to Pauly's car, I grabbed his arm. "I already feel at home with your family."

"Yeah, I can tell they like you too." Pauly started the engine. "My mom's aged ten years since my brothers joined the service. You're going to be a great distraction for her. It was genius to ask her to teach you to cook my favorites."

"I hope I get to meet both your brothers at the wedding." My ring sparkled for a second in a passing streetlight.

"What they didn't tell you is that we haven't heard from Tony in weeks. Every day my parents run to the mailbox in hope. Our biggest nightmare is that a soldier will show up at the door with news of his capture or death."

I sighed, suddenly sobered. "It must be so hard."

A sudden gust of wind and a spatter of rain hit the side of the car as we started across the bridge. Pauly steadied the steering wheel.

"Now that we're engaged, I hope you're free to share what you're learning at your job."

I stuttered, stunned. "I, I don't know." I hadn't heard that close relationships changed the secrecy rule. I distinctly remembered Mrs. Chase telling me I was to tell no one. A shadow fell over my happy mood. Why was he even asking? He knew about the document that Pat and I had signed.

Pauly sighed. "Those secrecy rules seem ridiculous to me. It's not as if telling your fiancé will make any difference in the outcome."

He might be right, but he might be wrong. Would he be able to keep the things I told him a secret? I stared into the darkness, trying to make out the Columbia River on its way to the ocean. I needed more time to figure out what to do. "Yeah, maybe. But I don't really know anything that makes sense to me anyway."

"But you must know something." He kept his eyes trained on the windshield. "You can't sit in meetings with scientists taking notes without figuring something out."

A car with lights sped toward us, its lights blinding. "Hey, jerk. Turn off your brights." Pauly flashed his high beams. The headlights weaved slightly into our lane as the car sped past. "That guy had to be drunk."

"I wonder if we should call the police. He could kill somebody." I looked out the back window at the red taillights speeding into the distance. We drove through the night in silence. Maybe the crazy driver was a gift that had wiped thoughts of secret sharing from Pauly's mind.

When he pulled up in front of my house and turned off the engine, he turned. "I'm sorry for pestering you. I don't want to put you in a tight spot. Forgive me?"

I nodded. "Of course, I do. I hope you understand that I can't tell you anything as much for your protection as my own. I know this sounds far-fetched. But what if a spy or an agent tortured you for information? If you caved, we'd both be in trouble."

Pauly laughed. "I know the government is wary of spies. But do you really think there are any around?"

I stared out the window, unable to join in his merriment. I knew informants were watching for spies. But this conversation was getting us nowhere fast. "I'd better go." I reached for the doorhandle.

Pauly wrapped his arm around me and pulled me close. "Please accept my apology. Sometimes it all just drives me crazy. But I'll quit with the work talk." His eyes were repentant as he kissed me, then rubbed my cheek. "You've got a stubborn spot of spaghetti sauce right there." He licked where he'd been rubbing. "Mmm. And another here." He licked again.

I laughed. "No! I looked at myself in the mirror when I used the restroom at your house."

"The light in there is pretty low. You must have missed some spots." Pauly licked me again. I laughed and struggled to look in the rearview mirror.

He licked my neck. "Mmm. You taste good. Just like my favorite meal."

All his fishing for secrets fled my mind and I shivered in delight. "Pauly Armstrong, you are impossible."

Pauly kissed me. "Mmmm. And you're absolutely delicious, my little Ally Oop."

Chapter 28

Dr. Jamison stuck his head in my office. "Miss Krepsky, I've called a meeting in the main meeting room in one hour. Put together some drinks and food and try to create a festive air in the short time you have." He gave me a winning grin.

I hoped today was the day we'd learn they had finished the job or maybe the war had ended. Excitement flooded my veins as I dug in my desk for Dots and a package of M&M's. I hurried into the break room, started coffee, and dumped the candy into a large bowl. On short notice, it would have to do for festive.

"Coffee and candy for all," I said when people started to file into the room. "Dr. Jamison says we've got something to celebrate."

The scientists and engineers brightened visibly and started filling coffee cups and passing around the candy bowl.

Dr. Jamison arrived and took his place at the head of the table. "I'm sure all of you have heard of the Japanese incendiary balloons that have landed in the Pacific Northwest. The theory is that they are trying to start a giant forest fire to refocus men and equipment away from the war." He cleared his throat. "Today, we got word that one of the balloons hit a power line running from Bonneville Dam to the Hanford Engineer Works. It could have been catastrophic. That particular line supplies the electricity necessary to run our cooling system. Thankfully, the never-before-used backup system kicked in so quickly the temperature didn't rise in the reactor at all." He smiled all around. "Colonel Mathias is tickled pink and wanted me to pass on his congratulations to you all for a job well done. If we hadn't created such a stellar system, we'd have lost power. And you can imagine the horrific results if that had happened."

Everyone clapped and congratulated one another. I hung back, honored to be privy to this strange moment in history, but discomfited on a new level. I had no idea that Japan was sending incendiary balloons over the U.S. There was no forest to burn around here. What other kind of havoc could the balloons wreak besides shutting down the reactor? I wanted to ask, but instead I busied myself with cleaning up the coffee area.

One of the scientists patted me on the back as if I'd played a part in creating the backup system. I smiled up at him and shook my head. I didn't deserve congratulations. I was just here to take notes about all their brilliant ideas and feed them coffee. But his pat highlighted one of the things I enjoyed about my job. I felt an accepted part of this brainy bunch. Me, the dumb one who barely passed high school. If Betty could see me now, she'd be shocked out of her shoes. I felt myself puff with pride.

When the meeting was over, I cleaned up the break room and hurried to my office to type up the meeting minutes. One copy for Mr. Dirk to carry to the main vault. One copy for the Change House and one for the file cabinet. I hurriedly aligned the carbon paper with one eye on the clock. Pat and I were meeting at The Donuts Diner when I got off work today, and I didn't want to be late. There was nothing worse than calling an establishment like The Donuts Diner to ask the wait staff to tell the person I was meeting that I was going to be late. Luckily, Pat was understanding about the unpredictable nature of my work. Pauly, not so much.

I sighed. I couldn't wait to see him again on Wednesday. It seemed forever since last Sunday when we'd had fun harmonizing to the music coming from the big Victrola in his parents' living room.

• • • •

WHEN I ARRIVED AT THE Donuts Diner, Pat was waiting by the doorway, looking up at the menu. When she saw me, her face lit up. "I can't believe it. You made it sort of on time."

"Yeah. Me either." I looked at the menu. Everything looked delicious, especially the BLT. But this restaurant was named The Donuts Diner for a reason. "Are you going to get a donut?"

"You betcha. Who can resist those sweet clouds from the heavens?" Pat stepped up to the counter. "I'll have a maple bar and a coke."

"I would like a glazed donut and a cup of hot black tea, please."

When we'd settled in a booth, Pat took a bite of her maple bar. "I don't think I've ever tasted anything more delicious in my life. Well, since the last one I ate, that is."

When I took a bite of my donut, the pastry melted in my mouth. "Mmmm. It's the best dinner ever."

"I met this guy." Pat's cheeks flushed happily.

"You're kidding?"

"Nope. He's a military man working as a guard at the station. Anyway, we're going out this Saturday night."

"Tell me more. How old is he? What does he look like? Where's he from?"

"His name is Jim and he's from Missouri. He's twenty-one with sort of dishwater hair and a bit of a paunch, but I love his accent. It's so cute."

"How did you meet him?"

"A week ago, a group of us went bowling. He was bowling one aisle over with his friends and we got to talking. He found out my number from Annette, and he called me the other day."

"I'm so happy for you." I smiled around my donut.

"Well, you never know how things will turn out. But at least I don't feel so hopeless."

I sipped my tea. "Maybe we can double date sometime."

Pat nodded. "This weekend we're going to a dance at the recreation center." She took a sip of pop. "So, how are the wedding plans coming?"

"Things are coming along. My mom knows this lady at church named Mrs. Durgy who is supposed to be this amazing seamstress. I guess she makes all the wedding dresses around these parts. Anyway, this Saturday we're going over to look at her selection of fabrics and patterns. I'm thinking a rose color for your bridesmaid dresses. After I pick out some options, you can go over there for a fitting."

"Ooh. That sounds fun too. Life is looking up." Pat polished off her donut and gave me a bumpy grin.

She was right. Everything was coming together beautifully. I loved Pauly with all my heart and soul. And thankfully, he hadn't pestered me about the secrets involved in my job since we left his parents' house the first time. I was an integral part of a team, and even if I had to work overtime, I liked my job. The place was interesting, and we were working together to save lives. The underlying danger of the project, while talked about often, seemed to be under control, thanks to the diligence of the engineers from Dupont. Soon the war would be over, and Pauly and I would be married. I couldn't wait.

Chapter 29

June 1945

My heart danced as I locked the filing cabinet for the last time. Pauly had surprised me with tickets for a spring band concert on my birthday, and tonight was the night. He was coming to pick me up at seven-fifteen. If I left at five o'clock, I'd just have time to get ready.

The phone jangled. I let it ring, hoping whoever it was would give up. When it didn't stop, I grabbed a notepad and pen and answered.

"Alice Krepsky, may I help you?" I put pen to paper.

"We need you at the 700 Area Clinic."

I stopped. "What?"

"Bring your ID and pencil detector. You'll get more information when you arrive."

"Uh. I, uh." I stuttered.

"When can you be here?"

"I can't be there." I crumpled onto my desk chair.

"If you don't come, we'll send someone after you. It's that important." He cleared his throat. "When can you be here?"

If I hurried, I might make it home in time for the concert. "Maybe by five-forty."

"When you arrive, stop at the reception desk and they'll direct you." The man hung up without saying goodbye.

I dialed Pauly's office phone number with shaking fingers. It rang and rang. Then I called his home number with the same result. I finally called home. Timmy answered.

"I'm going to be late. It's an emergency. Pauly is coming to pick me up for the concert at seven-fifteen. I hope to be there by then, but if not, tell him I'm so sorry." I wiped away a tear. "Tell him I'll be there as soon as I can, and if I don't make it to take someone else to the concert. I'm sure that Betty would love to go."

He yelled to Mother. "Ally is going to be late again and she's crying."

As I ran toward Clock Alley, my mind flashed back to my trip to the B reactor yesterday in my role as fill-in messenger. I'd gone in search of the women's restroom that had been built for the lone woman physicist who "babysat" the reactor. She was famously admired by all who knew her.

The restroom door opened into my face. I lost my balance, plunging through a roped off area and bumping against the wall.

A woman with a black mop hairdo and liquid brown eyes seemed surprised to see me. "Whoops, sorry there."

Flustered, I righted myself and attempted a smile.

She put out her thin hand to shake. "I don't see many other women around here. Leona Marshall."

"It's an honor to meet you, Mrs. Marshall. I'm Alice Krepsky, a secretary in the administrative office."

"Good to meet you."

I'd smiled, star-struck, and went on my way, marveling at having met her.

Now I wished I never had. Crashing into the wall at the B reactor had to be the reason I was now roaring toward the clinic on the bus. I must have come in contact with the dreaded substance that was the subject of so many of the safety memos I typed. I didn't feel sick. But if I had an unusual reading on my pencil detector, I might be sick and not even know it.

A tear dripped down my cheek. A couple of weeks ago, Pauly had been angry when I'd had to work on a Saturday. We didn't have specific plans and were able to spend Saturday evening and Sunday together, but it had created a jagged conflict between us. A conflict that still lurked around at the edges of our relationship. Today, I couldn't even explain why I was late. Nor could I ask him to pick me up at the clinic so I could make it to the concert. I wiped away my tears, feeling guilty and sad for breaking our date. Pauly didn't deserve this.

By the time I reached the clinic, it was just shy of six o'clock. A uniformed man at a desk peered at up at me through reddened eyes.

"I'm Alice Krepsky. I've been called here for a health check."

"ID please. And I need your pencil detector." He waited patiently while I removed my ID and pencil detector from my neck.

"Come on back. We've been waiting for you." He opened the door to an examination room. "Jump onto the table. The doctor will be here shortly."

The antiseptic smell in the tiny room reminded me of the sting of the Mercurochrome Mother dabbed on my scrapes when I was a child. Soft, sweet Mother. It was the only time she willingly hurt me. Fresh tears flooded my eyes. I'd give anything to hear her say that everything was going to be fine. Even when it wasn't. I climbed onto the examination table and watched the clock tick. It seemed mired in molasses.

Finally, the door sprang open and a doctor with wavy golden hair appeared. "How did you set off your pencil detector?" He sat on a wooden stool and tapped his stethoscope against his hand.

"I don't really know. Maybe when I bumped into a tiled wall in the restricted area at the B reactor yesterday."

"And how are you feeling? Any loss of appetite? Tiredness or fatigue?"

"I feel fine except for the fact that I'd rather not be here."

He chuckled. "I think we all feel that way on a Friday." He held the stethoscope to my chest. "Breathe deeply."

I could almost feel Pauly's excitement as he dressed in his suit and tie for the big evening. He'd run up the steps to my house, smiling from ear to ear until Timmy shouted the horrible news. In my mind's eye his smile drooped, replaced by that dark haunted look he wore when he was upset by something. Maybe I should have just let them all worry. It would be preferable to the sense of abandonment he must feel in thinking I was working overtime again.

"Your vitals look good." The doctor said. "Last thing is a blood draw, and then we'll have you on your way."

The phlebotomist directed me to lay on a bed. He joked about being a vampire as he poked the needle into my arm. I tried a laugh. It came out as a sob.

"Hey, don't worry. This is just a formality. I've never seen one person come in for a health check and end up in the hospital."

I wiped my eyes with my free hand. "It's just that I had a date with my fiancé. He doesn't work on the project and isn't very understanding when I'm late."

The phlebotomist tapped the side of the tube and blood poured in faster. "We'll get you out of here as soon as possible." When the tube was full, he ushered me back into the examination room.

I sat on the table in the cold room, bereft, unable even to pray. God had seemed so distant lately. Of course, I'd been too busy working to think about him much. Even when I was in church, my mind was on Pauly in the pew next to me. I wiped my tears and started praying.

A little before seven o'clock, the golden-haired doctor appeared. "Your blood draw looks good and you're free to go. If you feel fatigued, feverish, or lose your appetite, call the clinic."

My spirits dipped along with the setting sun as I waited with a cluster of people at the bus stop. When it finally arrived, the bus seemed to crawl through town as it stopped at every corner on its way south. My watch ticked to seven-fifteen. Pauly was at my house right now. I could imagine his shock at my absence. We had bonded over music—discussed our favorite records, gone to choir practice together, and even sang at his parent's house. Now I had wounded that bond. Hopefully, he could forgive me.

At home his car was gone. The windows in my house were dark, staring like disapproving eyes onto the street. I dragged myself up the front porch steps and opened the door. Daddy's pipe glowed. He switched on a light. "Where have you been? Paul was here and left for the concert with Betty. He was very hurt. What were you thinking?"

I whispered, "Where's Mother and Timmy? I have something I need to talk to you about."

"She's helping Timmy with his bath. What happened?"

"I had to go to the clinic for some tests because my pencil reader was high."

His frown deepened. "How did that happen?"

I sighed and collapsed on the couch. "You know I can't share anything, even with you."

"Are you feeling unwell?" Daddy pushed tobacco into his pipe.

"No. The last thing I wanted to do was hurt Pauly. I love him, but I had to go to the clinic, and I can't even tell him about it." I couldn't keep the sobs back.

Daddy handed me his fresh handkerchief. "Maybe it's time to quit your job and concentrate on getting ready for the wedding."

I sniffed. "It's tempting, but they're very close to finishing whatever they're making. It won't be long until I'm free." I sank to the couch and shook my head. "I like my job. Yesterday I even met Leona Marshall." I blew my nose.

Daddy shrugged. "At what cost?"

Timmy raced down the stairs in his red flannel pajamas. "Ally, you're finally here. Pauly took Betty to the concert. He was sad." He snuggled close. "And now you're sad."

"Yeah. I'm very sad. Too sad to talk right now." I started up the stairs and met Mother coming down.

"Ally, dear, you must be hungry. Your dinner is in the oven." Her soft, doe eyes held concern. "Are you alright? I know how much this concert meant to you."

"I'm not feeling well. I'm going to bed for a little while." I leaned in for a hug, then hurried up the stairs and shut the door behind me. The concert was supposed to last an hour and a half. At nine o'clock, I'd go over to Betty's house to apologize and try to make it right. But first, a little rest.

As I shrugged out of my work dress, the stack of records that I had borrowed from Pauly seemed to mock me. I climbed into bed in my slip and pulled the covers over my head. If only this day had never happened.

Chapter 30

I woke to gray dawn filtering through the curtains. The memory of the previous evening shot through me like a bullet, and I jumped out of bed, still dressed in my work slip. I'd been exhausted, but that was no excuse for not staying awake to apologize to Pauly after the concert. He was probably hurt to the core.

I peered through the curtains. Raindrops spitting out of the bleak sky meant another windstorm on its way. I shoved a towel along the bottom of the window to keep out the dust.

Maybe I should tell him a version of the truth. Tell him I'd felt sick and had to go to the clinic for a check. I found out I was fine, but I still didn't feel good, so I went to bed and slept until morning. It was all true, but I'd called Timmy to tell him I'd be late, not that I felt bad and was going to the clinic.

I paced my room, conflicted. More lies and half-truths would just create a greater sense of distrust between us. Perhaps to save our relationship, I had to tell Pauly the truth. I didn't have to tell him everything. Just that I had to go to the clinic because I'd been exposed to something dangerous. It was that or quit my job, and I couldn't quit. I rushed to the shower. I'd call him as soon as I was sure he'd be awake.

After my shower, I dialed Pauly's number and listened to it ring. Bea answered. "Hello?"

"Hello, Bea. This is Allie. Is Pauly there?"

"I haven't seen hide nor hair of him this morning. He got in late."

"Do you mind checking to see if he's awake? It's really important."

I heard her rapping at his door. "Pauly, Allie's on the phone." I heard rumbling. "He says he'll call you later."

A blast of rain showered against the window. "Please tell him it's important that I talk to him. It's about last night."

Bea relayed my message. "He says he's still in bed and will talk to you later."

"Okay. Tell him I love him."

"I'm happy to do that." Bea sounded warm and a bit sad.

I dialed Betty's house. "Hi, Uncle Pete. Can I talk to Betty?"

His voice thundered into the phone. "Bets, phone's for you. It's Ally."

I twisted the phone cord around and around my finger, waiting. Finally, Uncle Pete said, "She's in the shower. She'll be over when she's ready."

"Okay."

Mother entered the kitchen with a slight frown. "Hello, dear. Are you feeling better this morning? Our Pauly was so sad you couldn't make it home last night in time for the concert." She patted my arm. "Is everything okay?"

I nodded. "Everything is fine, Mother. I just got caught up in a problem that needed an immediate answer."

"Okay, dear. I'm sure everything will be just fine. How about we make him a nice batch of cookies? You can help." She smoothed my hair. Last night I had longed to hear Mother say everything would be okay. Today it just irritated me. Too many times she'd said the same thing as the world fell burning around our feet.

I pulled away. "No, I don't have time for that right now."

"Would you like a nice cup of tea?" She filled the kettle at the sink.

"No, thank you. Betty will be here in a few minutes." I retreated to the living room. For now, I'd stay near the phone listening for Pauly's call. I picked up the newspaper. On the front page, a list of local boys killed or missing in action was next to an AP article about the war in the Pacific. I scanned the list for familiar names. I didn't recognize any, but the seeing the names of the fallen reinforced my resolve to stay the course. We were on a mission to end the war. I couldn't quit now.

On the third page, Pauly's story about a new grade school in Richland made the project spring to life. I could picture him interviewing the workers and hopeful parents whose kids would be attending the new school. My heart swelled with pride.

Betty sauntered into the room. Her hair was in pin curls. "What happened to you?"

"I can't say without breaking confidentiality rules."

She shook her head. "It had better be good because you really missed out. The concert was great. Paul put on a good front, but I could tell he was hurt and angry. Everyone wore their best spring dresses, and the stage was decorated with flowers. He knew everyone and introduced me all around. Some people thought I was his fiancée, and he didn't correct them." Betty looked at me disdainfully. "Are you sure this job is worth it?"

I sniffed and shook my head, unable to speak. Why had I suggested that Betty accompany him? Of course, she had to lord it over me and make me feel worse than I already did.

She perched on the couch. "I thought you might come over to meet him afterward. Were you there till late?"

I choked out, "No. I fell asleep because I was so exhausted. I've been working overtime like crazy and..." The phone rang and I bolted. "Hello?"

"What happened to you?" There was an angry sneer in Pauly's voice. "More overtime?"

"No. I'm so sorry, Pauly. I couldn't help it. You know how much I wanted to go to the concert, and you know how much I love you."

The silence on the other end of the line was deafening.

My voice quavered. "Can you come over? I want to share some things that I've never told you before."

His voice was clipped. "Yeah. We need to figure out if this relationship is going to work or not."

Tears clouded my vision as I set the receiver back. I rushed past Betty to the stairs.

"Well, I was going to tell you my latest from Doug, but I'll just go on home now."

Mother said, "How is Doug?"

I didn't stick around to hear. I ran up the steps and slammed the bedroom door behind me. Face down on the bed, I choked out sobs.

I had to share the secrets I had sworn to protect. Or lose the man I loved.

• • • •

I SPLASHED DOWN THE wet sidewalk before Pauly had finished parking the car. He turned off the engine as I ducked into the front seat.

He glanced my way and sighed. "What happened?" His jaw was set at a pensive angle, his hands on the steering wheel.

I didn't dare scoot closer. "First of all, I'm so sorry. I wanted to go to the concert with you more than anything. I love you." I wiped at my tears.

"You've got a funny way of showing it." He shifted uncomfortably in his seat. "You've made it clear to me that your job comes first. I don't like playing second fiddle. So maybe..."

I sobbed out, "Before you say anymore, please listen."

Pauly nodded.

I tried to compose myself. "What I'm going to tell you is extremely confidential. I could get in huge trouble if anyone knew I was sharing."

Pauly stared at the raindrops smearing the windshield.

"Every day when I go to work, I expose myself to some kind of danger. I don't understand what it is, but I wear something called a pencil detector around my neck." I swallowed hard.

Pauly frowned and turned.

"As I was getting ready to leave yesterday, I got a call saying that the reading on my pencil detector had registered high. I had to go to the clinic for some tests." I reached for his hand. It hung limp and cold in mine. "I argued with them, but they said I didn't have a choice. They said they'd send security after me if I didn't comply."

He pulled his hand away. "So, what does that mean? Are you sick? Do you need to be in bed?"

"No. I'm not sick. The tests showed no problems. But they told me if I was fatigued or lost my appetite to come back to the clinic."

"What's a pencil detector? And what does it measure?" He turned to me.

I shook my head. "I don't know. All I know is that I'm a secretary for a team driven to end the war. I know they are close to finishing enough of whatever they are making. If I quit and they had to find and train another person, it could set the operation back by a couple of weeks. That means more American soldiers dead." I grabbed his hand again. "Can you view my absences when I have to work as your own way to sacrifice for the war effort?"

I watched Pauly's anger slowly evaporate like water off the sidewalk. He turned to me with concern in his eyes. "I guess so. But I should be the one putting my life at risk. Not my fiancée. I'm not a coward."

I shook my head. "I don't think there's a shred of coward bone in your body. I know your heart and what you're sacrificing for the sake of your family. As far as putting my life at risk, the man who drew my blood at the clinic said he'd never seen anyone admitted to the hospital because their pencil detector registered high."

"So, why did you even need to go?"

"I think because what they're creating is so new that they don't really know what the exact risk is."

"You're basically telling me that you're a guinea pig." Pauly barked a short laugh. "That's incredible. What did you do that made your pencil detector reading high anyway?"

"You know how difficult it is to share. After all the lectures about sharing information, secrecy is drilled into me. You know about the document I signed promising jail if I didn't comply. You must understand my predicament."

He turned away again. "You either trust me or you don't."

I sighed. I did trust him. Besides, I'd already shared one of the most important secrets of the whole operation. "I went into a restricted area with one of the scientists to take notes for a meeting, and I bumped into a wall of the reactor."

"Reactor? What's that?"

"I don't know. I feel like I'm working in the middle of a giant science experiment. And I know nothing about science. I'm sorry if that doesn't satisfy you, but that's basically all I know except a bunch of terms that I write down all day."

Pauly's face wore a fascinated expression. "What are some of the terms?"

I stared at my hands in my lap, suddenly angry as plutonium, radiation, and critical mass spun through my mind. I agreed with the idea of trust. But I could be jailed if they found out I was sharing secrets with Pauly. I felt torn in two as I reached for the door handle. If he couldn't accept the fact that I wasn't willing to share more, then maybe it was time to take a break from our relationship. At least until after the war. I couldn't speak it though and opened the door instead.

"Hey, where are you going?" He grabbed my hand.

Tears clogged my throat. "I can't share any more. I already feel uncomfortable. It's been a hard couple of days."

Pauly let go of my hand and turned the key in the ignition. The engine revved and then died. Outside, the wind had chased away the rain. It whipped my hair around my head and dried my tears. The car made another weary sound and died again. He rushed to open the hood.

Pauly's hair stood on end in the wind. "Of all the dadgum, cottonpickin'..." His eyes flashed in frustration. "Can I use your telephone?"

"Sure. Come on in." I started up the porch and held the door for him.

Daddy looked up from the newspaper. "Hello, Paul."

Pauly had composed himself and said politely. "My car won't start. I need to use your phone to call my dad so I can get a tow."

"No need for that. We can rig up something. Come on down to the basement and we'll see what we can figure out. It's not far to the Richfield service station."

When Pauly and Daddy disappeared downstairs, I ran upstairs to wash my face. Thankfully, Mother and Timmy had gone to Aunt Edna's house for one of her Saturday morning sweet rolls. The house was quiet except for gusts of wind against the side of the house.

A while later, I heard their voices moving through the house. The front door slammed. I slipped downstairs and watched them tie Pauly's front bumper to Daddy's back bumper with a thick rope. Finally, they each jumped into the front seat of their respective cars, and Daddy slowly towed Pauly's car down the street.

I stood at the window even after they had disappeared, confused. Did I honor the wishes of my fiancé or the requirements of the job? Should we call it quits and try again after the war was over? That would break my heart. Perhaps we needed to talk about it some more.

• • • •

A WHILE LATER, I HEARD the door open and ran downstairs. Pauly sobered when he saw me. Daddy, seeming to sense that something was amiss, sat down without speaking, and opened his newspaper.

"What happened?" I stood back.

"The car's in the shop. They're going to let me know what's wrong with it, but probably not for a few days." He grabbed my hand. "Where's somewhere private we can talk?"

"I guess we can go to my room for a while?" I shot the question in the direction of Daddy.

He nodded and lit his pipe.

My room felt tiny and girlish with Pauly's giant presence inside. He paced around for a minute and then settled at the window. "It hurts me that you think I would put your well-being at risk by spilling your secrets."

"You just don't understand what it's like. Somebody I rode next to on the bus told me that even the President of the United States doesn't know what's going on."

Pauly groaned. "And you believe that? Where would the army and Dupont get the authority to destroy White Bluffs and build this thing you describe as enormous? Trains moving supplies, people pouring into the area." He shook his head. "That makes no sense."

"I know it doesn't make sense. I'm just trying to explain how hard it is." I thought again about calling off our wedding plans until after the war, when I could comfortably lay myself bare before him. But the idea clogged my throat with tears.

Pauly sighed. "All right." He held my face in his hands. "I have to admit I admire your commitment to your job and your need to do it right, my little Ally Oop. But I can't wait until the lid is blown off this whole operation, so there won't be any more secrets between us."

I leaned in for a kiss. Suddenly, we were both overcome by passion. He pulled away reluctantly and looked at my bed.

"Somehow I don't think your dad would take kindly to the fact that there's a fox in his chicken house right now."

I laughed and wiped my eyes. "Tell me about the concert."

"Besides the fact that I was sore at you, it was good." Pauly rubbed my hand. "The band did some renditions of Tommy Dorsey songs. Betty is pretty, but she doesn't hold a candle to you." He laughed. "I have to admit I had fun making people think she was my real date. Rob Gunderson was home on leave, and you should've seen him checking her out. He kept looking between the two of us as if he couldn't believe it."

"And you didn't say anything to correct him?" I snatched my hand away.

"No, I was mad at you. But you know, even if she wasn't married, I wouldn't date Betty in a million years. She's too bossy and she talks too much. Whereas, you, Ally Oop, are as sweet and mushy as apple pie. I can't get enough of you." Pauly leaned in for another kiss.

I sighed and laid my head on his shoulder. "It can't be long until the war is over and then I'll never keep another secret from you again."

Chapter 31

Guilt followed me as I hurried down the dead and darkening street to Clock Alley. I'd been too exhausted and eager for home to wait for someone to walk with me to the bus. But I hadn't expected the thick cloud curtain obscuring the sunset. Daddy would be mad if he knew I'd broken my vow to never travel alone. My head pounded. The comfort of home beckoned.

I'd heard sparks of resentment in Pauly's voice when I'd called to tell him I had to work overtime again on a Friday night. But we had no special plans, and he'd calmed when I reminded him that we had all of Saturday and Sunday together. The same old, difficult dance had begun to soften. I yawned and my eyes burned. At least tomorrow I could sleep until eleven if I wanted. I just hoped a bus was waiting.

Footsteps crunched behind me. I turned with a smile, hoping to see a co-worker running to join me. Instead, a boozy stench assaulted me. A heavy hand slammed my mouth. The Coyote's voice was a growl. "Don't struggle and I won't hurt you." Pain shot through my shoulder as he twisted my arm behind my back.

"Ahhhh." I screamed a rabbit's sigh behind his iron grip. I kicked, and the sand tore off my shoes. I struggled and thrashed as he pushed me behind the unseeing concrete wall of the administration building. He pushed me to the sand, and the pressure of his gut stole my breath. I bit his hand. He slapped my cheek. "Bitch." His rough hand shoved up my skirt and tugged at my girdle.

Lights from a passing bus speared the place where I twisted and turned. "Help!"

"Shut up, or I'll kill you."

I prayed and wedged my knee toward his groin. The Coyote pinned it to the sand.

Panic suffocated me as I struggled to break free. Suddenly, a sense as quiet as a whisper, nudged at the edge of my consciousness–lie still. As death.

No. The Coyote would spear me with his poison. Then I truly would die. I struggled to peel his fingers from my throat as he pushed my skirt around my neck.

The sense hovered near my consciousness again: Lie still and I will fight for you. I continued to kick until finally, the sense overwhelmed my rational thought.

Summoning every shred of courage, I chose to lie as still as a rabbit hiding in plain sight. Every ounce of strength to lay weak. Eyeless. Boneless. Slack-jawed. Silent.

The Coyote released my throat. I felt him rear up. "Hey, wake up now." He slapped my face lightly. "Hey, are you alive?" He rolled off, his breath heavy as he reached to pull down my girdle.

"Yow!" He yelped, leaping to his feet. He danced around, slapping his back as if it were on fire.

Freed, I shot to my feet, wobbled, and then sprinted through the sand. Rocks on the road gouged my bare feet like diamonds. The white light of Clock Alley beckoned. I fell, sprawling flat, and listened for his pounding feet on the road. But only wind whistled around the corner of Clock Alley as I scrambled up and raced for the door. Light blinded me as I fell headlong inside.

"Help. Please help me." I cried out.

A guard's face was hollow with concern in the glaring light. "Hey. Are you alright?" He hurried over as I sobbed and stammered, shrinking from the gaze of workers who gathered nearby, staring.

"Can you stand?" The guard asked.

I nodded, and he took my arm. "Let's go see if the nurse is still here."

A large redheaded nurse in a white dress and peaked cap filled the tiny first aid room. Her voice was gentle as she led me to a cot. "Lie down. What happened to your shoes?"

I shook my head, sobbing too hard to talk.

She handed me a handkerchief. "Your stockings are torn, and your feet are red. You've skinned your knees."

She tore off my remaining stockings. "I'm going to bandage your wounds." I felt the sting of Mercurochrome as she doctored the cuts. Thoughts of Mother made me sob harder.

"You've got red marks on your cheek and neck. Do you hurt anywhere else?"

I shook my head again.

"Well, it doesn't seem that there's much wrong with you physically, although I'm sure you're going to have some bruises tomorrow." The nurse's freckled face was kind as sat next to me holding my hand. "I'm Margaret. When you can talk, I'd like to hear about it."

I shook my head.

"I'll be back with a cup of chamomile tea."

When she disappeared out the door, I panicked. The nurse had bandaged my cuts and scrapes. But she couldn't bandage my insides where I was wounded. And dirty. Dirty with the Coyote's smell, the touch of his hands. My stomach heaved, and I retched into a nearby trash can. If only I could purge the memory as easily as the small remains of my lunch.

I knew now that the overwhelming urge to lie still had come from God. He had fought for me. And if he was with me then, he was here now inside this little first aid room that smelled like Mercurochrome. Margaret appeared with a steaming cup. She cradled my hands around the cup. "I am here when you are ready to talk."

I took a sip of hot chamomile. She leaned forward in concern. Finally, I took a deep breath. "I was walking alone to the bus, and the Coyote grabbed me from behind. He pushed me down." I took a breath. "He pushed my skirt up and strangled me." Ashamed, I trembled, and the tea sloshed.

Margaret took the cup and set it aside. She wrapped her arms around me and hugged me close. When I'd calmed again, she handed me my tea back. I took a shaky sip. "I had an overwhelming urge to lie still. I almost couldn't do it, but I finally played dead. He rolled off me onto the sand. Then, all of a sudden, he started jumping around and slapping his back as if he were in pain. I ran as fast as I could to the Clock Alley." I took another sip of tea.

"A rattlesnake or scorpion probably bit him. They're all over the desert and they come out at night." She patted my hand. "What can you tell me about this person you call Coyote?"

"His name is Bart Bundy. I think he works at the pump house." I trembled so hard my teeth chattered.

She wrapped a drab wool Army blanket around my shoulders. "I'll report it to the police, but you weren't actually raped. And you know men..." She hugged me again. "They may do something about it, and they may not. It's best to try to forget it ever happened."

I tugged the blanket around my shoulders. "Right now, all I want to do is get cleaned up."

She stood. "And we need to figure out what to do about your shoes. Can you tell me where you lost them? I'll send a guard out with a lantern."

"He dragged me onto the sand on this side of the Administration Building. I lost them right away." I stood on shaky legs.

"Here's a towel and wash cloth. Go ahead and use the restroom to clean up. I'll help you walk. Come on." She took my arm.

Sand dribbled from under my skirt as I hobbled to a restroom. Sand poured onto the floor when I sat on the toilet. As I scrubbed, I shivered convulsively at the thought of his hand up my skirt. Thank goodness for the urging of God. And my iron-tight girdle.

A fresh sob grabbed my throat. Pauly. I could just imagine his rage. He could get in real trouble if he tracked down the Coyote. And I couldn't talk to my parents either. It was too embarrassing. Daddy would hit the ceiling and make me quit. Mother would somehow make it seem as if it hadn't really happened.

I was going to have to keep a stiff upper lip. And God was somehow with me. He had saved me. He would help me move beyond this.

The spots on my cheek and neck were an angry red, but they would fade. At home I'd tell them I'd fallen running for a bus. The fluorescent light above flickered and buzzed. I shivered. What if the Coyote was waiting for me outside? Tears started up again as I staggered back to the nurse's office. My dusty black pumps sat in front of the bed.

Margaret appeared. "Are you feeling better?"

"Not really. I'm scared to ride the bus home by myself. What if he's waiting for me?"

Her pale, freckled lips thinned. "I'll see if a guard can drive you home." She hurried out.

I slipped on my shoes and waited by the door. A guard with the rank of sergeant on his uniform filled the hall with his large frame. His gray eyes were kind in his wrinkled face. "I hear you need a ride home tonight, young lady."

I nodded and wiped at my eyes.

"Follow me." We exited a back door and ended up in a parking lot sandwiched between the Clock Alley and the Change House. "Hop in." He pulled out of the graveled lot onto the road. A guard opened the gate and waved us through. "I understand you've had some trouble."

I laid my head on the back of the seat, unable to speak as we gathered speed.

He said, "Security has done everything they can to keep our women safe. You've undoubtedly seen the barbed wire around the women's barracks. But sometimes things happen."

When I didn't speak, he went on. "I advise you to never travel alone. If you work overtime, get someone to accompany you or wait until there's a shift change."

I nodded. "I have learned my lesson. But I'm not sure I'll ever feel safe again."

The officer glanced sideways at me. "You can always call the guard station. I'll alert them to keep a special watch over you. Creating safety is my job, you know."

"That's very kind.," I choked out as tears flooded my eyes.

"I understand you normally work days."

I nodded and gave him a tremulous smile. When we got near home, I felt composed enough to speak again. "Would you please drop me at the bus stop? I can't tell my parents about this." I wiped my nose.

"Are you sure about that? I'd want to know if my daughter was in danger." He frowned.

Daddy would make me quit work immediately if he knew. "I'll think about it. For now, please drop me right here."

The guard handed me his card. "I'm serious about coming to your aid."

I studied his card, then climbed out. "Thank you so much for your help, Sergeant Joseph. I'll keep your card in my purse and call if I'm ever in need."

He waited at the bus stop until I opened my front door. Mother and Daddy looked up from their books and yawned almost simultaneously. I wanted to wrap up in their arms and never let go. Instead, I put on a false smile and showed off my bandaged legs. "I was running for the bus, fell flat on my face in the middle of the rocky road and got all skinned up."

Daddy stood and hovered over me. "It looks like you've been crying. Are you sure you're okay?" His frown was as sharp as a knife. "What happened to your neck? It's all red."

"Yeah, I fell really weird and shredded my stockings, but luckily the nurse was still there. She bandaged me up. I'm okay." I tried to sound lighthearted as I leaned in for a hug.

Mother headed toward the kitchen. "I've got some sausage in the oven waiting for you."

"I'm not hungry. What I really need is a shower. I'll come down if I feel like eating." I offered a smile and headed up the stairs.

The shower burned hot as I scrubbed. If only I could scrub away the red marks and the bruises. When the hot water ran cold, I turned off the faucet and grabbed a towel. It could have been so much worse. God had saved me. And now I had a whole guard crew on my side. I'd be safe. If the Coyote was around, I'd stick like glue to any safe person. The best thing was to tell no one and try to forget it ever happened.

I pulled my nightgown over my head, then combed and twisted my hair into pin curls. Tomorrow, I'd be fresh as a daisy for Pauly.

• • • •

I WOKE MEWLING IN DISTRESS, my dream crystal clear. A coyote was slinking through the sagebrush after me. I could see Pauly and my parents in the distance, but I couldn't get to them before it pounced, baring its teeth and growling.

Electrified with terror, I sat up and flipped on the light to look at the clock. It was three-ten AM. I peered out the window anxiously. Betty's backyard porch light shone, illuminating the quiet yard. In the next room, Daddy snored and then stopped. I was safe at home in my own bed.

I turned off the light and lay back down. Outside, a coyote howled. Then another. I shivered and pulled the covers tighter.

Timmy. He'd invaded my bed for years. Tonight, I needed him. I grabbed my pillow and blanket. My door squealed open, and I stilled. When the house stayed quiet, I slipped down the hall like a ghost.

Timmy lay curled on his side. As I fitted myself to his hot little frame, he squirmed. "Ally..." he whispered then quieted.

His soft snore reminded me of Sheboygan. Comforted by thoughts of our old house with Grandma and Grandpa next door and the church across the street, I drifted off.

Chapter 32

At first light, I tiptoed down the hall to my cold bed and pulled the covers over my head. Hopefully, when Timmy woke, he would remember my presence in his bed as a pleasant dream. My eyes burned. My body felt like I'd been hit by a train. More sleep. Please. I closed my eyes to the sounds of birds chirping. If only I were a bird, and my biggest worry was finding the next worm for breakfast. I drifted toward sleep.

When I awoke, the flat light of late morning lay on the curtains. I heard the sweep of the broom in the hall. My whole body ached as I heaved myself out of bed. New bruises covered my legs and arm. My neck flamed. A bruise stung my cheek. I gave into crying and then steeled myself to stop. Red eyes would only make things worse. I was going to have to conceal everything. That meant makeup. Lots of PanCake makeup.

Mother hummed when she reached the end of the hallway with the broom and retreated down the steps. I sighed. Secrets. Sometimes it seemed as if I might explode with them and detonate all the people I loved.

I swallowed two aspirin with a swig from the faucet. Then I set my record player needle on Chopin. It skipped, and the same chords started again. I lifted the needle as the telephone pealed downstairs. Daddy's voice rumbled.

If work was calling me for more overtime, I'd play sick. Soon Pauly would come over and I'd spend the whole day locked in forgetfulness. *Meet Me in St. Louis* was playing at the theater and rumor was that it was hilarious. Just what the doctor ordered. I examined the scratch on my Chopin record.

Daddy knocked. "Ally, Can I come in? It's important."

"Just a minute." I hurriedly applied PanCake to my bruised cheek and neck. "Okay."

His face was grave, distracted. "I got a call from Uncle Pete, and I'm afraid I've got some bad news."

"What happened?" I asked.

"This morning, a soldier visited Betty to tell her that Doug was killed in action."

Shock dropped me to the bed. "No. Doug? That can't be." Doug was too vibrant and deeply in love to die. "Are you sure there's not been some mistake?"

He shook his head. "Poor Betty is beside herself with grief. They've called a doctor to come and deliver a sedative. But I thought you might want to go over and keep her company until he comes."

"Yes, of course. Let me get dressed." When Daddy left, I threw on a long-sleeved muslin dress that went almost to my ankles. Then I limped painfully down the stairs. I spied Mother sitting at the table with her Bible. "I'm going over to see Betty."

"Okay, dear." She didn't even look up. Hopefully, everyone would focus on Betty's tragedy instead of my beat-up body.

I found Betty on the couch, the lap of her chenille bathrobe filled with sodden handkerchiefs. She sniffed and wiped her angry red eyes. Aunt Edna peered through the front window drapes. She turned. "The doctor should be here any minute. Can you let him in? I'm going to lie down."

Betty was shrunken. "There's no point in the doctor. No medicine can stop my grief."

I hugged her tight. "Oh, Betty. I'm sorrier than I can say."

She hung limp in my arms. Her voice held a bitter twist. "How could God let Doug die?" She dabbed at her eyes. "That is, if God even exists."

I sat down next to her and held her hand. "I don't know. But I do know that he is with us even in the middle of the worst pain." If only I could tell her about how God had helped me last night. His protection. He hadn't prevented the Coyote's attack, but because I obeyed his sense to be still, I was saved from the worst of it. Shame, anger, and guilt still smeared my soul. Fear had marked me in a way that I knew would forever alter my view of strangers. But God was with me. He was with Betty too, even in the middle of this nightmare.

A rap at the front door brought Uncle Pete out of hiding. "Come in, Dr. Duncan. I'm Pete Foster." His normally jovial voice was subdued, his eyes red around the rims.

Bald, stooped Dr. Duncan stepped inside, carrying his doctor's bag. He nodded and knelt beside my cousin. "And you must be Betty. I'm so sorry you must bear the grief of widowhood." He listened to her heart and laid his hand on her forehead. "I brought you a sedative." He opened a glass bottle, dropped a white pill into his hand, and looked at Uncle Pete. "We need water."

Betty shook her head. "A pill can't take away my grief. I don't want it." She turned her head away.

"You're right. It can't take away your grief. But rest will allow your body to absorb the shock of this loss. You'll be better equipped to deal with it when you wake again." He pressed the pill into Betty's hand.

Uncle Pete handed her a glass of water, and she sighed. "All right. Just this once."

Doctor Duncan set the pill bottle on the end table. "Take one every four hours as needed." He stepped toward the door and turned. "Betty, you're young and you've got your whole life ahead of you. I know it doesn't seem like it now, but you'll heal from this grief, and someday you'll start anew." He shut the door gently behind him.

Uncle Pete disappeared into the kitchen.

"Let me get you to bed." I helped Betty to stand.

She leaned hard on me as we moved to her bedroom. "Ally, I don't often tell you this, but I don't know what I would do without you. I love you, cousin." She sighed as I helped her lie down and pulled the covers up around her chin.

"I love you too," I said. And I meant it. Because even when I was mad at her, she was like a sister to me. And, despite my own trauma, I would do everything I could to help her stand strong through this sorrowful time.

• • • •

PAULY FROWNED WHEN I greeted him at the front door and said, "What happened to you? You look like your best dog died." He looked me up and down and touched my neck. "What's with all the makeup?"

I sighed, unnerved. Reporter Pauly never missed a detail. I shook my head. "Betty got news..." my voice cracked. "Doug was killed in battle." I grabbed his hand and pulled him to the couch.

Pauly sighed and pulled me into his arms. "Oh, no. What a horror. How is she doing?"

"As you can imagine, she's pretty beat up. The doctor came this morning and gave her a sedative. As far as I know, she's still asleep." I leaned into his wide, warm chest.

Timmy wandered into the living room. "Pauly, do you want to play trucks?"

"No, sorry little man. I need to spend time with your sister."

"Ally slept in *my* bed last night." His face glowed with pride. "But Doug died, and everyone is sad." He headed out the front door.

Pauly's face registered surprise. "You slept with Timmy? I thought you hated that."

"I was just feeling sort of lonely last night. It's hard to explain." I shrugged and avoided his eyes.

Pauly rubbed at my makeup. "What happened to you? Your neck is bright red. And you've got a bruise on your cheek."

"I fell running for the bus last night. A nurse bandaged me up, but I'm pretty sore." I lifted my long skirt and showed him my bandaged knees.

I saw hurt flash in his eyes, and he pulled away. "So that's what all the makeup is about. What's with you and secrets? You shouldn't have to hide your injuries from me. Unless there's more to it?"

I shifted uncomfortably on the couch. "No, I was just trying to look pretty for you, and hadn't had a chance to tell you about my fall yet."

Mother appeared. "Hello, Paul dear. It's good to see you. I'm sure you heard about our poor Doug. I'm going to make a casserole to take next door. You're welcome to stay for dinner."

Pauly glanced my way. "Thanks. I'll do that." When Mother disappeared, he grabbed my hand. "Thanks for trying to look beautiful for me." He sighed. "But I wish you felt comfortable showing me the real you – bruises and red marks and all." He frowned at my neck. "That doesn't look like you got it from falling."

I blinked back tears. "I fell really weird." I shrugged. "It's hard to explain."

• • • •

WE WENT TO SEE *Meet Me in St. Louis*, but the evening was strained. Pauly was decidedly cool and kept frowning at my neck. I couldn't see the humor in the movie even as the crowd around me laughed. The Coyote could be sitting right behind us. Or lying in wait outside the theater. He knew where I lived. He could be anywhere. I shivered even with Pauly's strong arm around my shoulder. He pulled me closer with a questioning glance.

Afterward, when we stood holding one another on my front porch, he said. "You're not yourself today."

"Yeah. I just feel so bad for Betty. As much as I get irritated at her, she's like my sister. Did I tell you that she told me she loved me this morning?"

Pauly's face cracked into the first grin of the evening. "Stranger things have happened." He kissed me lightly. "Betty will move on in time." Then he frowned. "I just have to say it. I'll be glad when you're done with that job. I can't shake my uneasy feelings about it." He gently touched my bruised cheek. "If found out anyone hurt you, I'd beat them to a pulp."

I wanted to blurt out *that's the reason I can't tell you*. But instead, I leaned my head into his chest. "Just blame my bumps and bruises on my exhaustion and a rough road to the Clock Alley." All of that was true. If I hadn't been so exhausted, I wouldn't have left work without a partner. I sighed. "I'll see you tomorrow. It will be good to see Pat too even though she'll be focused on trying to cheer up Betty."

Every cell in my body wanted to bolt into the house in fear as Pauly climbed into the car and drove away. Instead, I forced myself to wave until he turned the corner. Then I hurried inside and locked the door behind me.

Chapter 33

Singing in church together always seemed to draw Pauly and I closer and today was no exception as our fingers twined together.

After church, we drove home together. I climbed out reluctantly and hung on the car window. "Can't you come in with us? You can visit with Daddy while Pat and I go see Betty. We won't be gone that long."

His eyes shone as I leaned in for a kiss. "You and Pat need some time to reconnect, just the two of you. And I've got to get some things ready at the office. Besides, I'll be back for dinner in just a couple of hours."

"Okay," I said. I gave him one more quick kiss and hurried into the house with a sense of dread. I was glad that Pat was here today, but first thing, we had to go see Betty. I found Pat in the kitchen eating a snickerdoodle. Mother offered me a cookie.

I waved it away. "Are you ready to get this over with?"

Pat said, "Let's do it. Then I won't have to dread it anymore." Outside, she darted around a spraying sprinkler.

A sprinkle of water grazed my arm, and I sped up. Pat knocked on the door.

Aunt Edna opened it. "Hello, girls. Betty is waiting for you."

I tapped on Betty's door.

"Come in." My cousin sat in a desk chair by the window, her face pale. I recognized the faded black dress she wore, even with the bright pink belt and buttons removed.

"Betty, I'm so sorry." Pat gave her a hug. When she pulled away, a tear shone in her eye. "How are you doing?"

Betty shrugged. "We've scheduled the funeral for next Saturday. Even though Doug's parents never set foot in church, they've been planning most of it with Pastor Carver."

"Saturday, huh? I'll have to dust off my black skirt." Pat plopped herself on the bed.

"Mrs. Durgie is sewing a black dress for me. She said she'd have it done in time." Betty's eyes were dry and curiously devoid of emotion, as if she was already moving on. She looked at me. "I'm going back to Wisconsin. I'll live with Grandma and Grandpa and look for a job." She sighed. "This place will always be full of bad memories now."

"Oh wow, a while ago I would have been excited to go with you. But you know..." I shrugged, unwilling to go on. I'd heard enough disparaging words from Betty about my wedding. And after Doug's death, the idea of it had to be intolerable.

Betty propped her pale face on her hand. "I'll wait until after your wedding, though. I still look forward to being your matron of honor. It's going to be so pretty." She gave me a ghost of a smile. "Maybe I'll travel back to Wisconsin with family after it's over."

Pat opened her eyes in exaggerated surprise. A week ago, Betty had been criticizing everything about it, from my choice of flowers to the tiny chip of a diamond that Pauly was able to afford.

Pat said, "Wisconsin, huh? You're not going to be able to get rid of me that easy. You'll find me knocking at your door someday. Who knows, I may even stay forever."

"Really?" Now it was my turn to be surprised. "You'd both go off and leave me?"

"You're going to be a married woman. I love you, but you're not exactly going to be out having fun." Pat sighed.

Betty asked, "What about Jim? Last I heard, you liked him a lot."

Pat shrugged. "He's nice enough, but all he wants to do is go fishing." She yawned. "Boring."

"I absolutely forbid you to both leave me here in this horrible desert!" Of course, I'd have Pauly and both of our families. But what would I do when Pauly was working every day?

"You'll just have to convince my nosey cousin to move too," Pat said.

"That's not going to happen." I sighed and turned to Betty. "So how are you holding up?"

Betty stared out the window. "I just can't wait to get this funeral over. And I miss Doug so much, but that's nothing new. He's been gone almost as long as we were together." A tear slipped down her cheek. "Life isn't fair." She went on and on about the funeral plans and Doug's family in normal Betty fashion.

When she wound down, I asked, "Do you want to come over for Sunday dinner today? Timmy wants to play a round of Candy Land with us. And then we can play crazy eights."

"Sure." Betty's face brightened slightly. "I can't wait to get out of this morgue."

"Okay, let's go." Pat stood and headed toward the door.

"I'll be over there in a little while. First, I want to do something with my hair."

Outside, Pat said, "Maybe Betty won't play the widow card for too long. That's a relief." We headed toward my back door.

"Yeah, it was shocking that she was so nice about the wedding. I wonder what that was about?"

Pat sighed. "Maybe all this trouble is helping her grow up or something. My mom says after a sorrow you either get bitter or better. Maybe Betty is getting better."

A black spider scuttled up the outside of the house toward my bedroom. Suddenly, the memory of the Coyote came smashing back. His gut pinning me, stealing my breath. His hand up my dress. I shivered and bolted for the door.

Pat grabbed my arm. "Hey, what's the matter? You look like you've seen a ghost."

I shrugged. "I, um..." I struggled against tears. Maybe I should tell Pat about it after all. I needed to tell somebody who cared. And then I could talk to her whenever the spider in my soul crawled into view.

Pat followed me to my room and sat on the bed, tapping her toe impatiently while I paced, fighting tears. "So, what's going on?" she asked.

"On Friday night, I had to work late." I sighed and wiped my eyes. "I was too tired to wait for someone to walk with me to the bus, and when I was on the way..." I sobbed, unable to go on.

Pat hugged me and patted my back. When I calmed, she said, "Go on."

"The Coyote grabbed me and tried to rape me behind the administration building." A fresh wave of sobs poured out.

She shot to her feet. Her mouth dropped open in shock and horror. "What?"

"He didn't get too far, though. God gave me the sense to lay still. It was hard, but I did it. When the Coyote moved off, a scorpion or maybe a rattlesnake bit him and he started jumping around like he was on fire. I ran to Clock Alley." I hiccupped. "My girdle helped too."

"Oh, Ally. That's terrible." Pat's face had turned to ashes. "I hope you told someone in authority."

I nodded. "The Coyote slapped me and choked me. Then I fell in the road when I was running to the Clock House." I rubbed at my makeup to show her my bruise and the pink spot on my neck. "They took me to the nurse, and I told her all about it."

"I could kill the guy." Pat paced back and forth. Her voice raised a notch. "I hope he blew up like a balloon by whatever bit him, and that it festers so he dies a painful, horrible death."

"Shhh! My parents don't know, and they're not going to find out either." I sank to the bed. "The chief guard drove me home, so he knows, too. He said they'd all keep an eye on me."

"That's good, but they better throw the Coyote in jail." She stopped mid-stride. "You told Pauly, didn't you?"

I shook my head, and a fresh wave of tears began. "No. He'd just go after him and nothing good could come from that. He might get himself hurt or even killed."

Pat's eyes were blazing. "Do you know how hurt he would be if he knew you didn't tell him about it?"

I nodded. "But I love him too much to risk it. Once the war is over, and I quit working, I'll tell him all about it."

Pat's face was a question mark. "And you haven't thought about quitting now?"

"I have, but Sergeant Joseph said the security guards would watch out for me. And you don't know what it's like to be a part of my work team. They value me and my contribution. They rely on me." I shrugged. "We're on an adventure to save the world. That's heady for someone who barely got through high school. Plus, we're so close to getting it done. I just know it."

"You don't need that job to prove you're okay. It's not worth the risk."

"To me it is."

Pat looked at me quizzically. "What's this about God giving you the sense to be still? That sounds sort of looney, you know."

"I know it's hard for you to believe. But after I called to God for help, I had this deep sense in my soul that I was to play dead. It was hard, but I finally did it. And the Coyote rolled off me and onto something that bit him."

"Hmmm." Pat went thoughtful.

"I don't see how it could be coincidental because my instinct was to fight for my life. Being still was the last thing I wanted to do."

I stood when I heard the front door slam and Pauly's voice downstairs. "I'm going to go wash my face and get presentable. I'll be down in a few minutes." I stopped. "Pat, I really appreciate you listening. I know you'll keep my secret, won't you? We both know Pauly would do something foolish."

She sighed. "Yes, I'll keep your secret even though I don't agree."

Chapter 34

On Monday morning, fear held my breath as I climbed aboard the bus and bolted into the seat next to Dr. Holt.

He rattled his newspaper. "Good morning, Miss Krepsky."

"Good morning." My voice came out as a squeak. I hadn't seen the Coyote yet. Should I keep my head down to avoid the poison of his evil eyes? No. If I didn't know whether he was on board, the whole ride would be a torture. I'd watch people board the bus with my peripheral vision. I'd recognize his loping walk anywhere.

The first on the bus was a blond man with bucked teeth. Next was a woman with a kerchief tied around her head. Finally, the bus roared off to the 100 Area without the Coyote aboard. I sat back and stared outside at the monotonous gray desert sliding past in the early morning overcast.

I hadn't seen him today, but it was only a matter of time. I bit off a snagged fingernail, then sucked it when it bled. Maybe it really was time to quit my job. I could get ready for the wedding and spend more time with Pauly. The thought of him filled me with longing and a sense of unease. My horrible secret felt like a barbwire fence between us. I needed to tear it down, but not yet. When I got off the bus at the Clock Alley, I kept to the middle of the crowd and hurried inside.

Sergeant Joseph greeted me at the door with a kind smile. "Hello, Miss Krepsky. I hope you're feeling better today."

I nodded, relieved to see him. "I am. Thank you. Have you met Dr. Holt? He works in my building, and we often ride to work together."

"Good to know." He followed us to the doorway and spoke to a guard with sleepy looking black eyes. "Dave, this is Alice Krepsky.

You're to keep an eye on her. If she calls for an escort, go immediately."

The guard yawned and blinked as if he was coming out of a daze. "Will do, sir."

I smiled at Sergeant Joseph. "I can walk with Dr. Holt today. Thank you so much. I will definitely call on you if I need to, though." I hurried to catch up with Dr. Holt.

Stepping into the office felt like coming home. Dr. Jamison's hearty voice boomed out. "Ahh. My right-hand gal. Good to see you today. Good to see you. When you're settled, come into my office. We've got some work to do."

As I poured my energy and skill into the job, I forgot all about the Coyote. I loved every minute of the orderly and urgent process we had created. Even the constant need for secrecy and safety was as normal as oatmeal for breakfast.

I was cramming down my bologna sandwich at my desk when Mr. Dirk hung the Do Not Disturb sign on my door and locked it behind himself. "I hear you've had some difficulties." He sat down and frowned at me as if I were some sort of mistake he wished to erase.

I inhaled some sandwich and walked across the room to cough. I finally cleared my cough and wiped my watery eyes. "May I help you, Mr. Dirk?"

He had barely spoken to me in the past months as he'd collected letters and bulletins from the office to carry to the main vault in the 700 Area. Had I made a mistake of some kind?

"You've had some personal trouble." The creases in his forehead were hitched a notch higher than normal. "Care to tell me about it?"

"Um." I stared at my hands in my lap. "Did I do something wrong?"

"Friday night. What happened?" He waited, tapping a pencil on the desk impatiently. "I received reports from a Nurse Brown and

Sergeant Joseph that a man named Bart Bundy accosted you on your way home from work." He opened his briefcase and set a document on the desk. "I have to fill out an incident report, and I need your story."

When I didn't speak, his frown deepened. His eyebrow spiraled up. I interlaced my fingers to stop them from trembling. Unshed tears formed a knot in my throat.

"I have to make sure all accounts are corroborated." Mr. Dirk tapped his pencil.

When I finally opened my mouth to speak, it came out as a sob. He stood and began to pace the room.

I swallowed my tears and forced myself to talk. "I was leaving work after an overtime shift. It was darker outside than I expected. All of a sudden, Bart Bundy grabbed me from behind and dragged me behind the office building." I felt myself blush with shame. "I um... I finally broke free and ran to the Clock House. The nurse bandaged up my wounds. Somebody found my shoes, and Sergeant Joseph drove me home." I ran out of words.

"What kind of wounds did you incur?" He pursed his robot lips.

"He choked me and hit me on the face." Tears began to leak from my eyes. "Then when I was running to the Clock Alley, I fell and scraped my knees."

"Did he penetrate?" Mr. Dirk turned a bright shade of red.

I blushed to match his embarrassment and shook my head. The Coyote hadn't penetrated anything except my broken soul. "No, sir. When I played dead, he dropped to the sand then began jumping around, slapping his back as if he were in pain. Nurse Margaret said she thought he'd been bit by a rattler or scorpion." I stared at my hands.

"And you're sure it was Bart Bundy who accosted you. Any mistake and the man could lose his job unnecessarily." Mr. Dirk grimaced. "I understand he's been a reliable worker."

I nodded. "Yes. I know it was him for sure. I met him at the bowling alley one time. He followed me home that night even though it wasn't his regular route. One time on the bus, he sat next to me and fell asleep with his head on my shoulder." I shivered at the memory. I recognized his smell too, but that seemed too intimate to mention. Just the thought of it made me gag. I swallowed hard and hugged myself to stop trembling.

Mr. Dirk tapped his pencil on the report. "Did you do anything to entice him?"

"No. Not that I know of. I was just going about my business. I'd sort of forgotten about him until..." I stopped, unwilling to go on. Leave it to Mr. Dirk to think that I was a troublemaker. Angry tears spilled.

Mr. Dirk shuffled his papers back into his brief case and stood. "I'll give a copy of this report to employment services. Mr. Bundy will be questioned as well, but I expect he'll be given notice today. Do not leave the office unless accompanied by a guard until I inform you that he's been escorted out of town." His machine face registered nothing as he glanced at his watch and stood. "Starting today."

When he disappeared, the room began to swim. I slumped into my chair with my head in my hands. I had been contaminated in this strange place after all. Not by the toxic poison that the Dupont people worked so hard to contain, but by an evil man.

A rap on the door startled me. Dr. Jamison stuck his head in the door. "Miss Krepsky," He started to speak, then stopped. "You're white as a ghost. Are you feeling well?"

I tried to smile, but his eyes darkened in concern. "If you're ill, you should go home. We can get by without you if you need to go."

"Thank you, sir. Let me see if I feel better when I finish my lunch. I'll let you know soon."

Dr. Jamison withdrew, and I took a sip of water. The bologna sandwich that I'd shoved in my drawer when Dirt showed up turned my stomach. Maybe I should take time off until I knew that the Coyote was gone for good. It couldn't be long. I didn't want my co-workers to know I had to be escorted to and from work by a guard. They would ask questions. Questions that I was unwilling to answer.

More tears wet my eyes as I called Dr. Jamison to tell him I felt too ill to stay. "If I don't feel better by tomorrow morning, I'll call Mr. Dirk and see if he can take my place for a few days." Mr. Dirk would probably guess the real reason I wasn't coming in, but it couldn't be helped. Besides, I really did feel sick. I called Clock Alley to ask for an escort.

Mrs. Frank was dusting her spotless office. "Goodbye, Mrs. Frank. I'm not feeling well and am leaving early. I hope to be back tomorrow." I stepped outside into the blinding sunlight without waiting for her reply.

When the sleepy-eyed guard came into view, I hurried in his direction. "Hello. I'm not feeling well and am going home."

"I've been directed to make sure you get safely on the bus." Dave held himself erect and surveyed the street as we walked without speaking the rest of the way.

Thankfully, there was a bus waiting at the gate. The guard whispered something to a new bus driver and saluted a goodbye. The driver smiled; his yellow teeth lined up like a corn on a cob. "I'm Harry. Nice to meet you, Miss Krepsky. I'll make sure you get home safely."

"Thank you." I scooted over to the window in the first seat next to the driver and laid my purse next to me to discourage other riders. It was only one-thirty on a Monday, but I already felt as exhausted as if I'd worked hours of overtime.

If only I could unload my troubles onto Pauly's large, comforting shoulders. When the Coyote was gone, I'd do just that. He couldn't be mad at me for trying to protect him from getting hurt.

Chapter 35

Mother called. "Mr. Dirk is on the phone for you, Alice dear!"

I knotted the belt of my robe and hurried downstairs. Hopefully, he was calling with the news that the Coyote was gone, never to return, and I could go back to work. Playing sick was boring even with my record player for company. I hadn't been able to see Pauly and I missed him with all my heart.

"Hello, this is Miss Krepsky."

Mr. Dirk's robotic voice sounded far away. "Your story was corroborated by the fact that Mr. Bundy went to the hospital on Friday night with a rattler bite. He was escorted from town yesterday. If he shows up in Richland again, he faces jail time."

"I'm glad to hear that." Relief rushed through me. The only thing that troubled me was why Mr. Dirk had waited a whole day to call and tell me that the Coyote had been kicked out of town.

"I'm training a new secretary. If you come back, you can help with the process."

I sat up, alarmed. A new secretary? If I come back? It wasn't as if situations like this were going to be a regular occurrence. I hadn't missed a day of work until this week, and I'd proven over and over that I could do the job well. Everyone counted on me.

"I feel better and plan to be back at work tomorrow, sir."

"I hope to see you tomorrow, then." Mr. Dirk hung up without saying goodbye.

Mother appeared in the dining room. "I heard you say you were feeling better. I'm so glad."

"Yes. I'm feeling a lot better. In fact, I'm going to shower and get dressed right now."

I started up the stairs when the phone rang again.

Mother answered. "Hello? Yes, she's here. May I ask who's calling?" Mother covered the receiver, her doe eyes round with pride. "It's Matthew Ward from the FBI."

I doubled back to the phone, alarmed. "This is Allison Krepsky. May I help you?"

"We need you at Building 721 as soon as you can get here. I understand you've been sick." He waited.

"I'm better now." I glanced at the wall clock. "I can be there by two-thirty." My heart sped up as I raced up the stairs. Mr. Dirk had made the situation with the Coyote sound finished, but there had to be more to it. My trip to the FBI must mean that I had more documentation to sign. A ritual hoop to jump through.

Then a scalding thought hit me. What if the Coyote had somehow indicated that I'd been leading him on? Maybe they wanted to determine whether I was a temptress who might cause further trouble down the road. Whatever the case, it was more important than ever that I look and act professionally.

I raced for the shower and slipped on a shower cap. There was no time to curl my unruly hair. It was Mother's laundry day. When the water from the hot water faucet stayed cold, I stepped under a freezing stream and tried not to scream.

In my room, I dressed in my pale blue suit and white blouse. My Gatsby hat, trimmed with a rose covered my wild hair. A pair of white gloves would show them that with every word and mannerism I was circumspect, competent, and smart.

"I'm leaving for work. I shouldn't be long," I called to Mother before I slipped out the door. I snorted at the thought of the pride shining out of her eyes when she told me the FBI was calling. Today, her naivety was a gift. Daddy would be alarmed. Hopefully she'd forget all about the phone call before he got home.

The receptionist at the FBI office was a woman I recognized from the bus. According to Pat, she was a horrible snob. Today, her blue eyes were icicles.

I smiled. "I'm Allison Krepsky here to see Mr. Matthew Ward, please."

"Mr. Ward is expecting you." She stood, and I followed her to a room off the reception area. "Wait here."

The slamming door echoed behind her. I perched on one of two chairs at a gunmetal table. The walls glared white, bare even of the ubiquitous safety posters. Even though it was a warm spring day, heat poured out of a ticking radiator. I stared at my watch as fifteen minutes crawled past.

Where was Mr. Ward? More importantly, why had I been escorted to a hot, empty room? My hands grew wet, and I slipped off my gloves. Beads of sweat dripped out from under my hat. I longed to yank it off but didn't dare because of my unruly hair. If only Mr. Ward would appear. I could sign the necessary paperwork and get out of here. Maybe the icy-eyed receptionist had forgotten to tell him I'd arrived. I stood and twisted the door handle. The door was locked.

Suddenly, I felt as if I had sipped every molecule of air from the tiny hot room. Panic seared my veins as memories of the Coyote attack played in my mind like a horror movie. A sob escaped. My tears mingled with sweat. I was innocent of all wrongdoing. Why was I being treated like a criminal, shut up in this blistering, empty room?

The room began to spin. Just like Mr. Dirk, the FBI thought I had done something to entice the Coyote. They had lost a good employee and wanted to make sure it never happened again. Sweat coursed down my sides. I lowered my head into my hands.

If accused, I could call witnesses to my character. Pat, Mrs. Chase, and all my co-workers in the 100 Area would come to my defense. I had done nothing wrong. Perspiration soaked my clothes. I wiped my face and neck with a handkerchief and panted hungrily for air.

Then it hit me like a bomb. They had finally searched into my past. My old teachers and classmates had told them the truth—Allison Krepsky is stupid and incompetent. A fraud. The blistering hot walls seemed to echo every unkind word ever spoken about me, every angry red mark on my papers. The D's lining my report cards. I sweated as my daymare raged on.

Finally, the knob rattled. The door popped open. A weasel of a man in a baggy brown suit entered. "Mr. Ward, FBI."

My words rushed out in a torrent. "I didn't do anything to entice Bart Bundy. It wasn't my fault."

"Miss Krepsky, it sounds like you ought to change the kind of company you keep." Mr. Ward straddled the chair opposite me at the table, his sharp nose sniffing the air for evidence of my lack.

A bead of sweat poured down my forehead and I wiped it away quickly. "I was not keeping company with Bart Bundy. He attacked me when I was walking to the bus."

"Mmhmm." Mr. Ward rapped his knobby fists on the tabletop. "You're engaged to a young reporter in town named Paul Armstrong. Is that correct?"

"Yes. I fail to see what Mr. Armstrong has to do with any of this." I was suddenly angry.

"Shortly after you were admitted to the hospital for a health check, the *Walla Walla Union Bulletin* published an article about the dangers of working at Hanford." Mr. Ward's beady brown eyes were inscrutable. I looked away. "This information included some very intimate details about the health testing procedures that you experienced first-hand."

A knife point of fear speared me. "Paul works for the *Pasco Herald*, not the *Union Bulletin*."

Mr. Ward nodded. "We're aware of that. But he's been spotted on several occasions dining with the editor of the *Union Bulletin*, a Mr. Jeffery Davis." He stared into me, mining for secrets.

Pauly couldn't have been so careless of our relationship, so cruel as to put me in danger. Could he? "I've not met Mr. Davis, but

I do know that Paul is committed to reporting news about the community, not Hanford."

Mr. Ward's thin lips smiled derisively. "The same Paul Armstrong found soliciting information from workers outside the 700 Building in the interest of reporting it in the *Herald*? That very same reporter was warned to desist and threatened with expulsion if he didn't comply." The metal table reverberated when Mr. Ward slammed his fist. "Did you or did you not share with your fiancé details about your contamination and subsequent health check?"

I sobbed uncontrollably. "On the night I went to the hospital to be tested, I missed a concert date with Paul. He'd given it to me as a birthday present, and he was very angry that I couldn't go. I didn't feel I had a choice but to explain the reason. You've got to understand." But even as I explained, I knew it didn't matter. The fact that I was being grilled by the FBI meant I couldn't break confidentiality rules, no matter what. I wiped my eyes with my sodden handkerchief.

Mr. Ward's weasel lips smiled in satisfaction. "And instead of incriminating his own newspaper and running the risk of losing you in the process, he shared the information with Mr. Davis of the *Union Bulletin*."

Pure anger forced me out of my seat. "Do you have proof? Couldn't Mr. Davis have received the information through another channel?"

"That's no concern of yours." Mr. Ward said. "You've broken confidentiality rules." He held out his hand. "Hand over your identification badge. Your clearance is revoked. You are officially terminated." He stood. "Consider yourself lucky. You'll not be jailed. Mr. Dirk recommends that we release you to the care of your father." Mr. Ward's lips curled into a sneer. "But if you continue to share secrets, you will be jailed. Is that understood?" He pulled a temporary bus pass out of his pocket. "You may ride the bus home one last time, Miss Krepsky. I'll inform Mr. Dirk of what has transpired, and he'll make sure you get any personal items you may have left at the office." He stood and held the door.

The blast of fresh air did nothing to cool my humiliation as I rapidly made my exit. Blinded by searing pain, I shoved the temporary pass in the garbage. Someone called my name, but I didn't turn to see who it was. Instead, I ran out of the gate toward home, weighed down by sorrow and shame.

Could Pauly have betrayed me?

Chapter 36

I dragged myself onto my porch and stopped with my hand on the doorknob, bracing myself for the barrage of questions my family would launch my way. I could just picture the sorrow and disappointment on Daddy's face as I explained.

A fresh batch of tears flooded my eyes as I opened the door to an empty room and the smell of swiss steak. I heard the family laughing together about something in the kitchen and tip-toed up the stairs. Shutting the door to my room softly behind me, I ripped off my hat and blue suit and stuffed them in the trash. Stupid hat. Stupid hot suit. Stupid me. I dissolved onto my bed in silent tears.

I didn't want to talk to anyone right now except Pauly. Anger blazed a path through my heart. It was his fault that I'd been fired. How could he have betrayed me? Yes, I understood his desire to report the news, but to share my confidences with someone from a neighboring newspaper? His talk of trust had been nothing but a sham. He probably asked me to marry him just so he could learn Hanford secrets.

I curled into a fetal position as pictures of Pauly flashed through my mind. His warm kisses and loving glances. His acceptance of my need to stay on the job until the war ended. His apology for trying to dig up secrets.

I sat up and combed my fingers through my hair. Maybe he was innocent, and the *Walla Walla Union Bulletin* had come upon the information in a different way. One way or another, I had to find out. If I didn't, this newest secret would kill off our relationship anyway.

When I heard the clink of the family at dinner, I quickly dressed and tiptoed downstairs to the phone. Pauly answered on the first ring. I pitched my voice slightly above a whisper. "Pauly, I need to see you now." Hanging up softly, I slipped out the front door to wait. I'd stay outside until he came, even if it took all night.

Swallowing my tears, I wandered to the bus stop. If a bus arrived, I would hurry toward home as if I'd changed my mind about riding. I sighed. It was foolish to worry what others thought about me hanging around outside for no apparent reason. Soon everyone would know I'd been fired. Fired! I'd never be able to hold my head up again.

When Pauly's car pulled up in front of the house, I raced to meet it. He frowned as I climbed in the car. "What's up?"

"Mr. Ward from the FBI called me in for questioning today. I was fired because I admitted to sharing government secrets with you. He accused you of telling Jeffrey Davis from the *Walla Walla Union Bulletin* about the time my pencil detector read high, and I had to go to the clinic. Did you do it?" I started sobbing.

Pauly's mouth hung open in shock. "What? No. What are you talking about?"

I explained what happened at the FBI. "Mr. Ward said they saw you dining with Mr. Davis right after my experience, and then they published the article soon after."

Pauly slumped dejectedly against his steering wheel. "You believe that I would betray your trust?" He turned toward me with hurt shining out of his eyes, shook his head and started his car. "Ally, our relationship has some deep problems that I'm not sure we can fix. I think maybe we should call it off."

I could tell by his reaction that Pauly hadn't shared my confidences with anyone. Much less another reporter. "I'm sorry for doubting you. But I was bullied and fired by the FBI. The FBI! Can you even imagine how horrible that would be?"

Pauly responded by putting the car in drive.

"Can't we talk about it some more?" My voice come out as a shriek.

"Things have been difficult between us for some time now. This is just the final straw." Pauly reached across me grimly and opened the door.

I sobbed, set the ring between us on the seat, and stumbled out. It was all my fault. If he didn't want me anymore, I couldn't blame him. I really was the failure I'd always thought I was.

He drove away without a backward glance, and I ran weeping toward the house. Timmy was sitting between Mother and Daddy on the couch.

"My engagement to Pauly is off. And I've been fired because I admitted to the FBI that I breached confidentiality rules."

Mother and Daddy's mouths hung open in horror. Even Timmy was frozen silent.

"When did you talk to the FBI?" Daddy stood, his hands on his hips.

"Mother knew about the meeting. Oh Daddy, it's too complicated to explain right now." I glanced between Mother and Timmy. "I just wanted you all to know what was happening. Mother, please let the relatives know the wedding is off." Crushed, I rushed upstairs to my room.

I'd be marrying the love of my life if only I hadn't questioned Pauly. I could have lied and told him that I decided to quit my job to concentrate on the wedding. But then I would always wonder whether Pauly had shared my secret. No. Secrets were the whole problem with our relationship. Our marriage couldn't stand on lies and untold truths.

I climbed into bed and pulled up the covers. I smelled Daddy's pipe before I heard a tap at the door. "Come in."

"Tell me everything." He stared through the window while I talked through tears.

"You remember when I had to go to the hospital because my pencil reader was high?"

He nodded. I told him about the FBI visit. "I got fired on the spot because I admitted that I shared about my trip to the clinic with Pauly when I had to miss the concert. I'm surprised you haven't heard. Mr. Ward said I didn't have to go to jail because they could release me to you."

Daddy sat on the bed next to me. "I hadn't heard a thing. How did they find out you told him?"

"Pauly has a reporter friend from the Walla Walla Union. Shortly after I went to the clinic, the Union printed a story about an experience that was similar to mine. The FBI decided Pauly and I were the source of the information and came after me. They must have been following Pauly and probably me, too." I was riven by the horror. "When I asked Pauly about it, he was hurt that I didn't trust him and broke up with me."

Daddy patted my shoulder. "I understand why you'd have to ask. A marriage can't survive that sort of suspicion."

Suddenly, I felt disconnected from the world of my bedroom and Daddy, as if I was floating in space and looking down at the world below me. "I'm sorry for being such a failure of a daughter. I know how much you loved Pauly. You asked me to quit my job. I should have listened."

He sighed. Sadness tugged on his lips as he spoke. "Alice, we all make mistakes. Just get some rest. Things will look brighter in the morning. And don't give up on Paul yet. I know how much he loves you." Daddy patted my shoulder before shutting the door behind him.

I shook my head. Trouble had been brewing in our relationship for weeks. This was just the final straw.

Tomorrow I'd tell Betty I was going back to Sheboygan with her. At least I could leave behind this terrible desert that blew like a demon, smothering, choking, and creating blind walls that shifted and stung. This terrible place where secrets reigned over people's lives like a tyrant. I'd leave as soon as the funeral was over and run away from the pain of losing Pauly and the failure of being fired.

The word *fired* detonated in my mind, killing all the positive thoughts of work that I'd fed on over the past months. What must my co-workers think of me? Shame and humiliation scalded my memories. We were like a family, bonded together by our unusual mission. But I knew deep down I'd get over losing them.

Losing Pauly was a different kind of sorrow. One so deep I didn't dare touch it. For now, I would file it away and close that drawer in my mind. If I didn't, I'd be blown to bits so far and wide that I might never be put back together. As the night wore on, my bed turned to iron and my body ached. When the earliest birds started to screech, I pulled the covers over my head to shut them out.

• • • •

THE NEXT THING I KNEW, Betty was standing over me. "What's this I hear? The wedding is off, and you were fired?"

I cringed at her voice, wondering what her next words would be. *I always knew you'd be fired. They must have finally found somebody better. It's good you're finished with Pauly. He was too old and ugly, anyway.*

Instead, I felt her weight settle on the bed next to me. "What happened? I thought you were the best secretary since sliced bread. Pat told me how fast you were at typing, and I know from talking to people how hard it is to get a job as a secretary in the 100 Area."

I poked my head out of the covers to make sure I wasn't hallucinating. "I did love my job. And I was good at it." I would miss the hum and snap of the office as we worked together to save the world. "I liked the men at work, and they relied on me." Tears threatened as I dumped my story, starting with the Coyote attack and ending with my visit to the FBI. As I spoke, Betty's face turned white with silent outrage.

I went on. "They accused me of sharing work secrets with Pauly and suggested that he told another reporter who in turn, reported it in the *Walla Walla Union Bulletin*. I did share work secrets with Pauly. They were right about that, but he didn't tell anyone." I hid my head under the cover. "It wouldn't have mattered whether it was true or not. The FBI officer had me in such a dither by that time, that I'd have confessed to anything." A tear leaked, and I wiped my eyes with the sheet. "Pauly broke off our engagement because he thought I didn't trust him. But you know how difficult it is. He just couldn't understand." Too painful. I shoved the Pauly drawer shut again.

Betty held me in her arms and rocked back and forth as we wept. Finally, she stood. "I'm glad they took your story about the Coyote seriously and kicked him out of town. There's no point in ever thinking about him again. And maybe if I can make Pauly understand the pressure you were under, he will relent. I can vouch that you've never been a secretive person. You've always just been shy little Ally. The quiet one who never got in trouble and wouldn't hurt a flea if it bit her."

I sat up and shook my head. "Thanks, but I think it's a lost cause. Just the fact that the FBI brought me in for questioning should speak loudly to him about what I was up against."

Since Doug's death, Betty's face had been cast in shadows. Suddenly, her eyes glinted with humor. "I always thought you could find someone more handsome anyway."

I rolled my eyes and dried them with my sheet. She reached into the trash can. "What's your new blue suit doing in the garbage?"

"It's too full of bad memories."

"You'll forget. There's no point in wasting it." Betty started to hang it then stopped. "Phew! It needs laundering. I guess you weren't kidding about how hot it was in there. That creep." She angrily shoved it in the hamper. "At least you're not going to jail."

"Yeah. That's the one good thing." I sighed. "After the funeral, I'm going to move back to Sheboygan with you. Grandma and Grandpa will let us stay with them until we get on our feet."

Betty put her arm around my shoulder. "Are you sure you want to go back to Wisconsin? I think once Pauly realizes how much he misses you, he's going to come running back."

I shook my head. "I'm not going to wait around here for something that might never happen." I jumped out of bed. "Besides, I can't wait to get away from the coyotes, the rattlers, and the dust storms."

"Me too. We just have to get through the funeral." A big tear slipped down her cheek.

It was my turn to hug. "At least we have each other. And Pat said something about wanting to move. Maybe all three of us can go together."

Chapter 37

Except for the bright American flag draped over the coffin, the church was dark with sorrow. Doug's family wept in the pew across the aisle. Betty sat next to them, tearless, pinched, and pale.

My black-and-blue heart beat out its own painful rhythm. Pat had told me that Pauly was going to show up to pay his respects to Doug. Somehow, I had to get out of here without seeing him. Today was about Betty's sorrow. Not mine.

When Mrs. Dalgrin played the opening strains of "Leaning on the Everlasting Arms," I shut my mind to the music. Instead of singing with the rest, I thought about the next day. Our train left tomorrow evening, and Grandma and Grandpa were expecting us. My big trunk was mostly packed. I still needed to pack my carry-on suitcase with one change of clothes and all the sandwiches that Mother could stuff inside.

From the pew behind us, Pat reached forward and rested her hand on my shoulder. I grabbed and squeezed. My pure gold friend. I would miss her. She had listened to my side of the story with tears in her eyes and growled like a mother tiger. "Pauly is absolutely miserable without you. But he's stuck like glue to his viewpoint no matter how much I've tried to explain the hard situation you were in."

I asked her to come to Wisconsin with us, but she had just shrugged. "Maybe someday." I sensed that she didn't want to leave Pauly in his time of need.

Pastor Carver spoke. "When someone dies, we often think that God is absent or that he doesn't care about our suffering. But in Psalm 34 it says that God is close to the brokenhearted." His eyes radiated compassion as he scanned the audience. As he went on, I held his opening words over my heart like a bandage. God had saved me from the Coyote in this desert place. I would choose to trust that he was close to me in my brokenness, even though I could not see his blessings.

After the service, my heart dropped to the floor when I spied Pauly at the back of the church with his head bowed. I whispered to Pat. "I don't want people at the funeral to be whispering about my break-up with Pauly. This is Betty's day. I'm going to hide out in the Sunday school classroom for a while. Come find me when he's gone." I didn't wait for her answer, and she didn't follow as I stumbled out the side door to hide.

The classroom felt like a cage as I paced back and forth, waiting for Pat to appear. When people began to exit the church, I hummed tunelessly to muffle the sound of their voices. I'd be able to recognize Pauly's deep rumble even through a closed window. It was best just to forget him.

Soon Betty and I would be back home in Sheboygan. I pictured our quaint, settled town with church steeples anchoring everything in place. The park in summer and the bandstand. Grandma and Grandpa's smiling faces.

Finally, Pat appeared at the door looking sad and wan. "He's gone and you can come out now. You know, if you two set out to purposefully break my heart, you couldn't have done a better job."

"Oh, Pat. I'm so sorry." I followed her into the hall. "I'm going to miss you so much."

"Pauly is impossible. Maybe I will move to Wisconsin just to spite him." She tried to laugh, but it fell flat.

I followed her to her car. "I'd love you to you come, but not to spite Pauly. You stay here as long as he needs you." My love for them both threatened to spill over in more tears. I couldn't be responsible for hurting Pauly any more deeply. "Are you coming to see us off at the train station tomorrow?"

She jingled her keys and sighed. "Begrudgingly, yes. Ally, I'm going to miss you so much." She grabbed me in a hug.

"This isn't an end to anything, you know. We'll visit back and forth. And maybe you'll be able to move to Sheboygan sooner rather than later."

Chapter 38

The calm morning seemed to mock my inner storm as I stood next to the passenger train waiting to board. I couldn't wait to leave this painful place forever. But first I had to say goodbye to the people I loved, hopefully without blubbering like a baby.

Pat hugged me close. "You can't get rid of me, you know. And I'll try to knock some sense into that idiot cousin of mine, too."

I smiled. "Let's just say see you later."

When Pat released me, she nodded resolutely. "See ya later, alligator!"

Mother's doe eyes were dark with sadness as she gathered me into a hug. She whispered, "I wish I was traveling home with you. Give your grandma and grandpa a hug for me. I'll miss you, my darling girl." She patted my cheek and wiped her eyes with a handkerchief.

Daddy hugged me and said, "We'll come visit when the war is over. Until then, write home every day."

"I will."

Timmy squeezed my hand as if he would never let go. I leaned down to hug him. "I love you, little brother. Be good." Then I handed my ticket to the white-jacketed purser.

Betty was settling into seat 4A. "Ally, your seat is right here." She pointed at the cracked leather seat next to her.

As if I couldn't see. I sighed. Miss Bossy never quit. I closed my eyes against painful memories as the train chugged out of the Pasco yard and into the desert. It was better to focus on the future. Sheboygan beckoned. The cool, quiet, shady streets. The familiar house on Church Street. Band concerts in the park. Grandma and Grandpa. Rest and peace and safety.

As we traveled, we dozed, read, and talked intermittently about mundane things. Pencil detectors, poisonous metal, reactors, and my burning embarrassment at having been fired began to fade as we entered the prairie, still brown with winter's chill. Betty seemed as determined as I was to forget the past and move on. The ride home flew past in a haze of sleep and buried pain.

••••

GRANDPA MET US WHEN we stepped off the train at the Sheboygan station, his face wreathed in smile wrinkles. "You girls are a sight for sore eyes."

"Grandpa!" I hugged him hard. His familiar fishy smell was comforting. "Oh, I've missed you so much."

"Your grandma and I have missed you more than I can say, my sweet little Alice." His small blue eyes gleamed.

"My turn." Betty hugged him.

He embraced her. "Betty, we were so sorry to hear about Doug. We wish we could have met him." He patted her back.

"He was a really good guy, Grandpa. You would have loved him too. I know it." Betty pulled away, suddenly overcome by tears.

He led us to his weathered Ford and heaved our trunks into the bed of his pickup next to his tackle box and fishing poles. When we drove down the familiar street leading away from the train station, I sighed with pleasure. The leafy trees hanging over the smooth roads with sidewalks, and the stores advertising the best cheese in town, were a balm for my seared spirit. The air felt settled and temperate, with no scorching heat or wind to destroy the peace of the day. We turned onto Church Street and there was the stone church with its tall steeple. Across the street, Grandma and Grandpa's house sat dignified, permanent in the green yard.

When we stepped inside, Grandma hurried from the kitchen, wiping her hands on her apron. Her giant smile lifted the ripple of her cascading chins. "Come in. Come in. It's so good to see you." After hugs and kisses all around, she said, "You can pile your bags in the corner of your room. I know how much you girls like sleeping together, so I put you both in the guest room."

Betty spoke what I was thinking. "Oh, Grandma, that's so sweet! We liked to sleep together when we were ten. We've changed a bit." She winked at me. I smiled. It was good to be home. I drank in the familiarity of the knickknacks and photos crowding the ornately carved tables and the horsehair sofa with the big RCA radio sitting on the floor nearby. The table was set with a white cloth and Grandma's blue-and-white everyday dishes.

"Well, we can sort that out later. Dinner is ready." Grandma hurried into the kitchen.

While we ate Grandpa's freshly caught lake trout, creamed potatoes, and canned peas, Betty talked about Richland - the desert, heat, and dust storms, the buses and the square buildings with no character or charm. Grandma and Grandpa asked about our families and church.

After dinner, Grandma served slices of angel food cake with an icing drizzle. "So, your mother tells us you broke off your engagement to Paul, Alice."

I nodded, finding it difficult to talk over the giant lump in my throat. "Well, I didn't really..."

For once, I was grateful when Betty took over. "Paul is older, but he's a great guy. A reporter, you know. Ally had a top-secret secretarial job. He couldn't stand it because she couldn't share the secrets she was learning. Eventually he got so angry he broke off the engagement." Her eyes spoke her sadness.

Grandma and Grandpa looked at me for confirmation. I nodded. "It wasn't quite that simple..." I stopped, unable to go on.

Grandpa's eyes were troubled. "Our little Alice in a top-secret job. That seems like a horrible misfit for the quiet, sweet girl we know."

"I liked being a secretary." I felt tears forming.

Grandma patted my hand and frowned. "That's a fine job while you're waiting for a husband who can take care of you."

I set down my fork. "I'm sorry, I..."

Betty took over. "Ally was fired. She didn't want to lose Paul and shared some work secrets with him to try and keep their relationship alive. The FBI found out. They are crazy strict about it."

I shook my head at Betty and frowned. Grandma and Grandpa knew I'd been fired, but still, her telling the story felt like a stab wound. Besides, the Hanford secrets were meant to be kept even this far away. I didn't want Grandma and Grandpa to ask questions I couldn't answer.

They studied my face as if mining it for the truth. I nodded my head mutely. Grandma said, "Oh, dear, it sounds like you've both had a hard time."

Grandpa's face brightened. "I hear they're looking for a secretary at the marina office."

I nodded. Grandpa kept his fishing boat at the marina on Lake Michigan. He would put in a good word for me. It would probably be a sleepy place. Just what the doctor ordered.

As Betty talked on about the mysteries surrounding the Hanford Engineer Works, I excused myself. "I'm tired. I'm going to head off to a bath and bed."

The same old double bed with the sculpted headboard and pink bedspread sat against the wall in the guestroom. On the nightstand was a framed picture of Betty holding my hand tightly at a school picnic when we were in first grade. I examined it for nostalgia's sake and sighed. Our relationship had changed. And so had I.

In the bathroom, I set the rubber stopper in the drain and climbed into the old claw-foot tub. My tears mingled with the warm water pouring from the faucet. Safe in the privacy of Grandma and Grandpa's homey bathroom, I finally allowed myself to grieve for all I'd lost. My silent tears spilled as I buckled over in gut-wrenching pain.

When I was spent, I dried off, draped myself in a towel, and hurried across to the bedroom. My flowered nightgown, crumpled at the bottom of my suitcase, was soft from wear. The bed sheets were stiff with starch and smelled like bleach. I rolled to the wall and sealed myself against it—narrow and flat. At least I had a safe place to stay for now.

Chapter 39

August 6, 1945

I opened the front door to find the shades drawn against the heat, and the parlor a comforting cave. I sighed in relief and followed the sound of Betty's voice to the kitchen.

"How was work?" Steam hissed as Grandma ironed my yellow dress.

"It was fine." I sat at the kitchen table across from Betty. Luckily, my job at the marina was within walking distance from the house. I could live here until I got a car, and we found a place to rent.

This afternoon, I'd write a letter to Pat and Mother and Daddy. I sighed, longing again for Pauly.

"You must smell fish all day long. Besides being bored." Betty took a sip of lemonade. "A new clothing shipment came in today at JC Penney. You should come see all the latest styles."

I shrugged. "I don't have any reason to buy new clothes."

Betty nodded. "Yeah, but it's so fun to look."

Grandma's iron huffed as she shifted my dress on the ironing board. "You girls both have just the right jobs."

Betty loved seeing our old friends who shopped at the store. Every day after work, she told me who she'd helped and how they looked in the outfits they'd chosen. They'd be mortified to know how she analyzed and described their every fat roll and dimple.

I could do my job with my eyes closed. Mr. Dean, who owned the marina, was a distracted sort of fellow who seemed to live and breathe boats. The small office, with a window onto Lake Michigan, contained an ancient typewriter on a beat-up desk and a file cabinet in disarray—a world away from the Hanford Engineer Works. It hadn't taken me long to get things in order. And at least I had no Mr. Dirk slashing papers and barking out orders. No secrets to keep or deadly substances to avoid.

Grandma hung my dress on a hanger. "I've invited the Augers over for dinner tomorrow. You remember Gerald. He was two grades ahead of you girls in school. He's just been discharged from the Army."

I rolled my eyes at Betty. Grandma had been talking about finding me a husband since we arrived two months ago. I was glad to be back in Sheboygan, but they treated me as if I were the same age as the picture on the nightstand. I felt trapped under the glass of time. I had loved being a top-secret secretary. And though I didn't want to be a spinster, I wasn't ready to start dating again. Maybe someday. But first, I needed my broken heart to mend.

Betty smiled, "She doesn't—"

Grandpa slammed the back door and interrupted Betty. "I ran into Mayor Whitfield just now. He said President Truman is going to give some kind of special announcement." He disappeared, and a newscaster's voice poured out of the radio in the parlor.

"Thank you for ironing, Grandma. But you really don't have to do it. I'm a grown up now, you know."

"You'll always be my little girl." Grandma grabbed my cheek between her thumb and forefinger and squeezed gently.

I hung my freshly pressed dress in the bedroom closet, then went to the parlor to listen. The newscaster spoke authoritatively, "We interrupt our regularly scheduled broadcasting for an address from President Truman."

The radio scratched and hummed. Then the president's voice sounded over the speaker. "Sixteen hours ago, an American airplane dropped one bomb on Hiroshima, an important Japanese Army base.

I bolted to the edge of the sofa, on high alert.

"The force from which the sun draws its power has been loosed against those who brought war to the Far East. Before 1939, it was the accepted belief of scientists that it was theoretically possible to release atomic energy."

I stared at the radio, stunned. Atomic was one of the first words I'd learned to spell as a top-secret secretary. This bomb on Hiroshima was the result of our work.

President Truman continued. "But no one knew any practical method of doing it. By 1942, however, we knew that the Germans were working feverishly to find a way to add atomic energy to the other engines of war with which they hoped to enslave the world. But they failed. We may be grateful to Providence that they did not get the atomic bomb at all...we have now won the battle of the laboratories as we have won the other battles.

"We now have two great plants and many lesser works devoted to the production of atomic power. Many have worked there for two and a half years. Few know what they have been producing."

Betty's eyes were round with amazement. She let out a whoop. "Ally, that's us!"

All that I'd learned on the job flashed through my mind: Plutonium, radioactivity, the failsafe shutdown procedure, critical mass. It was all for the bomb.

President Truman went on. "What has been done is the greatest achievement of organized science in history. It was done under high pressure and without failure. We are now prepared to obliterate more rapidly and completely every productive enterprise the Japanese have above ground in any city. We shall destroy their docks, their factories, and their communications. Let there be no mistake; we shall completely destroy Japan's power to make war."

I felt a thrill curl in my belly. All that we had been working toward had finally been unleashed on the enemy. The war would be over soon. Our boys were coming home. Grandma and Grandpa looked between Betty and me with open mouths. When President Truman finished speaking, we all began babbling at once.

After everyone settled down, Grandpa said, "Ally, with your top-secret job you must have known all about this new atomic energy."

"Well, like the president said, Richland was just one place where they were engineering it and I only knew our small bit. What surprises me most is that our part of the process must have been completed before I left. But the urgency in production hadn't waned."

Grandpa said, "Well, you heard the president. They're probably producing more bombs. We're going to obliterate the Japanese people if we must."

Betty lifted her arms in a victory pose. "Just think of it. All those secret messages I carried made the atomic bomb possible. I helped to unleash the energy of the atom."

Grandma grabbed her hand. "Both of you girls had an important part to play in this."

Dr. Holt's words about being on an adventure to save the world came rushing back in force. If only I had been able to see my job through to the end. All the co-workers at the 100 Area that I'd tried so hard to forget paraded through my mind. Hard working, focused, kind, congratulatory, they had accepted me as one of their own. And I had respected and enjoyed working with them all.

As memories of my time spent at Hanford played in my mind, I sat at the edge of my seat waiting for word that the war was over. It never came.

Chapter 40

August 9, 1945

Three days later, I arrived home from work to find Betty at the door. "We dropped another bomb on Japan. They call it Fat Man."

"Oh, wow!" I thrilled in anticipation of the war's end as I stepped into the house. Even with the shades pulled shut against the sun, it was hot and humid. I smelled peach jam cooking on the stove. "The war's going to be over today then."

"We expect so." Grandpa's face was hopeful and tense as he looked up from his seat near the radio.

Betty plopped near grandpa, rapt with attention.

I stood for a minute, listening to the announcer. Soon our boys would be home safe. A mixture of pain and pleasure shot through me at the thought of Pauly welcoming his brothers back home. Bea would serve up a plate of spaghetti piled high with meatballs in celebration. Would they think of me?

Overcome by thirst and emotion, I headed toward the sound of banging pots and pans. In the kitchen, a row of glass pints filled with peach jam lined the counter. Grandma turned from the sink, where she was filling a pot with water. "I couldn't have picked a worse time to cook up a batch of jam. The news distracted me and now it's nearly dinner time. You must be starved after working all day." Her face shone red from the heat, and she wiped her brow with a rag.

"Don't worry about dinner, Grandma. We can eat cheese sandwiches while we're sitting around the radio." I reached in the refrigerator for a pitcher of lemonade and poured myself a glass.

"Good idea." She nodded and began setting the jam jars in the pot. "As soon as these have had their water bath."

I gulped down the lemonade and hurried into the bedroom to change. Pauly would finally be able to report the truth about Hanford. Did he think the bomb was worth losing his town or was he still angry? I sighed. Maybe he would forgive me if I told him the truth about every one of my lies. If only I had a chance.

I sat next to grandpa in the parlor, marveling that the radio announcer's voice held no emotion as he reported about the power of the bomb. The Japanese would be forced to surrender.

Betty's eyes reddened. "The first bomb was payment enough for Doug's death."

Grandpa's mouth was set in a grim line. "The fact that they haven't surrendered just shows how much the atomic bomb was needed. The Japanese leaders are evil."

Grandma stuck her head in the door. "I'm finishing up the jam. How about sausage and cheese for dinner? We can eat around the radio."

"I'll help you." Betty disappeared into the kitchen.

The announcer went on with news from around the country as Grandma and Betty carried in platefuls of gouda cheese, sausage, and cut up peaches.

When I dropped a peach slice in my lap, I carried my plate to the dining room where I ate alone with my thoughts. Dr. Jaimeson and the team at Hanford must be sitting on the edges of their seats, waiting for news. I wondered if Mr. Dirk would remain his robotic self and work as if nothing unusual were happening while the rest of them celebrated.

When I was done eating, I carried all the dishes into the kitchen where I washed and dried them with one ear tuned to what was happening in the parlor. When the radio programing shifted from news to *Fibber McGee and Molly*, I wandered in to listen.

The cuckoo clock on the wall near the front door chimed ten-thirty, and I yawned. "I'm going to bed. If they surrender, wake me up."

In my bedroom, I leaned my face against the open window screen for coolness and said a prayer for our country. When I was done, a picture of Doug grinning moonily at Betty flashed through my mind. Angrily, I threw my blankets to the floor, lay down and closed my eyes.

They popped open again as a new thought took root in my mind. I had helped to unleash this horrible destruction. Thousands of Japanese people had been slaughtered because of my work. How many more people would have to die before the Japanese government bowed their knee in surrender?

But closer to my heart, and devastating in its inky darkness, was the knowledge that my dedication to unleashing this horrible power had also killed my relationship with Pauly.

Chapter 41

August 15, 1945

Mr. Dean burst into the marina office. "They surrendered! The Japanese surrendered!"

"Hooray!" Relief and joy washed through me like a clean rain. I dropped the accounting book on the floor near the file cabinet and raced around the desk to hug Mr. Dean without bothering to pick it up. "I don't think I've ever heard better news." His fishy stink brought me back to my senses and I released him, embarrassed.

Mr. Dean grinned. "I know. I know. It's the best day ever, even though you're going to smell like fish the rest of the day." He picked the accounting book off the floor and opened the file cabinet for the cigars he kept in the bottom drawer. "I'd offer you one of these if I knew you'd like it. But I'll do you one better. Take the rest of the day off."

"Thank you, Mr. Dean!" I grabbed my purse from the desk. "I'll do double work tomorrow." On the way home, cars honked, and people cheered. I waved and whooped at everyone I saw, whether I knew them or not.

At the door, Betty engulfed me in a giant hug. Our tears of joy mingled together on our cheeks. She finally released me. "I don't know where Grandma and Grandpa went. But let's go someplace to celebrate. Grandpa won't care if we take his fishing truck."

When we saw knots of milling people gathered on Deland Park's grassy shore, Betty parked. As I climbed out of the truck, someone began belting out the National Anthem. We joined in as the song rapidly traveled through the crowd. Men removed their hats and we bowed our heads in reverence. When the song ended, a huge cheer erupted.

Betty dragged me by the arm to a group of our old classmates standing around a park bench near the water. She shoved into the middle of the crowd and interrupted their conversation. "You know

Ally and I worked at Hanford Engineer Works, one of the places where they made the atomic bomb. I was a messenger for information at the Hanford Engineer Works in Richland" Betty said preening with pride. "And Ally was a top-secret secretary for the scientists responsible for engineering the atom bomb."

I was grateful that she didn't mention I'd been fired. But when their eyes lit up with the admiration I had craved for so long, my joy in the celebration fell like a flat tire. I smiled and shook my head mutely.

Betty said, "Oh, you know Ally. She's too modest. She really did have an important job."

All the popular, smart classmates I'd wished so badly to impress when I was at Hanford began peppering me with questions. As I answered, the safety and security measures Mrs. Chase had drilled into me stayed at the forefront of my mind. I didn't even give a hint of the top-secret information about pencil detectors and the dangers of radiation poisoning that I had been privy to. These people didn't need to know details, especially about my role in it all. Only that our country had created and dropped the atom bomb that won the war.

The crowd finally broke up with promises to meet later to celebrate the night away at a band concert, and I took Betty aside. "I'm tired. Can I have the keys? I'm sure somebody will give you a ride home." When her old junior high boyfriend rushed up for a celebratory kiss, she dropped the keys in my hand without protest.

As I drove home in grandpa's old truck, I ignored the celebrations happening on every street corner. Why had I ever let my desire for admiration fuel my motivation? If I hadn't been so set upon proving myself, I would be marrying to the love of my life.

And love was immeasurably more valuable than proving myself. Pauly hadn't cared if I wore glasses, had klutzy spots on my clothes, and lacked confidence. He had loved me for who I was, and I had ruined it.

At home, Grandma and Grandpa were away celebrating and the house was quiet. Perfect for composing a letter. I couldn't be with Pauly. But maybe I could convince my best friend Pat to come to Sheboygan for a visit now that the war was over. I missed her with all my heart.

Chapter 42

I stood on tiptoe with excitement as Pat's train squealed to a stop near the station. I still didn't know how long she would stay, but I hoped forever. Men returning from war were taking most of the jobs in the area, but Betty said there was an opening for a clerk in the women's department at JC Penney.

Betty and I had found a two-bedroom house to rent just a block over from Grandma and Grandpa's. We each had our own room, but we agreed it would be worth sharing a room if Pat would come and live with us.

Finally, Pat appeared at the top of the stairs, her elfin face grinning even before she saw us.

"Pat! Over here!" I waved wildly.

She ran and we took turns engulfing her in hugs.

"I'm so glad you're here. I can't tell you how much I've missed you," I said.

"It's about time you got here. Now we hope you never leave." Betty looked around. "Hey, where are your bags?"

"Pauly's bringing them." Her eyes danced mischievously. "I got the knucklehead to come along with me."

"What?" I looked for him, suddenly charged with a combination of trepidation and joy.

"He's been pretty miserable, you know, even with his brothers back home."

A cart piled with trunks rolled up. Pauly peered around it cautiously. "Hi, I know you weren't expecting me, but I needed a vacation."

As I drank in his electric grin and warm brown eyes, my heart melted with love. Betty let out a whoop and gave him a hug. I held back.

"Alice, it's good to see you." His deep brown eyes registered reserve.

I wanted more than anything to twine myself up in his arms. To feel his sweet kisses and hear him call me his Ally Oop. I stayed silent for fear of choking on my words.

Betty took over. "We came in our grandpa's truck. But I'm sure all four of us can squeeze into it. Our house is small too, but you can sleep in the living room if you don't mind, Paul."

"I've rented a room at the Rochester Inn just a few miles from town. I can get a taxi." Pauly followed Betty with the bags.

My voice squeaked with nerves. "Grandma and Grandpa have a guest room, and I know they'd love you to stay with them. It's only a block from where Betty and I live."

Betty opened the driver's side and settled behind the wheel.

"I don't want to put anyone out." Pauly stood back and waited for Pat to climb in.

Pat said, "Hey, don't be so polite. It's not like you have money to burn."

Pauly stared at the one remaining seat in the truck. "Um, maybe I should ride in the back."

Betty said, "Oh no, you don't. It's filthy with all my grandpa's fishing gear back there. You'd smell like a trout."

He glanced at me uneasily. "I guess I'll get in first, then."

I felt my face get hot with remembered pleasures as I perched on his lap. "Um. I hope I'm not squishing you."

Pat said, "Oh, he likes to be squished, don't you, Pauly?"

"Hey, Pat. Mind your own business." His rumbly voice vibrated against my back.

"Well, if that isn't the pot calling the kettle black. You, the big reporter, telling me to mind my own business."

I laughed despite Pauly's frosty reception. "Oh, I've missed you both more than I can say."

As Betty started driving, she acted as a tour guide. I was so overcome by Pauly's nearness that I couldn't register a word she said. As usual, the familiar heat we made together began throbbing through my veins. I sighed, wishing more than anything that I could melt into him and kiss him endlessly. But we had issues to discuss and problems to solve if anything like that could ever happen again. I held myself tense as my body thrummed.

Betty asked, "So Paul, what's your favorite kind of cheese?"

He cleared his throat and shifted slightly.

When he didn't answer, Pat elbowed him. "Earth to Pauly. Are you there?"

Pauly sounded embarrassed. "I was just absorbed in the beauty of your lovely community."

"Oh, yeah. Cheese stores are beautiful all right." Pat laughed.

"Sorry, what was the question?" He asked.

Betty laughed. "I asked you what your favorite kind of cheese was."

"Oh, I don't know. Maybe Kraft American."

"Blasphemy!" Betty said. "You have never lived until you've had real cheese like Canaria or Gouda. Not to mention curds."

"Curds, hmm? It sounds like a nursery rhyme." Pauly shifted. "But I'm very teachable. Maybe I'll write an article and educate the cheese-ignorant side of the country."

I laughed, guessing that Pauly was as distracted by my nearness as I was by his. I couldn't get caught up in our crazy chemistry and lose all caution, though. His demands had put me in a tough spot, and we both had to prove that we could trust each other. Starting with me. I couldn't wait to get him alone and spill all my secrets.

Chapter 43

Betty parked the truck. "And this is Deland Park. Isn't it beautiful?" The red-orange leaves of the sugar maple stood out against Lake Michigan, bright blue in the September sun. "The weather is just perfect. No sign of a dust storm brewing on the horizon," she said.

Pauly and I spilled out.

"We'll see you two later." Pat's face gleamed with mischief, and Betty drove away laughing before we could say a word.

Pauly shrugged. "I guess they think we have some unfinished business. Let's go sit over there."

My heart beat like a wild bird as I followed him to a bench overlooking the lake. I hugged my cardigan close against the chill. "You deserve to hear the truth about everything I kept hidden from you. Before I start, though, I want you to know that I kept secrets to protect you. And, of course, because I was scared and because...you know." I stopped.

Pauly nodded as he stared out at the fishing boats plying the waters. "I do know. But before you tell your secrets, I have some apologizing to do." He turned to me, his eyes sore and pleading. "I'm sorry I pumped you for information. I put you in a tough spot and made you lose your job. I hope you can forgive me. I don't really have a good excuse, except you know how hurt I was because your job seemed more important to you than our relationship. And frustrated... Oh heck. It just makes me sad to go over all of that again." He sighed and looked away.

"Of course, I forgive you. And I even understand." I squeezed his hand briefly. "I'm sorry I hurt you, and I hope you can forgive me after you hear my story."

The nightmare of the Coyote came slamming back. I trembled with tears. He gave a sideways frown, his hands on his knees. I sighed and hugged myself tighter. "Do you remember when I got all beat up and tried to hide it with makeup?"

He nodded. I began telling him about the attempted rape. When I got to the part about the Coyote pinning me down behind the administration building, he stood up and turned away, his hands fisted at his sides.

My tears flowed as I told him about the nurse and the ride home with Sergeant Joseph. "I couldn't tell you because I knew you would have gone after him. You could have gotten beaten up or even killed." I sighed. "Thankfully, the security team and Mr. Dirk took me seriously and sent him away. I was going to tell you all about it after he was gone, but then..." I swallowed hard and went on.

"You know when I lived in Richland, I was out to prove that I was smart and independent after so many years of feeling stupid and living in Betty's shadow. Lately, I've been realizing that's not so important." I paused to gather courage. "Anyway, I want to apologize for letting my insecurity get in the way of our relationship. I realize now that I don't need to prove myself to anyone else. Except maybe that you can trust me to be honest."

Pauly sat down. "But how could you think I would tell..."

I held up my hand. "Wait. Let me tell you the rest of my story. I played sick for a few days because I was scared, and I didn't want to have to explain to my coworkers why I had to be escorted back and forth by a guard. I was an emotional wreck. Mr. Dirk told me he was training someone else. So, when the FBI called me in for questioning, I was sure they thought I had done something to entice the Coyote." I described the locked scorching room. "I became convinced that they had investigated my background and found out I was too stupid to do my job. I know. It was completely irrational." I shook my head, embarrassed. "But I was dizzy and disoriented. And by the time Mr. Ward had finished, I would have believed him if he told me that red was green. Of course, the fact that they fired me on the spot didn't help either. By the time it was all over, I was too shocked to think clearly." I hugged myself. "I'm so sorry I doubted you." Another tear escaped.

A fresh breeze wafted across the lake, and a single red leaf fell at our feet. Pauly removed his glasses and rubbed his eyes. After what seemed like hours, he spoke. "I'm so sorry you went through all that. I want to kill the guy who did that to you. What's his name?"

"Promise you won't go looking for him." I stared at his stony face and sighed. "His name is Bart Bundy, and he worked at the pump house. He's the same guy that followed me home on the bus that time."

He bowed his head. After a few minutes, he spoke. "God took care of you. I have to let it go." Pauly let out a deep breath. "As far as the FBI is concerned, Mr. Ward is the one who should be fired for bullying a young woman just trying to do her job and be faithful to her fiancé." There was steel in his voice, but his eyes were soft toward me. "After hearing President Truman speak about the scientific race with the Germans, I realize how dangerous it was for me to try to figure out what was going on." He shrugged. "I could have been a spy or at the least unlocked some secrets that informed the enemy about what was going on." He stared at the ruffled lake. "I never did find out where Jeffrey got his source for the incriminating article. When I called his office, they said he'd left the newspaper. I'm sure he was driven out of town by the FBI."

"Probably." I smiled, cleansed by my confession and his apologies. "There's one more thing I haven't told you, though."

Pauly frowned.

I laughed. "I don't know how to cook more than a bowl of cereal. I was embarrassed that my dad told you I was a good cook. And then I wasn't sure how to tell you without making him look like a liar. I was hoping your mom would teach me to cook your favorites."

"If I remember, when your dad said that Pat kicked you under the table and you turned red." Pauly laughed.

With the air clear between us, I wanted to kiss him until the trees stood bare. But I held myself in check. I had to show him I was an honest person. And we both had to prove that we respected each other's needs.

I recognized the look of longing in Pauly's eyes, and I was probably telegraphing my own desire. But he put out his hand. "Let's start over."

When I shook his hand, that jolt of shared attraction passed between us, and my heart danced with joy. Somehow, I knew we'd be up to the challenge.

Epilogue

My red roses trembled as I walked down the church aisle with Daddy at my side. I scanned the church for familiar faces. Outgoing Pauly had a guest list three times the length of mine, but strangely, I felt only a smidgen of dread at all the unfamiliar people. The sight of the tall man with glasses and an electric smile waiting for me at the front of the church would carry me through.

There were Mrs. Chase and Mary, smiling and sniffing back happy tears. Annette and her gang sat in front of them, pretty in their dresses. Mother, Timmy, Grandma and Grandpa, aunts and uncles and cousins, beamed at me with shining faces.

Pale winter light streamed in from windows above the choir loft, showcasing Pauly and the wedding party. Pauly's brothers stood next to him, serious and dignified in dress uniform. On the other side of the altar, Pat and Betty stood, both wearing midnight-blue silk dresses. The light set the gold in Betty's hair on fire. Pat, her elfin face shining, wiped away a tear as Daddy handed me off to Pauly.

Pastor Carver winked at us and began the ceremony. First, he spoke of the joys of marriage, and then the challenges. When he talked of the importance of grace and forgiveness, tears of thankfulness and joy spilled. I smiled tremulously at Pauly, whose love shone through his eyes like a beacon. Our relationship had already been tested by adversity. We knew that forgiveness was the glue holding our love together.

I held Pauly's warm, steady hands, and I recited my vows with a strong voice. "I Alice, take thee, Paul to be my wedded husband, to have and to hold from this day forward for better or worse, for richer, for poorer, in sickness and in health, to love and to cherish, till death do us part, according to God's holy ordinance; and thereto I pledge thee my faith."

Pauly's eyes were dark with emotion as he recited his vows and slipped the wedding ring on my finger. "I give you this ring as a symbol of my love; and with all that I am and all that I have, I honor you, in the name of the Father and of the Son and of the Holy Spirit."

Pastor Carver smiled. "You may kiss the bride."

Pauly kissed me hungrily and lingering. When the audience laughed, we separated and joined them as we raised our clasped hands in victory.

Pastor Carver boomed. "It's my great joy to introduce to you for the very first time, Mr. and Mrs. Paul Rodgers."

The crowd erupted in cheers, and we walked down the aisle smiling at friends and family. I was grateful for our upcoming honeymoon at an ocean-side cabin. Grateful for our home with grass and an oak tree growing in the yard. Grateful for my new job as secretary and proofreader at the *Pasco Herald*, where I'd start a new adventure to inform the world, one truthful story at a time. But most of all, I was grateful for love—a deepening love that had no secrets to hide and needed nothing to prove its worth.

The End

Don't miss out!

Visit the website below and you can sign up to receive emails whenever Janet Asbridge publishes a new book. There's no charge and no obligation.

https://books2read.com/r/B-A-TFBBB-TVOPC

BOOKS 2 READ

Connecting independent readers to independent writers.

About the Author

Janet Asbridge grew up in the shadow of the Hanford Nuclear Reservation. Her mother's stories about moving with her family to the new town of Richland, WA during World War 2 was the inspiration for *Atomic Secrets*. Currently, Janet lives in the shade of the Cascade Mountains on the rainy side of Washington State with her husband and spoiled cat, Salty. When she's not writing, she enjoys reading, walking in the woods, and creating mosaics. For her inspirational stories, check out her website @ janetasbridge.com. You can find her books for children at amazon.com.

Read more at https://www.jwasbridge.net.